## *Monstrous Creatures*

A tricorn could not be compared to its two-horned domesticated bovine cousins. None of the other denizens of the wilds of Raemllyn had the reputation for ferocity that this three-horned bull had.

"Easy," Davin whispered to Goran. They continued to step slowly away from the creature. Davin's back-stepping had slowed to a snail's pace.

The tricorn's head cocked to one side, as though uncertain what manner of creatures it faced. Then its head lifted, neck stretched, and mouth gaped to release a thundering bellow.

"Run!" Davin shouted.

The tricorn charged...

*Ace Fantasy Books by Robert E. Vardeman and Geo. W. Proctor*

## THE SWORDS OF RAEMLLYN SERIES

TO DEMONS BOUND
A YOKE OF MAGIC
BLOOD FOUNTAIN
DEATH'S ACOLYTE
THE BEASTS OF THE MIST
FOR CROWN AND KINGDOM
*(coming in January 1987)*

*Ace Fantasy Books by Robert E. Vardeman*

## THE CENOTAPH ROAD SERIES

CENOTAPH ROAD
THE SORCERER'S SKULL
WORLD OF MAZES
IRON TONGUE
FIRE AND FOG
PILLAR OF NIGHT

*Ace Science Fiction Books by Geo. W. Proctor*

STARWINGS

## 5
## SWORDS·OF·RAEMLLYN

# THE BEASTS OF THE MIST

## ROBERT E. VARDEMAN
## AND GEO. W. PROCTOR

ACE FANTASY BOOKS
NEW YORK

For Bob Wayne, fellow wayfarer of the fantastic

—*G.W.P.*


For Bucky Starr and his friend Martin Cameron

—*R.E.V.*

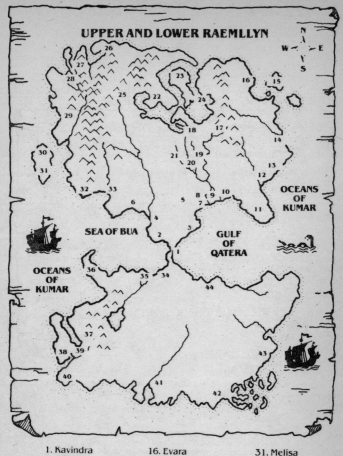

# UPPER AND LOWER RAEMLLYN

SEA OF BUA

OCEANS OF KUMAR

OCEANS OF KUMAR

GULF OF QATERA

1. Kavindra
2. Kressia
3. Sarngan
4. Amayita
5. Bian
6. Cahri
7. Chavali
8. Degoolah
9. Garoda
10. Jyn
11. Meakham
12. Parrn
13. Qatirn
14. Orji
15. Iluska
16. Evara
17. Salim
18. Yaryne
19. Leticia
20. Bistonia
21. Harn
22. Nawat
23. Vatusia
24. Rakell
25. Solana
26. Faldin
27. Weysh
28. Salnal
29. Yow
30. Litonya
31. Melisa
32. Delu
33. Jyotis
34. Initha
35. Zahar
36. Elkid
37. Uhjayib
38. Fayinah
39. Pahl
40. Rattreh
41. Ohnuhn
42. Gatinah
43. Ahvayuh
44. Nayati

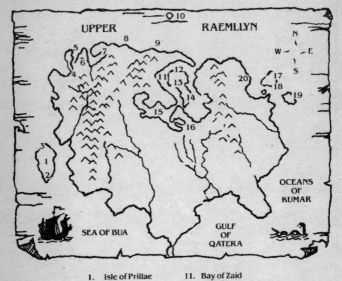

|     |                  |     |                  |
| --- | ---------------- | --- | ---------------- |
| 1.  | Isle of Prillae  | 11. | Bay of Zaid      |
| 2.  | Melisa           | 12. | Vatusia          |
| 3.  | Litonya          | 13. | Isle of Loieter  |
| 4.  | Weysh            | 14. | Rakell           |
| 5.  | Bay of Yper      | 15. | Bay of Pilisi    |
| 6.  | Agda             | 16. | Yaryne           |
| 7.  | Faldin           | 17. | Isle of Righden  |
| 8.  | Cape Terror      | 18. | Iluska           |
| 9.  | The Whirlpool    | 19. | Isle of Pthedm   |
| 10. | The Isle of Mists| 20. | Evara            |

# chapter

# 1

A BELLOW—A roar belched from the bowels of Hell itself—shook the Forest of Agda!

The heads of two stranded wayfarers jerked upright, the rabbit hole they squatted beside momentarily forgotten. Warily they peered at the wall of evergreens and winter-barren trees that hemmed the small clearing in which they crouched.

"Goran," the smaller of the two spoke as he pushed from the ground to a height of six feet, "that sounded like a tri—"

"Nay!" A barrel-chested giant, towering a full head over his companion, stood and shook a shaggy-maned head of fiery red. "Nay, Davin, it couldn't be. It's too far north. Such creatures prefer warmer climes, especially when winter's fangs bite through flesh to the bone! Were we near Meakham or even your own homeland of Jyotis far to the south, I would . . ."

Davin Anane no longer listened to his friend's words. Goran One-Eye's narrowly slitted good right eye said more. That single jade, gold-flecked orb bespoke caution.

". . . nay, I say." Goran scratched a hand through a tangled fire-red beard that covered cheeks, chin, and throat. " 'Tis merely the howly voice of Minima, Goddess of the Winds. If her stomach is half as empty as mine, I well understand her complaint. Come, we've a rabbit to prod from this burrow, a fire to build, and—"

"Your stomach! Is that all that ever concerns you?" Davin brushed aside a stray strand of shoulder-length raven hair the wind tossed across his eyes while he once more scanned the wooded perimeter of the clearing.

"Can you think of anything better to concern oneself with when you're lost in the middle of a godforsaken forest such as this?" Goran lowered his massive body, weighing a full twenty-four stones, to squat in the snow on haunches once again. Lifting a branch, he probed the rabbit hole. "Would you prefer

*1*

that I tortured myself with visions of fleshy, pink wenches awrithe with passion? Or perhaps it would be better to taunt myself with images of jewels and bists just waiting to be purloined by a master thief such as myself?"

"Goran..." Davin started, then swallowed the rest of his words; they would be wasted on his burly companion. Worse, they would provide fuel to fire Goran's tongue for the rest of the morning. Giving the forest a final perusal, Davin Anane crouched at his fellow thief's side.

A second roar shattered the forest's silence. Closer now! Accompanying the bellow came the rustle and snap of dry underbrush.

"Goran..." Davin leaped to his feet.

The remainder of the freebooter's warning drowned in a third thunderous roar. The owner of that deafening bellow crashed from the forest and skidded to a halt on four legs in the ankle-deep snow blanketing the clearing. Clouds of steam-like mist billowed from flared nostrils while dark eyes glared at the two men.

"A *tricorn!*" Goran One-Eye gasped while he cautiously stood. "And you doubted my word! Too far north for such a beast, indeed! Son of Anane, this shall be the last time I listen to you!"

Davin wasted no breath pointing out who had declared this clime too frigid for Raemllyn's wild three-horned bull. Instead he motioned his mountain-sized friend toward the trees behind them, his gray eyes never leaving the muscular creature.

"I've heard scholars claim the horn just above the snout is not a true horn, but a growth of hair," Goran whispered nervously as his hand dropped for a sword slung on his waist.

Davin's left hand closed around his companion's right wrist before fingers reached the blade's pommel. "Leave it sheathed. One blow would be all you could manage before the beast either gored or trampled you."

Goran swallowed and nodded without breaking his steady backward strides. Davin spoke the truth. A spear, or even better, a lance, might stand against the three-horned bull. A sword blade was far too short a weapon with which to face such a deadly animal.

And deadly it was! A tricorn could not be compared to its two-horned domesticated bovine cousins. While a multitude of fanged and clawed denizens populated the wilds of Upper and

Lower Raemllyn, none had the tricorn's reputation for ferocity and endurance. When men were forced into the woods to hunt a rogue—no man was fool enough to seek a tricorn for sport—at least twenty riders went armed with stout steel-tipped lances. Even those heavily weighted odds did not guarantee success.

"Easy," Davin whispered. His own backstepping slowed to a snail's pace.

The tricorn's head cocked from side to side, as though uncertain what manner of creatures it faced. Then its head lifted, neck stretched, and mouth gaped to release another thundering bellow.

Fifteen hands at the shoulders, Davin estimated the bull's height while he once more increased his retreat. If the animal had stood on a scales, it would have taken at least four men equal to Goran's girth to tip the balance. Nor was there a hint of fat on the tricorn's sleek black-and-brown dappled body, only rippling muscle.

The echoing roar died; the tricorn's head dropped. Three horns, two curved atop its head and the third jutting straight above its broad nose, dipped toward the two men. The muscular animal snorted while its left forehoof pawed the snow, an action that left no doubt that it intended to test the mettle of these two strange creatures it had stumbled upon.

"Run!" Davin shouted in warning while he spun about and sprinted toward a *morda* tree.

Behind the fleeing thief came the muffled pounding of cloven hooves tearing through the snow. The tricorn charged!

Although two strides behind his friend in his own start, Goran One-Eye moved with an uncanny speed that belied a ponderous mass that outweighed Davin by ten stones. In five strides the red-maned giant passed his companion, and in twenty he reached the *morda*'s bole. With the agility and lightness of a trained acrobat, Goran leaped high, caught a low winter-barren branch, and swung into the tree.

"Were I you, I would hasten my strides! The tricorn's horns are aimed directly at your backside and a mere four of the animal's lengths behind its target!" Goran called as he securely anchored himself with an arm about the tree's trunk, then held his free arm downward.

A long stride from the dangling hand, Davin leaped. He sailed through the frosty air with both arms stretched out, caught his friend's hand, and clung to it for his life. Goran wrenched him upward into the safety of the leafless branches as though he were no more than a child.

"There *is* occasionally a use for brainless brawn," Davin begrudingly admitted while he watched death charge below the limbs, three horns goring empty air which had contained him but an instant ego.

"Use for brainless brawn?" The bushy red eyebrow above Goran's good eye arched sharply in question while he peered at the beast as it swung about, searching for the two vanished men. "I see absolutely no use for such a powerful beast as a tricorn! Nyuria take the damnable animal, horns and all!"

Davin forgot his intention of correcting Goran's misinterpretation of his comment, when the tricorn's rolled upward. In the next instant the thief clutched at the *morda*'s branches to maintain his precarious balance. The tricorn charged the tree, slamming head and horns into the thick bole.

"Brainless is right! Look at the stupid animal! It believes its might greater than this ancient tree!" Goran shouted down at the three-horned wild bull. "Try again! Go ahead! Batter your brains out and save me the trouble! I can already taste fresh roasted tricorn steaks!"

With snorted clouds of mist billowing from flared nostrils, and snow flying from hooves, the rogue bull accepted the challenge. Bundled muscles unleashed like steel springs, and the tricorn rammed into the trunk of the *morda*, full weight of its massive body behind the blow. The vibrations of the impact still reverberated through the limbs of the tree when the beast threw itself against the bole again. And again and again and again!

"That's it!" Goran shouted with boisterous glee.

"Goran!" Davin made no attempt to hide the reprimand in his stern tone while he clutched at limbs with both arms to maintain his high perch. "Let the animal be! There's little chance he'll batter out his brains. The sooner you stop taunting, the sooner he'll grow bored and leave us in peace!"

"But Davin . . ." Goran glanced at his companion, read the irritation on his face, and shrugged like a scolded child before settling atop a wide limb with his back to the trunk of the *morda*. He looked down at the tricorn, who returned his stare. "We could be here all day, you know."

"Then we'll be here this day, and the coming night if the

Sitala so ordain!" Davin answered, his own attention returning to the tricorn.

The three-horned bull stood in the ankle-deep snow with its blocklike head raised to eye the two wayfarers. Its occasional snort and pawing of hoof offered no hope that the creature would soon bore of the treed pair.

"Meanwhile your precious Lijena and *our* horses will be a day farther from us." Goran idly surveyed the forest and clearing. A pained groan rumbled from his throat. "My rabbit! By Nyuria's scorched arse, my rabbit escapes!"

Davin didn't notice the white-furred snow rabbit that casually bounded from its burrow into the forest. The young adventurer's knuckles glowed white as his hands tightened into fists around the limbs to which he clung. His fingernails cut small crescents into the dark bark. A tremor of frustration quaked through his slender body. A single word pushed from his lips like a moan of agony, "Lijena!"

Goran One-Eye's shaggy head shook in pity. His young friend would never learn. "The skinny ones, Davin, it's always the skinny ones that get a man into trouble. Now, if you'd chosen better, we wouldn't be stranded on foot in the middle of the Forest of Agda with naught but our swords and what wit the gods gave us."

Imitating the tricorn below, Goran snorted and sent silvery plumes into the winter air. He didn't bother mentioning that he considered himself the only one who retained a shred of wit. The way Davin acted when it came to the wench from Bistonia displayed no sense whatsoever.

Adjusting a tattered fox-fur eye patch covering the empty socket that once had contained a left eye, he studied his fellow thief with his good eye. In truth it surprised him that Davin had held up as well as he had these past months, considering the distances traveled and the menaces overcome. Davin, after all, was only human.

And not Challing, like Goran One-Eye.

Another groan rumbled from Goran's throat when memories of Gohwohn—his homeworld in another dimension—crowded to the forefront of his thoughts. The sorceror Roan-Jafar had ripped him from that realm of existence, intent on enslaving the Challing and his magical abilities. For that perfidy the mage paid with his life. Goran's own hands had extracted the price.

But Roan-Jafar won the final victory. Goran was stranded in a strange dimension, on this world humankind called Raemllyn, with its boring political machinations.

The ultimate disgrace was being trapped in an unmalleable human body. His Challing form—or lack of any form, or the choice of any body that suited his whim, for a Challing was a being nine tenths mystical to one physical—suited him better.

The memories of Gohwohn parted, and the years of adventures he had shared as a thief at Davin's side in this world of humans paraded before his mind's eye. He smiled at the long line of lusty-eyed, amply endowed wenches who marched seductively by within his head. Each had introduced him to pleasures unknown on Gohwohn, delights of human flesh.

"By the gods, there are compensations," he sighed with gusto.

*"Compensations?* Have you lost what little is left of your senses? Damn it, man, Lijena took our horses, our supplies, everything! Even the jewels we stole!" Davin Anane cursed and the branches supporting him shook.

"The tricorn makes less noise," grumbled Goran. His friend had ranted about the skinny wench for the past four days. "Enough is enough! Your lovesickness is tiring."

"I'll find Lijena Farleigh," Davin continued, his anger undiminished. "Find her—and exact revenge!"

Goran heaved a weary sigh. He'd heard this before, at least a thousand times. "After the blond witch has stranded us—not once but twice, I remind you—after we've rescued her from the Narain and freed her of Lorennion's accursed demon,* you should be glad to be rid of her. Yet you pine after her, panting and tongue dangling like a dog after a bitch in heat." Goran punctuated his comments with a series of grunts and suggestive noises.

"Lijena wouldn't have suffered demonic possession if you hadn't cheated at the gaming tables and allowed yourself to be captured and sentenced to death. I had to buy back your miserable hide from Bistonia's Emperor of Thieves using Lijena as the coin!" Davin glared at the Challing in human form.

"Of course you did. Such is expected between friends," Goran said in an irritatingly innocent tone. "And *you* are responsible for her commerce with the Faceless Ones."

*To Demons Bound, Swords of Raemllyn #1

The taunt evoked an unexpected pensive note within Goran's breast. Even he feared the demons summoned from another realm by Raemllyn's usurper, High King Zarek Yannis. Not for ten thousand generations had those demons ridden across the face of this world. Now their fearsome presence manifested itself everywhere!

Goran grunted. In part the burden rested on Lijena Farleigh's shoulders. She had stolen the Sword of Kwerin Bloodhawk from Davin—the only weapon capable of defeating the Faceless Ones.

Along with the magic-forged blade, the blond-tressed wench had taken Davin's and his horses, leaving them stranded afoot. If there was one thing Goran One-Eye hated, it was walking! It wasn't fitting for a Challing, even in human form, to *walk*. But if he were to escape this miserable forest, with Lorennion's Blood Fountain*, the remnants of those mind-controlling demons the Narain, and the other too-well-remembered horrors, he had but one course—to walk.

"Forget her." Goran turned to Davin. "Back to Weysh is the path we should trod. It's near enough, and we had scant time to explore the seaport's more interesting niches."

"That jewel merchant—the one you said was old and slow, who turned out to be young and an excellent swordsman—will still be on the lookout for us." Davin nodded at the tricorn.

The three-horned rogue bull lowered its head, snorted, then trotted across the clearing. It paused when it reached the trees, glanced back at the two, then disappeared into the woods.

Neither Davin nor Goran moved, realizing the foolishness of abandoning their perches until the tricorn had time enough to place distance between it and the *morda* tree.

"Weysh," Goran repeated with determination. His good eye rolled to his friend.

Davin didn't answer. Standing on a limb, he surveyed the forest as though he expected to catch a glimpse of Lijena and their stolen horses.

Wishful thinking, Goran thought. The woman rode days ahead of them. With luck they would never lay eyes on her skinny backside again in their lifetimes.

"Weysh is such a fine place," Goran tried once more to draw Davin's attention.

*Blood Fountain*, Swords of Raemllyn #3

"It's a dull and dreary place that smells of sea and fish, or so you said when we first entered the town," Davin reminded the Challing of his earlier appraisal of the harbor town.

"Never would I say such a thing about that fair city." Goran shook his head in denial. "I don't suppose I've ever told of how I lost my eye in Weysh."

*"What?"* This claim startled Davin from his thoughts of Lijena. "You lost your eye ... you said you had never been to Weysh until you and I—"

"In Weysh I lost my eye," Goran said firmly. "Such woe I have never known, not even from your scrawny wench."

Without warning Goran bellowed a bull-throated roar that echoed throughout the Forest of Agda. Davin jumped, hand dropping to his sword.

"That was the sound I heard one humid summer night." Goran smiled at his companion. "As best as I can reproduce the sound, that is. A wench, one with meat on her bones, and I had been enjoying one another's company through the evening. I had worn her out with my amorous abilities, and the poor thing rested before another bout of arduous lovemaking."

"What was the poor thing?" Davin cut in. "The woman or your—"

Goran ignored him. "The cry awoke me. In a flash I whipped out my sword and ran to the window. Peering—both eyes, mind you—across the Bay of Yper, I saw a sight that even until this day fills me with dread."

"The wench's husband?" Davin attempted to bring the tale to a quick end.

He failed.

"Worse," Goran solemnly assured his friend. "Though that puny merchant later showed more wrath than I'd thought him capable of. But that's another story. No, Davin, I saw a sea wraith. It towered well above even the tallest masted cargo ship in the harbor. And none save I foolishly answered its hunting cry."

Goran paused dramatically, then continued in a whisper. "Because only I saw it, it came for me. Sea wraiths are blind, you know."

Davin didn't, nor did he wish to admit he cared. But in spite of himself he felt himself expertly drawn into Goran's farfetched tale. In the five years they had roamed across Raemllyn, he had heard a hundred—more!—stories of how the Challing had lost his left eye. Each tale proved wilder and more outrageous than the prior, but still Davin listened. He hoped for Goran to repeat himself just once or to hint at a story that might be true.

"Yes, sea wraiths are blind, and there is nothing they covet more than sight. I had the misfortune to unknowingly respond to the wraith's challenge. I should never have gone to the window. Sword drawn, both eyes fixed on its fearsome form, I didn't know what to do."

"You could have gone back to bed." Sarcasm dripped from Davin's words.

"You might have. Not I! I am a Challing from Gohwohn. Such craven behavior never occurred me." Goran sighed. "I wish now that I had been around you so that it would have." He gently touched the battered eye patch. "Two eyes are *far* superior to one. Far superior."

"I think we can climb down now. I see no sign of the tricorn," Davin suggested. When Goran made no move, he began to pick his way to the ground.

"The sea wraith stole my eye!" Goran roared when he dropped lightly to the snow beside his friend.

The outrage was so real that Davin almost believed he had wrongfully doubted the Challing—were it not for the smirk that rippled across Goran's lips. With a shake of his head, the last son of the House of Anane turned and began walking southward into Agda's wood.

"It came for me," Goran said. "It came, and we fought. Never fight a sea wraith, Davin. Never. They are implacable! My finest sword thrusts availed me naught. My cleverest parries failed to stop it. But I fought because I do not quit. Naked in the night I fought."

"Didn't the din of this titanic battle awaken the woman?" Davin continued to poke holes in Goran's cobbled yarn.

"She slept through it all," Goran said. "I told you I'd worn the poor thing out with my prowess. She snored so loudly it masked the swish my sword made as it repeatedly cut through the wraith."

"The blade didn't affect the wraith?" Davin arched a dubious eyebrow.

"It held the monster at bay, but little more. Lacy tendrils, finer than any fog, leaked out of every cut I made. This mist took form and reached for me." Goran's voice dropped so low that Davin strained to hear.

"Those tendrils writhed like human fingers, probing and gripping, tearing at my beard, working to pluck out my precious gold-flecked orb!"

"It obviously succeeded." Once more Davin tried to end the wild tale.

"It did, to my eternal sorrow, it did! When I saw that I worked against myself by slashing at the wraith, I stopped battling," Goran went on, undaunted by his companion's words.

"To run?"

"To find a better weapon! But that damned wench stirred on the bed. I turned when she distracted me with her passionate moans," Goran replied.

"What?" cried Davin. "Wait! What passionate moans? You said she slept."

"She did. But the wraith's tendrils had formed more than groping fingers. I was so startled, my jaw dropped and I gaped. Quicker than a striking *pletha* snake, a tendril slipped behind my eye and popped it out. I screamed, but it was too late. The sea wraith had my left eye. Through tears of pain I focused my right eye on the monster and found myself staring at . . . my own eye! The wraith winked at me, then slipped back through the window and into the night."

"What happened then?"

"There was nothing else I could do but return to bed." Goran managed a barrel-chested sigh. "But it wasn't the same with the wench after that. Not when she awoke fully and thanked me for such loving care. I had not the heart to tell her she had been ravaged by a ghostly monster."

Davin laughed. For a moment Goran's improbable bawdy yarn erased the pain left by Lijena Farleigh's abrupt departure and the theft of their horses.

His somberness returned when he thought of the powerful Sword of Kwerin Bloodhawk in the woman's hands. Prince Felrad was the sword's rightful owner. Felrad's sole hope of deposing the Velvet Throne's usurper, Zarek Yannis, lay with that ancient ensorcelled blade.

"Davin!" Goran's fingers tightened like steel bands on Davin's arm. He jerked the smaller thief to one side and tossed him into the snow behind a row of low shrubs.

"What're you doing?" Davin tried to shake free of the Challing.

Goran's meaty hand clamped over Davin's mouth. Davin nodded to indicate he wouldn't call out. Goran's hand relaxed, and Davin peered out through the shrubs. He felt the blood rush from his brain. He wobbled slightly, then sank behind the relative shelter the shrubs provided.

"The Faceless Ones!" Goran whispered, unable to hide the fear contained in those three words.

# chapter
## 2

*FACELESS ONES!* DAVIN Anane's brain reeled in panic. His heart felt as though it would explode from his chest. In spite of the winter's cold a prickly sweat broke over his body.

"We must make a hasty retreat, friend Davin. No mere man, or even a Challing, can stand before hell riders!" Goran's single eye went saucer wide and darted about in search of an avenue to conceal their escape.

Davin drew a steadying breath. Twice before he had faced the hellish warriors Zarek Yannis drew into this realm to aid him in the conquest of Upper and Lower Raemllyn. During the first encounter quick wits, a hollow reed, and a river allowed him to evade the Faceless Ones' houndlike ability to track spoor. On the second occasion he wielded the Sword of Kwerin Bloodhawk and sent the souls of four of the demons back to the hell that spawned them.

This morn the legend blade rode with Lijena Farleigh!! Without the spellbound steel no man could defeat the black-cowled horrors Yannis unleashed on Raemllyn.

With another breath to quell the panicked race of his heart, the last son of the House of Anane lifted cheek from snow and peered through the foliage of broad-leafed evergreens.

No one could mistake the two demonic steeds that met his eyes for ordinary horses. Tall and muscular, they stood like mounts bred to bear the ponderous burden of knights in full armor. Even beneath the gray overcast sky their jet coats shone as though they had been groomed with oil.

These might have been the attributes of earthly horses, but it was here the comparison ended. Snow sizzled, instantly transformed into steamy vapor, with each rise and fall of the demon mounts' hooves—for each of those hooves burned with flames of red and orange. Fire, too, came from their nostrils within a swirling shroud of dark smoke. Nor were the eyes those of ordinary steeds, but glowing orbs of fiery crimson.

"Davin!" Goran tugged at his fellow thief's arm. "We tarry here overlong. The Faceless will descend upon us ere we move a muscle to escape!"

"There are no Faceless Ones, only two of their mounts," the young Jyotian replied.

"Only horses?" Goran's shaggy red-maned head poked up, and he stared in disbelief. "By Nyuria's pitchfork, does my eye deceive me?"

"If it does, then both my eyes also lie." Davin pushed to his knees to peer over the tops of the evergreen scrubs. He saw no sign of black-robed riders with skeletal talons and silver scaled tails.

"No Faceless?" Doubt creased the Challing's brow when he cautiously rose. "This makes no sense."

"Something is awry." Davin felt as befuddled as Goran sounded. "Why would Faceless Ones leave their horses? I've seen them on foot. They travel slowly, hunched over as if in pain."

"You ought to know," Goran said disdainfully. Davin claimed he once eluded three of the Faceless—one of the few mortals to ever do so. Goran maintained his open skepticism, thinking the tale no different from those he spun about his lost eye.

"Wait here."

Goran's mouth opened in protest, but before he uttered a sound, Davin dropped to his belly and wiggle-crawled through the snow until he crouched behind a thick-boled fur tree. Warily he peered about, shrugged, then motioned for his friend to join him. The Challing moved lighter than a shadow across the glade to Davin's side.

"The Faceless Ones are nowhere near, only the horses." Davin glanced back to the fire-hooved creatures, then scanned a windblown, treeless knoll to the right. "We can get a better view from atop the hill."

"Aye, and the hell riders will get an eyeful of us if we climb the rise," Goran objected. "There's no tree or bush to hide us. . . ."

Ignoring the changeling's protest, Davin stood and started up the hill. Only the sound of the wind and the sizzle of the demonic horses' hooves in the snow reached his ears.

"I feel magicks a'dance," Goran announced in a low voice

when he trotted to his companion's side once again. "I like this not."

Davin's head jerked around to the Challing. The green light of witch-fires flickered in Goran's good eye—certain omen spells played here. Did they stem from some external source, or Goran himself? "What do you sense?"

Goran shook his head and heaved broad shoulders helplessly.

Davin frowned while he continued the climb. The magicks reawakening within the Challing worried him nearly as much as the possibility of openly confronting the Faceless Ones.

When Roan-Jafar bound Goran to human form, the mage had stolen away the Challing's mystical powers. During the two adventurers' last visit to the city of Leticia, the sorceror Masur-Kell brewed a potion that returned a portion of the changeling's natural abilities. The trouble was, the effects of the potion were random. At times Goran controlled them, at others they controlled him!

Davin knew Goran could alter his form and psyche to that of a female who called herself Glylina. And the Challing assumed the shape of a Narain to save Davin from those winged-demon pets of the master mage Lorennion. But what other powers lurked within the Challing's breast? Davin had no desire to even guess.

Reaching the crest of the knoll, Davin stared out over the Forest of Agda. Trees, snow, and distant mountains met his gaze. "Still no sign of the Faceless. The demons weave a riddle, but I see no thread."

"No riddle, but the site of a heroic battle."

Goran's voice came hollow and distant from his lips, a sound that sent a shiver up Davin's spine. Once, when they chased the demon-bound Lijena across half of Upper Raemllyn, he had heard that voice, and he swore the Challing had glimpsed the future.*

"Battle?" Davin stared at his friend, uncertain of the changeling's meaning.

"There, there, and there you'll find remnants of the battle." Goran pointed to three spots in the snow. "Dig, son of Anane, and understand the strength of she who wields the Sword of Kwerin in Bloodhawk."

*A Yoke of Magic, Swords of Raemllyn Book #2

With bare hands Davin scooped away the snow in each of the spots and uncovered three sword hilts of gold and bone—hilts that once held blades forged of crystalline flame! "These belonged to Faceless Ones! How?"

In truth Davin knew the answer to that single question. One weapon existed with the power capable of shattering the blades of hell riders—the sword of Raemllyn's ancient hero Kwerin Bloodhawk. The same sword Lijena stole from him four mornings ago.

Armed with the spell-endowed blade created by the legended mage Edan at the dawn of Raemllyn's history, the frosty-tressed daughter of Bistonia had faced three of Zarek Yannis' most horrifying warriors on this spot—and defeated them.* Of that Davin was certain; no other explanation accounted for the bladeless hilts and the demon horses at the foot of the knoll.

That Lijena had prevailed, even with the Sword of Kwerin in her hands, sent the Jyotian adventurer's head aspin. The young woman had never displayed any prowess with a sword. He remembered seeing a weapon in her grasp but four times—twice when the demon possessing her attempted to drive a steel into my heart!

"There, too, lay the remains of the defeated Faceless Ones."

Goran's distant voice intruded on Davin's bewilderment. He looked up to see the red-bearded giant pointing to a copse of cherry laurels below the rise. There, half covered by the snow, he saw what appeared to be a bundle of black cloth.

"What is it?" Davin glanced back at his fellow thief.

"What is what?" Goran blinked and shook his head like a man pushing aside the veils of a deep trance. His voice lost its distant hollowness. "What are you staring at, Davin?"

"The bundle of black you pointed at after showing me the hilts of the Faceless Ones' shattered swords." Davin started down the hill toward the evergreen cherry laurels.

"Sword hilts . . . black . . . oh . . . yes, of course. Quite observant of me, wouldn't you say?" the Challing muttered as he tramped after his friend.

The dubious expression etching uncertain furrows in the Challing's face belied the self-praise in his voice. Davin grimaced. Goran had no more idea how he had known of the hilts than he did, the Jyotian realized.

*Death's Acolyte, Swords of Raemllyn Book #4

Davin shuddered as the skin at the back of his neck came alive, as though crawling with myriad slithering worms. Once again the young thief had witnessed the Challing's undelved powers thrusting forth to dominate their owner. Davin shivered again, doubly. He had little use for magicks and liked them even less when they were as unpredictable as Goran's.

Reaching the dense clump of cherry laurels, Davin eased his sword from its sheath and carefully probed the coarsely woven black cloth entangled in the branches. The snow clinging to the blackness fell away to reveal not one, but three cowled robes.

"By Nyuria's shriveled staff!" exclaimed Goran when he bent closer to peer with his good eye. "Davin, these cloaks belonged to Faceless Ones!"

"Aye," was all the Jyotian could mutter.

The robes confirmed his earlier suspicions. When he had defeated the four Faceless who pursued Lijena, Goran, and him following their escape from the mage Lorennion, only the demons' robes remained after the Sword of Kwerin had bitten into their unholy flesh.

"Three of them," Goran said with obvious awe. "It appears the Bloodhawk's blade is just as potent in the wench's hands as it was in yours!"

"Lijena, who else could it be? Naught but Kwerin's blade could have done this." Davin replied, confirming Goran's conclusion.

"The skinny ones are always trouble," muttered Goran.

*Lijena!* Davin repressed a shiver that attempted to climb his spine. How he feared for her! How he longed to hold her again!

At the same time anger flared within his breast. He wanted to rip the magical sword from her grip and return it to Prince Felrad, the rightful heir to Raemllyn's Velvet Throne. In the Bloodhawk's sword lay the prince's sole key to defeating the usurper's dark hordes and regaining rule of the realm. Didn't Lijena recognize the power she inherited with the blade?

"Here, Davin." Goran reached out and lifted one of the Faceless Ones' cloaks from the limbs.

"By the Great Father Yehseen, what are you doing?" Davin jumped away as the cloak fluttered out, opening like the dark wings of a giant bat.

"You humans show such odd fears." The Challing shrugged and swung the cloak about his shoulders. The blackness lay in sharp contrast with the brilliant crimson tunic and green breeches Goran wore. Turning his head, he sniffed disdainfully at the coarse cloth. "It smells of a Faceless, but it offers protection from the elements. See how it repels the snow's wetness. You should wear one, Davin."

"I'll freeze to death before I'll don a demon's weave." Davin spat and pivoted, stalking toward the shrubs where the Faceless Ones' mounts stood.

"So be it," Goran answered, and tugged the remaining robes from the branches, tossing them over a shoulder. "Three robes and only two horses. I wonder what became of the third mount?"

Davin shook his head. The same question plagued him, but until his and Lijena's paths crossed once again, he doubted he would have an answer.

"And what of these two fine steeds?" Goran asked when they approached the fire-hooved horses. "Will you cast aside such good fortune like a fool, simply because the steeds were spawned in another realm?"

Davin arched an eyebrow. He had not considered the possibility of mounting the Faceless Ones' horses; he had been too concerned with the whereabouts of their owners. He studied the two saddled creatures, telling himself that aside from their fiery hooves and the smoke and flame they snorted, the two animals were merely horses. The question was, would they allow mere mortals to sit astride their backs?

There was one way to find out.

"Wait here," Davin said, and slipped around a pine tree, then hesitantly approached the demonic horses.

The nearest of the two black creatures reared and savaged out with flaming hooves.

His question answered, Davin hastily retreated to Goran's side. "Such steeds were never meant to carry mere men."

A loud snorting neigh from the second horse emphasized the thief's pronouncement.

"Perhaps," Goran replied, then winked. "Then it might be those fine-looking horses just might not like you, Davin. After all, you've never had a way with animals."

"Never had a way with . . ." Davin swallowed the rest of his words.

"I am tired of walking. Challings were never intended to walk like peasants, like mere *humans*." Goran's inflection turned the word into an insult.

Goran casually strolled toward the nearest of the Faceless Ones' mounts. The beast snorted fire from its nostrils and backed away a half step to eye the changeling. The Challing held out his hand.

Davin caught his breath, expecting the horse to rear again, pawing the air with fire-engulfed hooves.

The animal did the opposite; it quieted and allowed Goran to place a hand on its broad muzzle.

"Come along, friend Davin, or I'll leave you behind. By the time you reach Weysh, I'll have tupped every wench in the port!"

"Goran, this can't be." Davin's curiosity did not overcome his caution. He remained by the pine's protective bole. "Why does it let you approach and not me?"

"Mayhap it senses that I am also a being from the realms of magic," Goran suggested, then added, "On the other hand, it could be the black cape. It smells of a Faceless One." The Challing tossed his friend a cowled robe. "Now by Nyuria's roasted haunches will you put it on?"

Reluctantly Davin did as told, and hesitantly walked to the demon mount Goran held by its bit. The horse displayed no sign of fear when Davin took its head and Goran mounted. Nor did the beast offer protest as the Challing's massive bulk settled into the saddle.

"It's safe. As long as you confuse their pitiful senses by wearing the cloak, it's safe." Goran laughed, jerked hard on the reins, and wheeled the horse about. He set off at a gallop, the horse's fiery hooves sizzling as they touched the snowy carpet.

Davin hugged the Faceless One's cloak tighter around his body and approached the remaining mount. With a quick movement he vaulted into the saddle. The fleet animal leaped forward, following Goran One-Eye through the forest.

Davin Anane did nothing, merely clung to the saddle horn and reins with frightened intensity. So it was he rode west through the Forest of Agda toward the sea and the town of Weysh, uncertain whether he or the demon horse was in control.

# *chapter*

# *3*

MOUTH GRIMLY SET, and with a silent prayer to Yehseen—
Father of Raemllyn's Gods—perched on his tongue tip, Davin
Anane clung to the saddle horn and reins of his demon-spawned
mount as it bounded through the Forest of Agda after Goran
One-Eye and his fire-hooved steed.

The wind, razor edged with bitter, lacerating cold, stung
his face, to bring tears welling in his eyes. Nor could he close
them to keep out the icy needles. To do so would have meant
the loss of his seat astride the fire-snorting beast—or worse.
He vitally required his eyes as he lunged and ducked beneath
overhanging boughs thick enough to take off the top of a head,
should constant vigilance falter for an instant.

Even pressing low against the hellish horse's broad neck,
with the Faceless One's cape cracking and snapping from his
shoulders like a garrison flag, did not seem to help. He bobbed
and weaved each time the steed raced beneath fir, pine, and
*morda*.

But the mount! Davin never conceived, even in his wildest
imaginings, that such a powerful animal could exist. Every
stride of the creature's muscular legs drove flaming hooves into
the blanketing snow; steam hissed and billowed in the horse's
wake.

Untiring, the beast galloped with a smooth, flowing rhythm.
For its rider the sensation was like floating, flying, being on
the back of a giant wingless bird. Minutes and hours lost meaning in the wild rush through the tangled wood of Agda.

As the black steed broke into a wide clearing, Davin lifted
his head and shouted, "Goran! Slow your pace."

The red-maned Challing tugged slightly at his reins, allowing the Jyotian thief to ride beside him. "Is this not glorious,
Davin! This is the way we were born to travel! We'll walk the

streets of Weysh ere the sun sets beneath the waters of the
Oceans of Kumar."

"We should ride southward after Lijena," Davin called out.
"With these mounts we can catch up with her by the morrow."

"We go to Weysh!" Goran replied, his eye patch flapping
in the wind.

"But the Sword of Kwerin Bloodhawk! We must retrieve it
for Prince Felrad!"

Davin panted from the dual exertion of shouting into the
wind and staying in saddle. A league of full canter tired a horse
of ordinary flesh and blood. Not so with these magic-bound
beasts. Davin now fully appreciated the threat the Faceless Ones
presented to Raemllyn's rightful ruler. The demons easily offered a match for a hundred or more human warriors, and these
war-horses gave the Faceless a mobility undreamed of in all
Raemllyn.

Although the young freebooter could only guess at the animals' endurance, he feared the horses were capable of tirelessly
racing the wind every hour of the day—and night. But he
realized that if the creatures maintained this easy pace for ten
hours a day, a company of the hell riders might span the breadth
of the continent in less than a week.

"Oh, no, you Jyotian lowlife!" roared Goran. "We go to
Weysh. We've followed that skinny hussy of yours for the better
part of half a year. No more will I go achasing across the face
of Raemllyn like some tired old hound. Not until I've had my
fill of wine and decent meat—and sampled *all* the other pleasures Weysh has to offer—will I even consider tramping off
after Lijena again. And even then I promise you nothing!"

"You let your gonads think for you," grumbled Davin. "We
can catch Lijena, recover the Sword of Kwerin, *and* arrive in
Weysh before we would have on ordinary steeds."

"*I* let my gonads think for me? That's a rich one!" Goran
put his heels to the demonic horse's flanks. The sleek black
mount lunged ahead, doubling its already prodigious speed.

Davin's heels answered in kind, urging his flaming-hooved
steed after the Challing. He tightened his grip on the saddle
horn to maintain his balance. The lack of a steady seat stemmed
not from the horse's uneven strides, but from the rider. Although an accomplished horseman, Davin bordered on exhaustion. Scant opportunity for rest had presented itself between
battling the Narain and Lorennion's horrors. Nor had three days

of tracking Lijena on foot provided needed sleep.

His own weariness convinced Davin that Goran spoke the truth. If he couldn't stay erect in the saddle, how could he hope to wrest the Sword of Kwerin from Lijena? She had proven herself more than a match for three Faceless Ones. Better to rest, Davin told himself, *then* seek her out.

"Aye," Davin called to his friend. "We ride to Weysh, tarry there for..."

Davin's words trailed off and a frown creased his brow. Goran appeared curiously hunched toward the neck of his mount when he disappeared behind a screen of trees then rode into sight once again. Davin wiped wind-whipped tears from his eyes, thinking the light and the moisture played a trick on him.

It didn't.

Nor was the rider ahead of him the shaggy-haired Challing!

"Goran!" Davin drew his sword as his heels dug fiercely into the horse's sides. "The Faceless Ones!"

How or why, the Jyotian didn't know, but one of the Faceless had intercepted them. The hell-spawned demon now spurred his mount after the changeling!

With a glance over his shoulder to make certain a second Faceless One didn't ride at his own heels, Davin leaned from one side of the saddle to the other. He craned his neck to its limits, but was unable to see Goran beyond the hellish rider. No doubt Goran reined his mount in a reckless headlong drive, attempting to elude the monster behind him.

The heels of his boots digging into his horse's flanks again, Davin hefted his sword and swung it in a flashing arc above his head. There he held it poised for the downstroke while his fire-hooved steed gained ground on the hell rider ahead.

Patiently he held himself ready for the one blow that might—just might—take the demon unaware. Squarely he eyed the back of the black cowl which hid a face and head no man had ever seen. His horse edged beside the Faceless One's mount; Davin swung downward with every ounce of strength he could muster.

And missed!

Beneath him the unearthly horse bobbed to the left to avoid two waist-high saplings in its path. The slight jerk to the side was enough to spoil Davin's aim. Instead of tempered steel landing squarely on the demon's neck, the blow sliced through empty air.

The element of surprise was lost!

An eye burning like a red coal snapped around to glare at the Jyotian from beneath the woolen hood of black—an eye that seemed to pierce his soul. A skeletal hand dropped one rein and pointed at him, as if the Death God, Black Qar himself, beckoned.

Battle cry roaring from chest and throat, Davin swung his blade a second time, intent on slicing into that seething orb.

The hell rider's skeletal hand rose and deflected the blow with contemptuous ease.

In the next instant Davin's mount shied to the left once more, to avoid a row of low shrubs. Human and demon parted, each swinging in opposite directions as they circled to face one another.

A cold fear filled the young thief when his gaze lifted to meet the creature who approached. Within the pitlike blackness of the cloak's cowl the coal-red eye burned with magical intensity.

Davin frowned. Something was amiss!

It struck him like a blow from a smith's hammer—*coal-red eye!*

"Goran?" Davin called, uncertain of himself. "Goran, is that you?"

Within the cowl's blackness he barely discerned a fox-fur patch where a left eye should have been. The glow of the demon's remaining eye dulled to an orange ember.

"Of course it is I. Who else would it be?" came a cracked, rasping voice. "Though I'll be damned if I know why you try to kill me!"

"You . . . you're in the guise of a Faceless!"

"Eh?" A skeletal hand lifted. One flickering eye fixed on the bony parody of a hand. Then the hand vanished beneath the crimson tunic and ripped its front to reveal a scaly chest oozing yellow pus from a dozen ichorous sores.

"This is truly amazing," came the grating voice that Davin now recognized as Goran's. "I seem to have transformed into one of them. Amazing—even for a Challing."

The laughter that erupted from the demonic throat echoed through the forest. Crepuscular animals both large and small stopped in their food gathering and froze, remaining silent until the danger from the lowest depths of Peyneeha passed.

"Change back," Davin said. "Now. I won't ride with you in that form."

In the past Goran displayed the uncontrollable ability to transform himself into female form. Goran-Glylina had tried to seduce Davin, and for that the Jyotian might never forgive his friend. But this! To turn into their demonic foe!

"I hadn't noticed the change come upon me," Goran admitted. "I prefer this form for riding. My arse had started to sprout blisters, but the transformation made that particular pain vanish."

Goran rose in black iron stirrups and swung to one side. A short, stocky tail whipped out from beneath the long cape.

"Goran!"

"All right, all right. Let me concentrate. This is difficult for me. I have little control over the transformations, even after partaking of the mage's odious potion."

The Challing's head drooped forward. When he lifted it again, Davin cried out in alarm.

The glowing eye had been replaced by a more familiar jade one with gold flecks. Even the face was Goran's, but the rest of the body remained demonic!

"I know," sighed Goran. "There seems some small problem with my control. It is as capricious as before."

Davin watched while Goran struggled with his shape. Scales bulged, rolled, melted to smooth, unblemished flesh of milky white. The Challing's hellish shaped altered, growing more compact and curvaceous. Not Goran, but the beguiling Glylina sat astride the Faceless One's steed.

"Satisfied?" the Challing demanded in a voice octaves higher than Goran's. The tone gradually deepened as the changeling's body once more began a metamorphosis, swelling and expanding until Goran One-Eye sat before his human friend. "I feel as if I'd been riding for hours now. I hope you're happy."

"You *have* been riding for hours. And you're supposed to feel tired. You're no demon."

"No," Goran said haughtily, "but I am Challing."

The flame-bearded giant swung his steed around and set off again at the breakneck pace. Davin heaved a sigh and followed, glad that the broad shoulders and flowing red hair of his friend now showed above the dark cape of the Faceless.

• • •

Davin Anane wasn't sure when he drifted to sleep. One moment he rode, rocking with the motion of the racing horse. The next he toppled to one side, his equilibrium gone. The demonic mount never slowed or heeded its rider's troubles. Davin yelled as he tumbled from the saddle to land heavily on his backside.

Groaning, Davin carefully tested arms and legs to assure all bones remained intact before shoving to his elbows. He winced, not in pain, but from the sight of the flaming heels of his demon horse disappearing into the forest. In a few seconds the forest swallowed the sizzling sound of the horse's passage.

"Goran!" he called. "Goraaan!"

The Challing did not answer.

Muttering a curse that maligned his friend's parentage, Davin rose and brushed away the snow caked on his backside. With another curse he started after the vanished horse. Finding the trail proved easy; all he had to do was follow the icy puddles of melted snow left on the forest floor where the demonic steed had trod. Less than a minute after he'd begun his on-foot trek, the pounding of hooves sounded ahead of him. Hand on sword, Davin stepped to one side, half hidden by the bole of a towering ironwood tree.

"Where are you, Davin? Did that horse kick out your brains?" Goran shouted.

Davin heaved a sigh of relief and stepped out to greet his friend.

"I fell asleep," he explained. "When the reins slipped from my hands, the horse took the bit between its teeth and bolted. He left me asprawl in a snowbank."

Goran roared with unbridled delight. "You humans never were much as horsemen. Come along now. Climb behind me, and I'll show you how to ride a real horse."

Davin hugged the cloak tighter around him. The long plumes of fire gusting from the horse's nostrils, and the pure hatred in those wild eyes, did little to dispel Davin's worry about riding double. A hasty sidestep save him a seared foot as the horse tried to plant a fire-wreathed hoof atop his boot.

"Hurry up." Goran leaned down and stretched a hand toward his companion.

The movement was a mistake.

With back arched and all four feet leaving the ground, the black horse lunged upward. Goran flew through the air, tumbling head over heels. Only his plowing into the snow ended a bellowed string of curses.

The demonic horse hit the ground running. In a matter of seconds the forest swallowed its dark form.

Davin shook his head when he turned to his companion. "Yes, that's something to admire in you Challings. Your wondrous ability to soothe horses. Almost magical, I'd say."

"Sarcasm ill-becomes you, Davin Anane," growled Goran. He pushed to his feet and peered into the wood. Fingers of steam rose from the ground, marking the hell horse's path. "Too bad it didn't bolt in the direction we head. Weysh lies yonder." Goran pointed to the left, then started off, lumbering along in silence for a hundred paces.

Davin trooped beside him, secretly glad to be afoot. Although their progress toward Weysh had been spectacular, and now his feet would be hurting like a million fire ants nipped at them before arriving, Davin preferred this to the presence of the hell-spawned mounts.

Or he was glad—until Goran began singing a bawdy ballad concerning a winsome wench, her cuckolded husband, three sailors, and a large dog. Before Goran completed the second verse, Davin longed to have the Faceless One's horse beneath him once again.

"There. At last." Davin Anane dropped atop a smooth boulder and rested.

Spread at the base of a low, forested hill sat the bustling seaport of Weysh. The young thief pulled off his boots and wiggled his aching toes. The rush of relief almost overwhelmed Davin. They had slept soon after losing their hell horses, awoke at dawn, and spent the entire day walking.

Now they arrived at their destination, the sun in their eyes and Weysh inviting—as much as any wilderness town with buildings constructed of unpainted logs could possibly be.

"I'm for a large tankard of ale," said Goran. "*Two* large tankards. Two *very* large ones."

"I'll match you drop for drop," declared Davin, "but there's a small problem facing us."

"Ah, yes, your skinny wench. She stole everything but a few paltry rations." Goran patted his empty money pouch.

"We'll have to ply our trade," Davin replied with unashamed

relish. It had been overly long since he pitted his wits against a merchant with more coin than caution. Davin sobered a bit when he realized that it had been in Weysh where he'd last worked—and the outcome had been a close one.

"What was that jewel merchant's name?" Davin asked. "The one you claimed would never notice a few gems missing from his trove?"

"Parvan Weeselik. Yes, Weeselik. Peculiar name," mused Goran. "Do you think he has replenished his supply? We ought to be able to make off with them and never break into a sweat. After all, we've already scouted his establishment."

"Let's pass Weeselik by this time and work on others more likely to forget a few coins missing." Davin remembered too well the gem merchant's ability with a blade.

"You're turning into a spoilsport," Goran said. "It must be the way you moon over that blond wench. But that'll change. I'll find you a lusty woman, one with meat on her. Lijena will be but a vague wisp of a memory ere the night is through."

Davin wished that it might be as simple as Goran's words. But love was not a simple emotion. And he now knew that he *did* love Lijena Farleigh.

"Hurry, Davin!" Goran urged. "I long for the pleasures of civilization."

Davin tugged his worn boots back on and started down the hill toward the dish-shaped depression that held the port city. In less than an hour they passed the city guard and slipped through streets shrouded in darkness.

"They seem active this eve." Goran eyed two passing guardsmen. "See how they patrol in pairs? Some come and go in squads."

Davin nodded. The city guard stayed to the brighter lit regions of the city, but such activity boded ill. A multitude of guardsmen could respond quickly, should the cry go up.

"There looks like a rowdy gathering." Goran pointed ahead. The giant smiled broadly and started off, arms swinging, arrogance etched along every line of his face and in every movement.

Davin watched as the Challing stopped beneath a torch hung from the side of a building and hunkered down just outside a circle of dice players. When none moved to permit him entry into the circle, Goran shifted first to the left, then to the right, wedging forward. Two men went sprawling to either side of him to open a gap large enough to accommodate the change-ling's bulk.

"Ah, a friendly game. Hurry, man, don't let the dice grow cold and unlucky," Goran said when Davin stepped behind him to peer over a shoulder.

Several of the men exchanged glances, then looked to a sapling-skinny man with thinning brown hair and a ragged scar beneath his left eye.

"What say you, Elozzi?" a blond gambler asked.

"A silver eagle to ante," the skinny man answered with a shrug. "Money is money whether from friend or stranger."

"Goran—" Davin began, in an attempt to steer his friend away from the game of chance.

"Come now, what do you take me for?" bellowed Goran, rising to his full height and puffing out his immense chest. "A brigand? No! I am a gentleman. Does one gentleman ask an-other to show his coin before play?"

Several of the players drifted back. Elozzi boldly eyed Goran. "Aye, stranger, that's what we do in Weysh. Too many damned sailors hereabout. They play and lose, promise to pay and then sail with the morning tide, never intending to harbor here again. Cash and nothing else will do in this game."

"But it's just a *friendly* game!" protested Goran.

"Nothing friendly about it, stranger. We play high stakes. Ante or move your carcass." The words came from a man to Goran's side.

"A rude one, wouldn't you say, Davin? I must teach him a lesson in polite behavior!" Goran grabbed for the man, but Davin interposed his body between Challing and victim.

"A moment, Goran. These are good people," Davin said, then turned to the intended victim. "Excuse him. We've been on the trail for many days. Civilized behavior needs cultiva-tion." He held out his hand.

Hesitantly the gambler took it, and they shook. Davin smiled and slapped the man on the shoulder in a comradely fashion, then turned back to Goran. "Go on, play, Goran. And do show the color of your coin."

As Davin released the man's hand, the gambler edged back and slipped into the darkness with a cautious glance over his shoulder.

"It seems there'll be one less player to try for your purse, my friend." Davin slapped Goran on the shoulder. His hand smarted from the impact; it was more like hitting a tree trunk than a human being.

However, the action allowed Davin to pass the Challing the purse he had filched from the gambler when they had shaken hands. Although the Jyotian preferred honest thievery to gaming, Goran was known to be lucky with dice—especially when his magical abilities were aplay, as they had been this day.

Goran grinned broadly while he dug into a pocket, produced the leather pouch Davin had placed there, opened the drawstrings, and dropped a coin into the center of the ring. "Let's play."

Elozzi passed the Challing the dice and began the pot with his own coin. The remaining ten men tossed in their own money, calling out their bets.

Within an hour Goran had rolled Emperor's Eyes five times for big pots and managed to drive away all but four of the original eleven players.

"A tidy winning." Goran's chest swelled as he raked in the last pile of coins.

"No more," Elozzi declared with a shake of his head. "My purse grows too light, and the winter is too cold to go without food."

The three other players nodded in agreement, tucked lightened pouches in belt or pocket, and left. Elozzi rose and walked beside Goran to pat the Challing on the shoulder.

"You play well, stranger," he said. "Now let me have half the take."

"What? Why should I? I won and—"

"But not fairly. You are slick, but I am better at cheating. You worked them well, from the time your friend lifted Chesso's purse to the way you manipulated the dice in your favor. But I watched, and I knew."

"It's a fair trade, Goran," Davin spoke up. When in a strange city one played by the street rules, if he intended to survive. "He helped us out. Several times I saw him switching the dice so you'd win."

"You have sharp eyes, too," said the man, "as well as good judgment."

Elozzi motioned to an alley behind him with a tilt of his head. From the shadows emerged a half-dozen brigands, all armed with drawn short bows. If either Goran or Davin had made a wrong move, those arrows would have feathered them like birds.

"A fair trade, as I was saying," said Goran. "And do allow us to buy you a tankard of ale." Goran slapped the man's back as though they had been lifelong friends.

"I accept your generosity," Elozzi replied with another nod, which sent his men back into the veiling shadows. "I would like to talk with both of you. I like the style you displayed tonight and might have use of men with such skills."

"Need of us?" Davin arched an eyebrow.

"I, shall we say, control matters in Weysh. Especially along the docks." Elozzi flashed a sly smile.

"A good man to know. Let us buy you *two* tankards. We can discuss this after our thirst is slaked." Goran almost lifted Elozzi off his feet as he steered the smaller man down the street.

Davin followed a few paces behind, aware of their silent cortege. Elozzi didn't trust them any more than Davin trusted the self-proclaimed ruler of Weysh's docks. On either side of the street moved a score or more armed men.

"Here," Elozzi said. "A good place." He indicated an inn, the Broken Mast.

Of all Elozzi's henchmen who followed, Davin noted only one entered to seat himself near the door. The Jyotian decided most inside the inn were also Elozzi's minions. The others could forego their bodyguard activities and return to cutpursing.

The unlikely trio sat in the center of the room, an open position that left Davin feeling uneasy and vulnerable. Goran seemed not to notice, and Elozzi smiled broadly—too broadly for Davin's comfort. If anything happened, they had to cross several rows of low, battered oak tables to get to either window or door. Similar tables separated them from a flight of wooden stairs leading to the inn's second floor. Worst of all, Davin couldn't sit with his back secure against a wall.

"Ale! For the three of us," cried Goran.

He pinched a buxom brunette serving wench on the bottom when she answered his call. She squealed, but displayed no sign of taking offense as she hurried to fill the order with three foaming mugs of ale. Davin drank slowly, worrying over poison. Elozzi quickly finished his, Goran only a fraction of a second behind.

"Another!" demanded the Challing.

"You are a gracious winner," said Elozzi. "I like that. As I said, I can use a pair like you. Quick fingers," he eyed Davin's hands, "and brawn able to turn aside any challenge." His gaze shifted to Goran. "You would provide me with skills desperately needed along the docks."

"You think to recruit us?" asked Goran. He downed another tankard and motioned to the serving wench for a third.

"Why not? You are new to Weysh."

The tone caused Davin to stiffen. There was something in the way Elozzi spoke that said the wharf thief recognized them. Had the merchant Parvan Weeselik offered a reward for the capture of his elusive jewel thieves?

The question resolved itself quickly. Davin heard the door open. He turned to see Chesso, the man he'd robbed. Davin had wondered why Chesso hadn't noticed the lightening of his purse and returned to the gambling ring. Now he knew. Chesso had summoned the city guard.

"There," cried the man. "They're the ones Merchant Weeselik's offered the reward for. Don't let them escape!"

Four city guardsmen pushed into the room, swords drawn, cutting off escape into the street!

# chapter

## 4

DAVIN ANANE TOOK in the situation with one sweep of his gray eyes. To make a stand against so many amounted to suicide. But to sit motionless while the trap snapped shut would result in the same end.

The last son of the House of Anane had no intention of dying this night.

With a smooth swipe of an arm, he sent the tankards flying from the table. A curtain of blinding, frothing ale showered the air before him. Halting shouts of surprise rose from guardsmen and tavern patrons alike. In that instant of hesitancy Davin jammed an elbow into Goran One-Eye's ribs to alert the Challing, then leaped to his feet, grasped the edge of the wooden table, and upended it.

A menacingly bestial growl in his throat, Goran shoved from his chair. The growl transformed into a deafening battle cry when the barrel-chested changeling hefted the table and charged toward the inn's door.

The guard sergeant barked a warning—too late! Table held before him like a massive shield, Goran plowed into the guardsmen. Swords, arms, and legs helplessly flailed the air; with cry and groan the four weaponsmen crashed to the stained wood floor. All lay pinned beneath the table, squirming, Goran's weight holding them securely to the floor.

Steel hissed on leather as Davin freed his sword. His wrist flicked and the blade's tip leaped up to nip at Elozzi's throat. "You betrayed us!"

"Not I." Elozzi eyes went round and wide with fear. His Adam's apple bobbed nervously. "Chesso . . . Chesso was the one. I have nothing to do with the city guard. Less than nothing."

"Bah." Davin lashed with his right foot.

The toe of the young Jyotian's boot connected squarely with

the Weysh thief's crotch. Elozzi screamed in agony as he reeled
back to collapse amid a table of bystanders.

"The back door!" Goran nodded to an exit beneath the stairs
at the rear of the inn.

Giving the table one last hard downward shove, the Challing
spun and charged through the room, scattering drunken patrons
to each side. Obstacles cleared from the escape path, Davin
followed in his friend's wake.

The red-maned titan's stride quickened as he approached
the rear door. With a bull-throated roar, he tucked chin to chest,
hunched massive shoulders, and charged straight through the
barrier without pause to see whether the door was locked or
not.

Davin threw left arm across his face to protect it from flying
splinters, but neither faltered nor slowed his pace. He didn't
dare. Angry shouts from behind him announced that additional
guardsmen entered the tavern from the street to aid their companions.

Goran roared again, war cry rebounding from the stone walls
that hemmed both sides of the narrow alley behind the Inn of
the Broken Mast. The cause of the gargantuan's distress—two
city guards that attempted to bar his escape!

A mistake for which both guards paid dearly. A
sledgehammer-sized left fist smashed into the face of the first.
The guardsman toppled, blood flowing from crushed nose and
shattered teeth. Of the two, fortune rode on his shoulders.

Goran's sword flashed past the falling man, driving tempered tip into the chest of the remaining guardsman. Steel drove
straight and true. The second city guard also fell, not in howling
pain, but in death, his soul tendered to the god Black Qar, who
men call Death.

Another chorus of barked orders and shouts came from the
street at the end of the cramped alley. Human and Challing
skidded to a halt atop cobblestones. Guards would soon swarm
into the narrow passage before and behind them, trapping them
between naked sword blades!

The two adventurers' heads jerked from side to side, seeking
an avenue of escape. Davin cursed Raemllyn's gods and this
fish-stinking seaport that once again sought to rob their lives.
The last time he and Goran had entered Weysh, they had burned
down half the wharves to elude the city guards.

"The wall, Goran!" Davin pointed to the top of the stone

wall that rose eight feet into the air. "From the wall to the roofs!"

Together they leaped. Their hands deftly found holds atop the wall and they scrambled upward. Along the wall they ran, jumping onto the roof of an adjacent warehouse and from there to the roof of another building. Behind them in the night the startled cries of the city guard rose, unable to comprehend how the two strangers had slipped through their hands.

Knowing the guards would eventually place the pieces of the puzzle together and realize the fugitives had taken an aerial route, Davin and Goran pushed on. With footfalls softer than fog, the pair of thieves made their escape over the rooftops. Only once did Goran pause. When Davin turned to see what stayed his friend, he bit at his lower lip to stay the barrage of profanities that tried to spit from his tongue.

With obvious delight, Goran peered through the upper story window of a bawdy house.

"Ah, Davin, the Sitala are so cruel. Except for the fate those five gods have dealt us, we might be in there enjoying the pleasures that fire a man's veins!" Goran gusted a huge sigh that wracked his entire frame.

Davin snaked out an arm, snagged his friend's collar, and yanked the Challing after him. If the entire city guard of Weysh had been alerted—and Davin saw no reason to believe otherwise—being caught on precariously sloping rooftops would be as dangerous as being trapped in an alley with guardsmen on both sides.

A half hour and fifteen buildings later Davin paused to search the ground below the roof of the home on which they stood.

"A garden?" Goran asked while his good eye took in the expanse of manicured grass, shrubs, and trees spread two stories below.

"Too big for a garden. One of Weysh's parks perhaps." Davin estimated the area below covered a square equal to eight of the town's blocks. Flickering light from torches and braziers on the surrounding streets reflected from a small statue near the center of the park.

"A monument of some sort," said Goran, having noticed the same statue. "A bit sparse for any true honor. But then I might be wrong. Imagine the spring sun shining down on this tribute to a great man, families with food spread before them on the ground, a veritable feast! All the sweet, young girls flirting with their suitors. Ah, this place is a wonderment to me, Davin. Truly it is."

Davin frowned. Sometimes the Challing's thoughts wandered. Davin wished Goran would go join them. All he wanted was freedom from pursuit, not high-flown words about imagined Weysh social customs. His attention returned to the park. City guards were neither to be seen nor heard.

"It looks safe enough. That knoll and those shrubs yonder might provide a bit of cover." Davin pointed beyond the statue, to what appeared to be a well-concealed hiding place.

Goran didn't answer, but stared dreamily at the statue, lost in woolgathering. Once again applying an elbow to the Challing's ribs to awaken his attention, Davin turned to walk along the edge of the roof until he reached a drainpipe. Like a spider moving in the night, the young thief agilely shinnied to the ground, waiting for Goran to join him before hastening across the street and into the park.

"Covered with bird shit," Goran grumbled when they reached the statue. "And so small! No bigger than an ordinary man! What sort of tribute can that be?"

"A deserved one." Davin read a bronze plate attached to the base of the figure. "Seems he was a traitor. Betrayed Weysh to pirates some fourteen years ago."

Goran grunted with disgust when they started toward the knoll. A noise like a muffled cough or the clearing of a throat spun the two companions around. Both wrenched swords from scabbards.

"What was that?" Davin whispered. "I heard no one come up behind us."

"Nor did I, and my night senses are sharper than a mere human's." Goran's head swiveled from side to side. No one was anywhere to be seen.

A plaintive whimper disturbed the night. Both thieves' heads jerked to the right. Their gazes homed on the statue.

Or what they believed to be a statue.

"It's alive!" Davin gasped in disbelief.

"Help me," a weak plea touched their ears. "Th-they ensorcelled me. I meant nothing by my deeds. Nothing. Pray, good sirs, help me. Save me from this awful magic."

A sea bird dislodged from its perch atop the statue's head and fluttered off into the night. Davin climbed onto the statue's base and stared directly into the face. Eyes blinked at him, eyes that contained infinite agony. Lips moved so slightly Davin would have missed it if he hadn't been so close.

"If you can't free me, kill me! I beg you!"

"Did you truly betray the city to pirates?" Goran inquired before Davin could recover from the shock that the statue lived.

"I did. I make no false pleas. But they've held me prisoner for fourteen years! Fourteen years of suffering and humiliation!"

"Not long enough!" Davin jumped down and shook his head. "The pirates who sail along the coast of Upper Raemllyn are vicious. To turn them loose on an undefended town is a crime rivaling anything Zarek Yannis has done."

"No, I beg you—"

"At least he gets plenty of fresh air," remarked Goran. "When Velden held me prisoner in his odious sewer, I sorely lacked for gentle sea breezes and the sight of any living creature that was not a rat."

"*Please!*" the statue pleaded. "Please aid me."

Without another glance or word, the two thieves turned broad backs to the ensorcelled traitor, slipped over the low knoll they had spotted from rooftop, and hid among the shrubs growing there. Nor were they the first to seek concealment in the park. The remains of several small cooking fires bespoke others who once found refuge behind the knoll.

"Do you suppose our frozen friend might turn us over to the city guard if they happen to ask?" Davin wondered aloud.

"No doubt. But would they believe him, is a better question. I suspect the guards come along and leave seed at his base to entice the birds. What a fate!" Goran chuckled.

"We shouldn't take the risk." Davin glanced around. The hiding hole looked far more secure from the rooftop. "This might be the first place they'd look also."

"Let's not be hasty." Goran settled down on his haunches and studied the area. "We have good views to all sides. It would take a small army to roust us. Why not rest for a few hours, then press on? There must be good people somewhere in Weysh willing to put us up for a price."

"You still have your dice winnings?" Davin lifted an eyebrow in question.

"And some additional," boasted Goran. "When I knocked Elozzi over again as I dashed from the inn, I just happened to get tangled in his money pouch. Strange how it came free to weigh me down."

The Challing laughed, obviously delighted at his own exploit; Davin joined him. This was the best he'd felt in months. They had returned to their old, familiar ways. Living by their wits, taking their pleasure when and where they could. It was a good life; one Davin enjoyed.

Not like they'd endured since Lijena had been kidnapped, demon-possessed and driven across Raemllyn into the hands of the master mage Lorennion.

"You take first watch. Wake me in an hour." Davin settled atop the grass, folded his arms across his chest, and rolled onto his side.

Goran grumbled something about his own weariness. His complaints fell on deaf ears. In minutes Davin Anane slept soundly.

## chapter

# 5

"DOUBLE THE REWARD." Parvan Weeselik could not conceal the disgust in his voice.

The young gem merchant was usually a patient man, but now he struggled to control his mounting anger. The two thieves who had possessed the temerity to rob him—*him!*—had returned to Weysh and once again eluded the city guardsmen. It was as though the two brigands were smoky phantoms rather than flesh and blood. Weeselik chafed at the guards' lack of skill and the thieves' obvious overabundance of the same.

"But Parvan, you already offer five hundred gold bists. Isn't a thousand too much, even for such dangerous criminals?" A honey-haired woman with a full figure, lounging on a sleeping couch, paused from the jellied fruits she popped into her mouth to eye the merchant.

Weeselik watched enthralled for a moment as varicolored fruits vanished behind lips as honeyed as the sweets the seductress ate. He shook himself free of the spell the woman wove around him.

"Not at all, Holimma. Allow one rogue to steal my gems and all will flock to my door like crows to a corpse. This is prevention." Weeselik rocked back in his chair and glanced at the nervous guard captain standing before his desk. "Go and find them."

"Yes, lord." The officer snapped to attention with a smart click of his heels.

When the guard turned to leave, Weeselik called after him. "And remember what my father did to Partal-syn-Mor."

The soldier blanched and hastily retreated.

"Why must you always bring up that moldy old statue?" Holimma asked. "You know your father had little to do with it. If anything, he shouldn't have sentenced poor Mor to such

37

a fate. After all, your father made a fair living selling supplies to the pirates."

"No one ever claimed my father wasn't hypocritical. He had the spell placed on Mor to keep the man from revealing everything about his own dealings with the pirates. But, dear Holimma, that is history. We have only the present to occupy us." The gem merchant grinned.

"Then let's make the present memorable." Holimma held out slender arms to her handsome companion. The movement opened her thin gown, and it fell about her slender waist, revealing flawless white skin. The courtesan shifted slightly, allowing the gown to slip even lower. She smiled, and the merchant was lost.

Parvan Weeselik went to her, the two thieves momentarily forgotten.

"This isn't the best place in Weysh to hide." A disembodied voice spoke.

Davin Anane and Goran One-Eye jolted upright, the sun of new morning in their eyes. Davin shook his head to clear away sleep cotton. He had been on watch, but had slowly drifted until he was more asleep than awake. Even with senses fully alert, he saw no source for the voice.

"Elozzi," Goran growled meanacingly. "The bastard's found us!"

"Of course I have. I told you that this was *my* city. I control movement all along the docks, and you're scarcely a bowshot away," Elozzi answered, but did not step into view.

Davin blinked again. Masts of ships rose just over treetops masking the harbor from direct view. He shuddered, thinking of what could have happened had a sailor found them instead of Elozzi. The merchant Weeselik might want them, but his wrath would be nothing compared to the outraged captains whose ships Goran and he had set afire during their first visit to the seaport. Escape had been easy, but it had left behind a boiling wake of destruction and resentment. Davin wondered how he'd ever let Goran talk him into returning to Weysh so soon.

"You are quick fingered, that I'll grant you." Elozzi's voice hardened. "If you don't return my share, plus a full half of all remaining, you'll end up like Mor, the statue man you met last night."

"To end as a statue with a bird-shit crown!" Goran groaned. "Is that how criminals are dealt with in Weysh? How barbaric!"

"But effective. We keep crime well organized and within bounds. You two disrupt our orderly system. For that you'll have to pay—dearly."

Elozzi rose as though he pushed from beneath the ground itself. It was mere illusion. Davin scanned his surroundings in the light of the new day and understood. The Weysh thief had wiggled on his belly along a gulley that had been hidden in the night's darkness, when they first sought shelter here.

"You are valuable to Lord Weeselik. I wonder why?" Elozzi eyed them as if they were prime cuts of meat presented for the High King's approval.

"Lord Weeselik?" asked Goran. "He rules Weysh?"

"His wealth does. The city guard has been alerted to a fine reward for you." Elozzi idly picked at his teeth with a dirty fingernail.

"How much?" The Challing's curiosity was obviously piqued. "What are we worth?"

"Not worth the bird dung mounded on Mor's skull, if you ask me," Elozzi answered. "But Lord Weeselik has offered the princely sum of five hundred silver eagles, or so say the guardsmen."

"So the actual amount is greater." Davin knew how guardsmen operated. A few coins would change hands at each level of command. The actual reward might be as much as a hundred gold bists.

"I have my sources of intelligence," bragged Elozzi. "A hundred bists is the true price on your heads. What makes you worth so much?"

Davin relaxed. Elozzi would have turned them in directly to Weeselik for the full amount if he'd been interested only in reward. The man no doubt saw other opportunity in the situation. A chance to gain more information about Weeselik's business and profit by a safer future robbery of the merchant's trove? Or was it something Davin couldn't guess?

"Weeselik cannot stand to know that there is a man handsomer than he in Weysh." Goran tilted his head toward Davin. Before the Jyotian thief could even laugh at such a wild claim, Goran added, "Or one such as myself, who is both handsomer *and* more intelligent."

"More puffed up with his own vanity," muttered Davin.

Louder, to Elozzi, he said, "We seem to be obligated to you. Pay him, Goran. And perhaps friend Elozzi will be able to arrange a method for us to elude the net Weeselik casts around the city."

"You have found the proper one to furnish such a service." Elozzi smiled broadly, showing yellowed, cracked teeth. Elozzi leaned his head to one side and studied the two fugitives. "For a price."

"Thief! Brigand!" roared Goran. "You take all our coin, then demand more!"

Elozzi shrugged. "If it is too big a burden..."

"How much for passage out of Weysh?" Davin asked, recognizing the futility of their position.

"Depends on your destination."

Davin thought hard. Upper Raemllyn abounded with pirates preying on trade along a northern sea route. The northern route past cold Faldin to Rakell was the worst stretch of all, fraught with both pirates and fearsome demons.

"Faldin," Davin answered. "That'll be far enough."

"By Nyuria's scabrous organ, no!" yelled Goran. "Why pay this weasel only to go a few leagues? We go to Evara on the eastern coast or nowhere."

"Goran—" Davin began.

The red-bearded giant cut him off with an obscene gesture.

"Evara, eh?" mused Elozzi. "That's a long and arduous journey, especially now."

"What do you mean?" asked Davin. "The worst of the winter storms are past."

"Are you completely unaware?" Elozzi asked, eyes widening in surprise.

Davin couldn't decide if this were an act or Elozzi was truly shocked at their ignorance.

"Zarek Yannis mobilizes for the coming battle. All Raemllyn buzzes with the war cries," Elozzi continued. "Prince Felrad has fortified the city of Rakell. He has shouted his challenge from the Tower of Lost Mornings in Kavindra."

"Prince Felrad went to Kavindra?" Davin didn't have to feign shock. The High King's capital of Kavindra was securely under the usurper's thumb. For the prince to go there to make the formal challenge spoke much of Felrad's courage—or did he only bluff? It mattered naught to Davin. If Yannis moved his legions—and the Faceless Ones—toward Rakell and Prince

Felrad, then the rightful heir to the Velvet Throne needed the Sword of Kwerin Bloodhawk all the more.

And Lijena held the spell-forged blade!

"You look startled. Is this unknown to you?" asked Elozzi.

"It is," Davin admitted. "Are you saying that Yannis is strong enough to patrol the northern waters of Upper Raemllyn and prevent passage?"

"Hardly, but he has dealings with the pirates. Free of any of the High King's constraints, they sail and plunder at will. Prince Felrad's ships seldom get through."

"You're saying we'd have to book passage on one of Yannis' war vessels?"

"Not necessarily," Elozzi said, with the sly smile of man who knew more than he said. "For a price, anything is available in Weysh."

"How big a price?" Goran asked.

Davin Anane groaned when Elozzi told them. To obtain the price, they might as well turn themselves over to Parvan Weselik and collect his lofty reward. Even with a hundred bists from such a suicidal act, Elozzi's quote would leave a huge deficit and no coin for Evara.

The man dressed in the guard uniform bowed from the waist and waited for Parvan Weeselik to notice his presence. After a pause long enough to assure the underling knew his proper place, Weeselik looked up and nodded.

"Lord Weeselik, there is success in our dealing."

"You have them?" Weeselik's brow lifted with interest.

"No," the guard said uneasily, knowing the merchant's temper. "Not precisely. But there has been contact. My spies reported the terms of a deal made, and from this, well . . ." He shrugged thin shoulders.

"One thousand gold bists," Weeselik said coldly. "That will be your reward when you deliver their heads to me—separated from their worthless bodies, of course!"

"Lord," the guard said cautiously, "I have a better plan."

"What?"

"Allow me to explain."

The guardsman did, and at first Weeselik frowned. But as the onionskin layers of the plot peeled back, a smile curled his lips. He finally broke out in laughter.

"Do it. This appeals to my sense of justice. Yes, yes, do it as you've explained." The merchant waved the guard away and turned back to his books, with their long columns of figures.

A thousand-bist reward would injure his profits for this month, but not seriously. And he might even be able to get enough enjoyment from those thieves' fate to offset the loss.

His father had ensorcelled Mor and turned him into a living statue. Parva Weeselik's revenge on Davin Anane and Goran One-Eye would be even sweeter. He chuckled as he worked far into the afternoon.


"Look at my hands," complained Goran. "Bloody! My fingers are bloody from lifting purses like a petty criminal! It's a crime, I say. A damned crime."

The Challing sank to the ground and leaned back, supported by the gentle knoll a few paces from the ensorcelled traitor Partal-syn-Mor.

"Of course it's a crime," Davin replied, studying his own hands in the dusky light of evening.

Although Goran exaggerated about bloody fingertips, his words rang far too close to the truth. Davin's fingers threatened to draw together and cramp in knotting pain from the rigors of the day. Neither Goran nor he worked cutpurse well—not one purse after another. Their talents lay more in the quick smash and run, the subtle entry and theft, the duping of the greedy to separate them from surplus coin.

Those approaches to easy money took time, and time was one thing that rapidly grew short. Everywhere they turned they saw patrols of the city guards. If they thought the guardsmen had been alert when they entered Weysh, those minions of law and order now slept with one eye propped open to assure they missed nothing. Such was the power of a big reward from a prominent citizen.

All that was left to Davin and Goran was working the marketplace crowd, taking a few coins here and there. They had both purloined so many pouches this day, they lost count of the drawstrings they had yanked open.

"There must be a better way," Goran moaned pitifully.

"There is, but we didn't have time for it." Davin's ire had been raised by Weeselik's reward. He longed to return to the merchant's jewel shop and pilfer the bounty of riches contained within. But one look at the security had forced him to drop

thoughts of petty revenge. Weeselik had patrols of private guards
pacing the front and rear of his store. Several more sat on the
roof and inside.

"We have enough," said Goran. "I got a full two hundred
bists."

"And I another two-fifty. We can pay Elozzi for our passage
and still have a pair of coins to rub together for luck."

"Luck?" muttered Goran. "What's that? We have offended
fair Jajhana. No longer does the Goddess of Fortune smile on
us. We are doomed, Davin, doomed!"

"Then be doomed elsewhere, for I have arranged your passage to Evara." Elozzi's familiar voice floated on the evening.

Again neither Davin nor Goran had heard or seen the man's
approach. Yet Elozzi stood before them, a dark brown cloak
tightly drawn about his thin body. "The passage is arranged.
That is, if you have the four hundred bists."

Davin silently threw the heavy pouch to Elozzi. The Weysh
thief opened the drawstring and quickly counted the coins inside. A smile on his thin lips signaled his satisfaction, and he
motioned for the two to follow.

Jyotian and Challing trailed Elozzi, checking the route for
any sign of treachery. They found none. When they set foot
on the rickety wooden dock, evening had turned to night.

Elozzi pointed. "That one. A cargo ship bound for Faldin
and Evara. It leaves with the tide, so you must hurry. Take the
small boat and row out."

Davin lowered himself to hands and knees to peer over the
edge of the dock and into the inky blackness underneath. He
heard a small boat knocking loudly against the pilings.

"Row?" grumbled Goran. "We have to row? With our hands
left in bloody tatters from stealing your damned passage money?"

"Oh?" Elozzi said mildly. "You wish someone to help you
out to the *Twisted Cross?*"

Davin, still on hands and knees, glanced over his right
shoulder at the changeling. His gaze froze before reaching
Goran. A dozen armed guardsmen swarmed from out of the
night's blackness. Ere he could shout a warning, a heavy blow
to his shoulder drove him to the wooden pier. The young Jyotian
rolled to one side, numbed right arm useless. He fumbled at
his sword with his left.

The effort was wasted.

A moan came from above him, and in the next instant

Goran's falling bulk pinned him securely to the dock. Davin peered up, and his heart turned to a lump of ice. Elozzi threw back his brown cape. Under it lay the uniform of a city guardsman.

The treacherous Elozzi turned to a newcomer and said, "Lord Weeselik, they are yours."

Davin saw Parvan Weeselik smile. He would have preferred rage. That he would have understood.

"Well done, Elozzi. Here's your reward. One thousand gold bists."

_A thousand!_ Davin's mind cartwheeled, startled by the princely sum. No wonder Elozzi had betrayed them.

"Now, get these mongrels out to the _Twisted Cross_. Captain Iuonx awaits them," Weeselik commanded.

Davin struggled to shove the unconscious Challing aside. None of this made any sense. It sounded as if Weeselik ordered them to the _Twisted Cross,_ their original destination. Before he could wiggle free of the Challing's bulk, Parvan Weeselik walked beside him, and with great deliberation, slammed a booted foot into the side of the Jyotian's head.

Stars spun in wild new constellations before blackness deeper than the darkest night consumed Davin Anane.

# chapter
## 6

A TIDAL WAVE of water as cold as the heart of Ianya, that legendary northern realm of perpetual ice and snow, broke over Davin Anane. He jerked and groaned; both were mistakes!

In the Jyotian's head a devilish demon awoke armed with a smith's hammer. The damnable creature worked from within, attempting to take off the top of his skull with pounding blows that reverberated through the brain and down the spine.

Nor did the vibrations stop there, but spread in quaking circles that set his stomach to churning. Bitter bile pushed from gut to throat and into mouth. Davin fought back with a gagging cough that equaled the hack of a man with a tubercular lung, an action that began the cycle anew.

"This'un'll live, Cap'n Iuonx," a man cackled with unrestrained delight.

*Captain Iuonx?* The name wedged into Davin's throbbing head, but he could not place it. He tried to turn without increasing his agony. He failed. His eyes shot open, searching for this Iuonx and the owner of the cackle.

For a heart-stopping second, he thought a new woe had been added to those assailing him, and that he'd been struck blind!

Gradually his vision focused on a strangely bouncing, swirling world. Yet another ache invaded his body. His shoulders and wrists cramped. The cause—two cold, iron bracelets locked about his wrists, and an attached thick-linked chain that hung from the darkness above. Davin half stood and half dangled in the bonds.

Wincing, he got his feet under him and stood to relieve the knives of pain in his shoulders. He blinked. The floor under boot was wooden, as was the curving wall he discerned through bleary eyes. Both floor and wall glistened water!

"What about the other man, the big one?" a voice that sounded like the grating of boulders asked.

"I've another bucket to wake that'un, Cap'n!" the other cackled his answer with relish.

Davin turned slightly to see the shadowy forms of two men, one who lifted a wooden bucket and flung its contents onto the sagging body of a one-eyed, red-haired giant.

*Goran!* The Jyotian thief's fuzzy brain cleared when he recognized his friend dangling from chains similiar to those binding him. Goran's bulk neither quivered nor shook when the icy water splashed over him. He simply hung there limp and lifeless.

*Dead?* Davin's heart tripled its pace; could the Challing be dead? *How?* The thief could find no answers in his confusion.

"This one's in worse shape'n I thought, Cap'n," came the first voice. A note of concern replaced the cackle. "He's still out. No more response than we get off the Cape Terror lighthouse."

"He'd better not be as dead as everyone at the light," the second voice answered with a grunt of disgust. "If he's dead, I'll have Elozzi's black heart. I paid *good* coin for *two* ablebodied sailors! See if he breaths, Arkko."

"Aye, Cap'n Iuonx!"

*By Yehseen's poxied staff!* Davin silently cursed as memories deluged his pounding brain. Elozzi, that treacherous mongrel, was a city guardsman who profited from all sides. The whoreson robbed Goran and him of passage money, sold them to the jewel merchant Weeselik, *then* got crimp money from Captain Iuonx!

Threefold profit from a single transaction! If there were a master thief in the port of Weysh, it surely had to be the skinny scar-faced Elozzi. Davin longed for a word and ten minutes alone with the misbegotten swine. He had another payment he wished to deliver to the bastard-born snake!

"This'un's heart still beats, and I can smell his foul breath, Cap'n," said the sailor called Arkko. "But it'll be hours 'fore he comes around. Perhaps Elozzi had to drug one so large?"

A sigh of relief escaped Davin's lips. *Goran still lives!*

"Mayhaps, but I like it not. Nothing was mentioned of drugs," Captain Iuonx answered with another grunt. "At least the other one is coming around. The *Twisted Cross* needs another pair of hands on deck. Get him down, Arkko."

The two turned from Goran and stepped back to the young Jyotian. The smaller of the men, Arkko, unhooked a brass key from a broad belt about his waist and reached up with hands as rough and twisted as driftwood. When the man unlocked the manacles, an evil grin split a face crisscrossed with scars that a thick beard failed to hide.

The smell of rotting fish was on his breath when he spoke: "Welcome to the crew of the *Twisted Cross*, sharkbait! I be your worse nightmare come to life—Arkko, first mate to Cap'n Haigex Iuonx, the bravest man ever to sail the northern waters of the Oceans of Kumar!"

Davin ignored the mate and stepped before his superior, while he rubbed circulation back into his throbbing wrists. "Captain Iuonx, there's been a mistake. I paid Elozzi for passage. We had a small disagreement and—"

Davin gasped—groaned! The captain of the *Twisted Cross* drove a short wooden stick into his seasickness-plagued belly. The Jyotian doubled over, clutching his gut, trying not to retch.

"Speak when you're spoken to." Captain Iuonx stiffened to a height that equaled Davin's own six feet. The sailor's features visible beneath a salt and pepper beard that bushed over chin, cheek, and neck darkened. The man's coal-black eyes narrowed. "I'd as gladly rip your tongue from your mouth as to listen to ye prattle!"

Davin swallowed the protest on his lips. The captain's tone left no doubt that he was a man of his word.

"Have ye ever sailed before?" Captain Iuonx lifted Davin's chin with the stick.

"Yuh, yes . . . sir." The young adventurer cautiously added the *sir*. "Years ago I sailed a merchant vessel bound from Jyotis to Weysh."

"Good. Did ye work the riggins?" Captain Iuonx pursed his lips when Davin nodded in the affirmative. "Then ye've saved yourself from swabbin' the decks—this day at least. Get him topside, Arkko."

The first mate eyed the Jyotian. "He's a mite under the weather, from the look of him. Ain't got the sea under his step yet."

"Get him to work. That'll put him right. We don't want him getting sick all over the decks when we hit the Near Point whirlpool." Captain Iuonx stalked off without another word, climbing a ladder to the deck above.

Arkko glanced back to Davin. "Come along, landlubber. We'll make a seaman of ye, or ye'll die tryin' to learn."

For an instant Davin considered jumping the mate. He quickly pushed aside the idea. What if he overcame the man? Davin was without sword, and there was a whole crew to defeat above. An impossible task for one man. And one Davin doubted could be accomplished even with Goran at his side.

The thief cringed when he glanced back at the unconscious Challing. Manacles designed for wrists of ordinary thickness bit into flesh. A rivulet of blood trickled down each of the changeling's forearms.

"Don't worry so much about him when it's *your* worthless hide that'll be flayed off if you give us any trouble," Arkko said when he noticed the Jyotian's interest in the flame-bearded gargantuan.

Davin said nothing, but followed the *Twisted Cross*'s first mate up a narrow ladder into the light of day. No land was visible off either side of the three-masted vessel.

"Here!" Arkko popped an oil-treated thick hide slicker against Davin's belly. "Ye'll need this up there. Else ye'll freeze off your jewels ere the sands of an hourglass pass."

Davin donned the waterproof fur-lined coat, then walked toward the riggings Arkko pointed to.

"The bastard Arkko'll kill us all 'fore we reach Cape Terror," to Davin's right a gnarled sailor with white hair and beard grumbled beneath his breath as he dipped a cup from the water barrel.

"Cape Terror?" a crewmate muttered. "We'll be sitting in Jajhana's lap if we make it that far. Pirates'll take us first!"

"If we're lucky," broke in a third sailor.

"You deem a pirate attack lucky?" Davin could no longer hold his tongue, as he dunked his own cup into the barrel.

"We'll be dead—and the demons will suck our souls from still living bodies," the sailor answered without a glance at the newcomer.

"What demons, Gagno?" demanded the first sailor. "What demons are these ye speak of?"

"Ones even Black Qar and his demon Nyuria fear," Gagno replied solemnly. "Ones so fearsome you die of fright just gazing on their evil visages!"

Both of the man's companions voiced their opinion of Gagno and his wild tales. Not so Davin. Since Zarek Yannis had summoned the Faceless Ones from their dark realm, Raemllyn had been plagued with myriad grotesque creatures not born of this world.

Lifting the cup to wind-chafed lips, the Jyotian slowly drank. His gaze darted about the *Twisted Cross*. During the long day above he had been permitted no time to study his situation. Now he realized how desperate it was. Twenty sea-hardened men, those loyal to Captain Iuonx, stood positioned about the ship's railings, armed with sword and whip, ready to deal out agony to anyone who faltered to heed an order. The remainder of the crew—thirty to forty additional hands, he estimated—were like him, men kidnapped and sold into temporary slavery.

"Wouldn't drink all that, if I was ye," Gagno warned. "It's all the fresh water ye'll be getting this eve. And ye'll be needin' something to wash down the muck that passes for food on this ship."

Davin glanced at the older man and saw him turn and walk to a line forming near the stern. At the head of the line stood a steaming black pot and stacks of wooden bowls. Realizing dinner was now being served aboard the *Twisted Cross*, Davin followed Gagno's lead.

"To the end of the line." Arkko shoved the young Jyotian aside when he finally reached the pot and bowls.

Davin's protest was cut short by a sharp blow to the side of his head. Groaning, he staggered a moment, then dropped to the deck on hands and knees. Through the haze of pain he saw Captain Iuonx and his swagger stick.

"Do as the mate orders or ye'll find yourself chasing the ship." Captain Iuonx turned and left.

"Chasing the ship?" Davin mumbled amid a spinning daze.

"I put a rope around ye waist—or maybe your worthless neck—and then heave you behind the *Twisted Cross*. With luck ye might last a few hours before ye drown. Otherwise the sharks . . ."

Davin needed no further explanation. Standing on rubbery legs, he managed to stumble to the end of the line. When he again faced Arkko, the mate scraped the bottom of the large pot and managed to dish two small spoonfuls of thin gruel into his bowl.

"You'll have to be quicker next time," Arkko said with a sarcastic grin slipping across his lips.

"How?" Davin cried out, angry.

Arkko turned and sneered. Holding out a hand, he rubbed fingers and thumb together. Davin recognized the gesture from long years of bribing officials.

With a silent curse the Jyotian thief took his bowl and settled cross-legged on the deck beside a grate-covered hold. If he wanted to eat aboard the *Twisted Cross*, he had to bribe the mate. *But with what?* Elozzi had taken all their money before sending them to the ship.

The few drops of gruel did little to satisfy Davin's hunger or mounting frustrations. Wiping the bowl clean with a finger, he set the bowl aside. He froze before his fingers released the wooden container. His gaze probed the hold beneath the metal grating. Below, two sets of manacles and chains dangled from a beam. The same chains that had held Goran and him. Both were now empty. Where was Goran? Had the Challing somehow managed to free himself?

Picking up his bowl, Davin returned it to a stack beside the now empty pot. Instead of returning to his place on the deck, he angled to the right and hastily disappeared down the ladder leading to the hold. Quietly he called out; the Challing didn't answer.

Soft moans came from a small rope locker at the back of the hold. Davin silently moved through the stacks of cargo until he saw a partially opened door. A thin yellow beam of light sneaked from the room. Davin moved closer and peered inside.

A startled gasp pushed from his lips! Within the locker a grizzled sailor and a beautiful raven-haired woman were locked in a passionate embrace. The voluptuous seductress the Jyotian well knew from Agda's wood!

Yanking open the compartment door, Davin bellowed, "Black Qar take you! How dare you do it again!"

The startled sailor rolled off the half-naked woman, eyes wide. "Didn't know she was yours," the sailor said, a crooked smile on his lips. "However, I enjoy Glylina's charms so much, she's going to be mine from now on!"

In the batting of an eye the man whipped out a dirk hidden from the top of a high leather boot and lunged for Davin.

The Jyotian adventurer sidestepped and landed a hard fist on the sailor's neck. The seaman stumbled and fell to one knee. A knee to the man's chin, with all the force of Davin's pent-up frustrations, finished the lusting seafarer, leaving him unconscious amid coils of rope.

"I do so love it when men fight over me," dulcet tones chimed behind Davin.

"I'm going to slit your throat from ear to ear," the heir to the House of Anane said. Retrieving his dirk, he spun about. "I warned you to never again change into female form."

"Nay, Davin, nay. You warned me not about my female form." Glylina modestly clutched an oversize crimson blouse to her pillowy breasts. Coral nipples poked through open folds of fabric. "Don't, Davin. I didn't do this to mock you. It—it was the only way I could escape my chains. This is just part of my Challing nature. You can't hold that against me."

"Nyuria take you!" Davin cursed and spat. "Glylina, there's no use for you here!"

"You *do* remember." Glylina coyly batted long, dark eyelashes at him. "I said I'd never attempt to seduce you again. I said nothing of abandoning that gross Goran body for this one when necessity demanded it."

"Why was it necessary?" asked Davin.

Glylina held up her slender wrists. Davin saw where tender Challing flesh healed itself from the cruel bite of iron. The hands attached to those wrists were small enough to slip free of the iron shackles without opening them. He tucked the dirk into his belt with a grunt of approval.

"And there is . . . or was need of Glylina's services," the temptress said. "There are other benefits to be gained from this shape."

"What do you mean?" Davin glared at her.

"How much money do you have?"

"None," Davin said in disgust. "Elozzi robbed us both before selling us to Captain Iuonx. You know we both came aboard the *Twisted Cross* as paupers."

Glylina reached under a thin pad of burlap and pulled out a bulging pouch. She tossed it to Davin, who caught it. Frowning, the Jyotian opened it. Silver eagles shone in the dim light of the rope locker.

"There must be fifty eagles!" Davin exclaimed. His surprise faded and anger replaced it. "You've whored yourself! That's how you got this!"

"Nay, not whored myself—though I would have, had you not entered so rudely." Glylina shrugged. "I lifted the purse when he first embraced me."

"Change back. Into your Goran shape." Davin's disgust

grew. If Goran's actions were unpredictable, Glylina's were doubly so!

"It's not that easy. You know that, Davin." A look the young thief couldn't interpret passed over Glylina's face. "I seem to be trapped in this fine body for the moment. Why not take advantage of it?"

Slim hands opened the dirty tunic. The two perfectly shaped breasts revealed jiggled temptingly before Davin's amazed stare.

"Goran, uh, Glylina, I warned you. . . ." He advanced.

"Davin, please! I didn't mean it! 'Twas only a jest between friends!" Glylina hastily closed Goran's blouse, which swallowed her diminutive form.

There was no hint of sincerity in the Challing's tone, which Davin ignored. What bothered him was the strange attraction Glylina held for him. Worse was the surge of lust that stirred his loins when she batted those wondrously long eyelashes in his direction. Nor could he disregard the curve of her sleek, comely—

"Change. Now." Davin's hands balled into tight fists, knuckles glowing white. This *was* Goran! He forced himself to repeat the thought again and again.

"I'll try, but I have little control. Masur-Kell's potion returned some of my power, but not enough. Not enough to— *Aaiieeee!*"

Davin's gray eyes widened in horror. The beautiful Glylina transformed into a hideously twisted beast. Joints cracked and supple limbs elongated in a sickening parody of human form. He blinked; as quickly as the awful change had come, it passed. Goran lay gasping on the pallet, his mighty chest struggling to supply enough air to his lungs.

"Are you all right?" Davin mumbled the first words that penetrated his brain.

"I was better as Glylina." Goran pushed to his elbow with a throaty growl and glanced around the cramped compartment.

Davin's gaze followed his to the sailor crumpled among the ropes. "What are we going to do with your paramour?"

"Throw him overboard. He's of no use to me now! Who'd notice one less scurvy knave in this crew?" Goran waved away his companion with disdain.

Davin decided leaving the sailor where he lay was as wise a course to follow as any. Glylina would vanish, and neither Arkko nor Captain Iuonx would believe there actually had been a woman on board the *Twisted Cross*. Davin looked questioningly at Goran. He didn't believe the Challing would shift form again—if he could help himself. To do so now might mean they'd both "chase the ship."

"At least we can eat," Davin said, balancing the money pouch in his hand. He explained the first mate's toll on meals aboard the vessel.

"I should have continued my little enterprise," said Goran wistfully. "That pouch hardly contains enough for one good meal at those rates."

"We can make more. The sailors don't look as if they understand odds. I'm sure there are games of chance running constantly." Davin hoped the lure of dice would entice the Challing more than further exploration of Raemllyn's oldest profession. There were few things in this world Goran liked better than gambling—especially when the dice were weighted in his favor.

Goran gave a noncommittal grunt.

Davin changed the subject, feeling it better to put Glylina far behind quickly. "How long have you been free? Have you explored the hold? What cargo does the *Twisted Cross* carry?"

"I awoke and freed myself less than an hour ago." Goran rose and buttoned the shirt over a hairy chest. He found his discarded eye patch and tugged it over the hollow socket of his left eye. "Don't you know anything about this vessel? What information have you gleaned?"

"I've been above all day, working in the rigging. Doesn't it show?" He held out wind- and sunburned hands and gingerly rolled back the collar of his tunic for Goran to see what damage the elements had done.

"You humans are definitely an inferior life-form," Goran commented without a trace of malice. "Change your skin. A Challing can."

"Repair your damned eye," Davin flared. For whatever reason, Goran had both eyes when he altered form, but was unable to replace the lost eye when in his Goran shape.

"The potion has curious effects. When I return to my full power, I shall repair the lost orb. Until then I think the eye patch gives me a dignified aspect."

Goran tossed his red mane back and struck his interpretation of a regal pose. Davin laughed. The Challing's vanity definitely had a human quality.

"Did I ever tell you how I came to lose my precious left eye? It was shortly after I was yanked from my beloved realm of Gohwohn. I was serving as the captain of a—" Goran began.

Davin cut off his friend before the changeling filled the *Twisted Cross*'s sails with gusty hot air. "Time would be better spent examining the cargo to see what Captain Iuonx finds worth risking pirates and Zarek Yannis' war vessels to sail this northern route."

"Aye, and the sea monsters," Goran added while he followed his companion from the rope locker. "Poor Byatt spoke of them before your arrival. Said they were vastly more dangerous than anything Zarek Yannis might set afloat. That a man's life might be so short created a burning passion in his breast, or so he told Glylina."

Davin said nothing. Even Gagno's frightened telling of demons in these waters hadn't fully convinced Davin they existed. To be certain, Raemllyn's oceans and seas spawned gigantic serpents, but they ordinarily shied from the ships of men. The Faceless Ones, the Narain, those were real. Sailors' tales of monsters set lose by Nalren, God of the Seas, always abounded. Those yarns were usually born out of one too many mugs of ale or spiced wine.

Most of the cargo hold was filled with bales of textiles that were of little importance except to merchants awaiting their arrival in distant ports.

"Cloth? For cloth Captain Iuonx risks his life?" Davin shook his head, unable to comprehend why the captain would even consider setting sail with such a cargo.

"We didn't even find any food," complained Goran. He rubbed his growling belly. "I'm inclined to find this Arkko and buy supper. They must keep the food under lock and key to prevent filching."

"Cloth?" Davin wondered aloud. It was ridiculous for any captain to brave the waters of Upper Raemllyn with inferior grade cloth filling his hold. There had to be something more; something hidden from a cursory examination.

Tugging the stolen dirk from his belt, the Jyotian leaned to the nearest bale and slit it with the double-edged blade. Only the tatters of severed cloth fell out of the cut.

Undaunted, he thrust his hand into the bale. Nothing. He shoved harder, his arm vanishing all the way to the shoulder.

A knowing smile uplifted the corners of his mouth when he looked at the fire-beard titan and winked. He pulled out his hand and held it before Goran. Clutched in his palm lay a small packet wrapped in heavily oiled cloth.

"Ah, this is more like it!" Goran eyed the bundle with greedy interest. "What have you discovered, my quick-fingered friend?"

Davin opened the heavy parcel. Small gold disks tumbled forth. He turned them over and examined each side of several disks. Blank face and obverse and milled edges told him nothing.

"What kind of cargo is this? A bist without a dead king's portrait?" Goran scoffed. He lifted a coin-sized disk and felt it with fingertips, as though unable to accept what his eye perceived.

"A bist in appearance," Davin said slowly. He hastily used the tip of his dirk to scratch a disk. A dull sheen like that of lead marred the disk's surface. "A thin sheath of gold on the outside—base metal inside. These are fake planchets."

Goran scowled.

"Look," said Davin, warming to Captain Iuonx's scheme as he saw it. "What would you do if I gave you such a disk? It looks like a gold bist, although it contains only cheap metal. But in all other respects it is identical to a bist—size, weight, color, milling."

"But it's not," protested Goran. "There's no official portrait on it."

"All it needs is to be stamped with the proper dies. Stamp it, cut in a portrait, and what do you have? Counterfeit coins worth a hundred times the cost of manufacturing," Davin explained.

"Why doesn't Captain Iuonx do the stamping himself?"

Davin smiled. "Bistonia is the center of banking for Raemllyn. What if a set of dies was stolen and taken to, say, Evara?"

"Then those with the dies would need the raw materials for their counterfeiting," finished Goran. "Ah! There is genius at work here. Almost equaling my own! What better way of getting the counterfeit coins into circulation than to have a ship's crew spend them in every port city along the way."

"Or have the captain sell them," Davin suggested. Another thought occurred to him. "You could finance a considerable army with fake coins."

"Zarek Yannis?" Goran's good eye narrowed.

"It's possible. Captain Iuonx need not fear the usurper's warships if this is true."

"I could toss Captain Iuonx overboard and end this scheme."

"No!" Davin shook his head. He doubted even Goran could get past Iuonx's armed gorillas on deck. "Let me think on it. We might be able to turn this to our own advantage."

"There's no way we could spend so many bists without attracting unwanted attention, even if we had the dies," Goran said with a disappointed sigh.

"But Prince Felrad might find it possible. How many fake bists would it take to undermine Yannis' treasury?"

"By Nalren's seaweed beard, I'll find those slackers," came Arkko's booming voice. Davin hastily thrust the planchets back into the bale, smoothed over the cut, and motioned to Goran. The Challing already stretched out on a soft bale, eye closed and feigning sleep. Davin mimicked his friend's repose.

"There they are," came the grating voice. Harsh hands pulled Davin and Goran erect. "To the deck or I'll cut your throats. Ye've watch to stand this eve."

"Wh-what's happening?" Davin stammered, trying to sound as if he'd just been awakened.

Neither Arkko nor the sailor with him answered. Davin and Goran were roughly shoved on deck.

The tiny dot on the horizon held Davin's full attention. He couldn't identify it, but a coldness formed in his gut. In a few seconds a sailor perched high atop the main mast confirmed his suspicion.

"Pirates!" went up the cry from the lookout. "Pirates sailing down hard upon us!"

# chapter 7

"ARM THE MEN, Arkko!" Captain Iuonx shouted above the clash of waves against the hull and the stiff wind that billowed the sails.

Confident and firm was the sound of that command, but the two-fisted, white-knuckled grip with which the *Twisted Cross's* captain grasped the ship's rail, belied the tone of his order. As did the way Iuonx's eyes betrayed flickering fear when they fixed unwaveringly on the vessel that sliced through the waves on a direct course for the merchanter.

"Pirates!"

The single word ran like a shudder through the crew. Davin's head, like those of the others, turned to the lone vessel rising to challenge the cargo ship's right to sail Raemllyn's seas. Through a squinted gaze the Jyotian saw the long, thin green pirate flag aflutter from the tallest of its masts. Like a great wooden shark that tasted the scent of blood, the craft's sleek prow cut through whitecapped waves with unerring certainty.

Nor was there hope for escape, the young thief realized. The elements that had so aided the *Twisted Cross* in her journey northward, now allied themselves with the pirate ship. To flee the attack meant Captain Iuonx would have to tack against the wind. By the time the merchant vessel reset its sails for such maneuvering, pirates would be swarming over the decks. If ship and crew were to survive, the challenge had to be met and overcome.

"I pray to the gods your wrists and arms are as stout as they look!" Arkko slapped the flat of an off-balance sword against Davin's stomach.

Before the adventurer could answer, the *Twisted Cross's* first mate strode to Goran. He hastily eyed the muscular titan, then shoved a gnarled double-spiked war club into his hands.

"At least we have weapons!" Bulging muscles of his right

arm aripple, Goran swung the two-handed club with contemptuous ease and decided relish. "All we need now is a head or ten to bash."

"Brave words from the mouth of a walking dead man!" This from Gagno, who stood white and shaking with a rusty harpoon clutched in his hands. The sailor leaned over the railing and looked as if he were about to lose the pitiful gruel meal he had bought from the first mate. "It's said no mere men sail these waters! I've heard the tales—ships of demons that beset merchanters! Demons seeking souls for Black Qar as well as common booty!"

"Yon ship appears substantial enough to me," Goran said, disregarding the man's fear with a toss of his fiery mane. "'Tis no phantom vessel assail there. Nor are those wraiths crowding her deck, but men of flesh and blood. And men can die!"

Two ships' breadth away from the *Twisted Cross* the grimy faces that stared at Davin *did* appear to be human—almost.

Something was out of kilter.

For a moment that something eluded the Jyotian, then it penetrated. The pirates' expressions were not what Davin expected from ruthless sea brigands. Rather than howling masks twisted in bloodlust, these were the visages of men lost in ecstasy.

"Prepare to repel boarders!" Captain Iuonx's booming command drove the strange thought from Davin's mind. The captain thrust a thick bladed cutlass toward the pirate vessel while he clutched his wooden swagger stick in the other hand.

Like striking snakes, grapnel hooks trailing stout lines arced through the air from the attacking ship. A scream jerked Davin's head to the left. Rather than wooden rail, a three-clawed hook found flesh. Snagged back to gut, a sailor writhed and twisted to free himself as the line tautened; he was wrenched overboard, lost in the foaming brine.

A multitude of other steely points bit into deck and rail. Here and there sword and dirk managed to sever line from hook; the effort was an exercise in futility. From the deck of their craft the pirates hauled on their well-placed lines. Hand over hand they worked, drawing the two vessels together in a bone-jarring impact.

Prepared as he was for that clash of wooden hulls, Davin's feet flew out from under him, sending his weight tumbling into Goran. Together the two impressed sailors spilled to the deck.

By the time they untangled themselves and recovered their footing, pirates leaped over the rails. The cacophony of cold steel meeting cold steel rang through the air.

Still no battle cry tore from the invaders' throats. Nor had the pirates' expressions changed. They appeared driven by religious fervor rather than greed or savagery. If anything, they seemed *happy* to be off their ship and onto the decks of the *Twisted Cross*.

Again Davin shoved aside the pirates' puzzling visages, leveling his own blade to meet a blond-bearded brigand who ran forward with cutlass raised.

Yet it was with words rather than flashing steel the pirate met the young Jyotian!

"Lay down your blade, friend," the man's voice gently pleaded. "There is no need for spilling blood. We come to offer you untold bounties of the spirit!"

Davin didn't listen. The blond man's words simply provided him the opportunity to strike first. His wrist flicked and the point of his blade leaped up, meant to skewer the attacker's throat.

With lazy ease the pirate's blade fell, batting away the deadly tip.

"Friend, hear me. Do not deny yourself the chance to bathe in the golden light of the Gods. Lay down your ..."

Davin didn't hear. Forcing strangely sluggish muscles to respond to his mental commands, his arm and wrist twisted his sword in a semicircle to dance above his opponent's blade. Like lead his hand once more lifted the sword tip toward blond beard's throat.

Again the pirate brushed the weapon side like a man flicking away a bothersome fly.

"You cannot—" The pirate's words ended abruptly. Goran's spiked club bashed into his temple, sending him reeling to the deck—dead!

"Davin!" The Challing scowled at his companion. "What's wrong with you, man? Use your sword. These men are no match for two such as we!"

Davin blinked and stared into Goran's face. The lead in his arm slid into his feet and legs, and that transformed into a treacle-thick lethargy that seeped through body to brain.

"Why fight?" Davin asked, as if he had posed the single question that would unlock the wisdom of the gods themselves.

"For your life!" Goran roared as his club shattered the skull of a pirate who stepped before him with sword and dirk in hand. "Why else would you fight?"

Davin lowered his guard while his gaze roved over the decks of the *Twisted Cross*. Around him officers and crew of the merchanter reached the same conclusion he had—there was no reason to battle these men from the sea who offered them peace and friendship. Davin tossed aside his sword and threw open his arms. Joy filled his voice when he called, "Welcome!"

"Are you mad?" Goran spun about, jaw sagging in disbelief. "They pour onto the *Twisted Cross* like ants onto honey!"

"They mean no harm, Goran," Davin replied with a gentle smile. He held out a hand to the nearest pirate.

The man grinned and accepted his hand, not in anger, but in friendship.

"What kind of witchery is this?" The changeling's single eye narrowed suspiciously. "What spell robs you of your senses?"

Davin's smile only broadened. The Challing was a fool. Couldn't Goran see that they were among friends? These weren't bloodthirsty pirates, but new companions.

Even . . .

"A *god!*" Davin gasped. "A golden god graces us with his presence!"

"What nonsense are you babbling?" came Goran's querulous voice.

Davin didn't bother with his friend. He had no time for the Challing's irritating arguments. Not now—not when a golden-haired god with billowing white wings stepped aboard the *Twisted Cross*. Davin dropped to his knees to worship the deity. It was the only fitting position with which to receive one who cloaked his body with the very clouds.

"Black Qar!" Goran's single-eyed gaze darted from the in-sane Jyotian to the monster that crossed between the pirate vessel and the merchanter. "I thought we'd rid ourselves of *them!*"

"Down, Goran, down onto your knees. Worship our new God." Davin banged his head against the deck in his haste to abase himself before the golden-tressed deity. Never had he seen such eye-searing beauty as radiated from the being who now graced the *Twisted Cross*.

"Davin." Goran dropped beside his friend. The source of the young thief's madness was all too clear. "Don't you recognize *it*? Don't you *remember* what happened in Mapalah?"

"Quiet, the god speaks. He grants us a glimpse of his infinite wisdom!" Davin whispered.

"Black Qar take all the Narain!" But Goran bit back further angry response.

The Challing silently cursed the human weakness that allowed their minds to be easily clouded and ensorcelled. No god strolled across the ship's deck, but a gray-skinned, leather-winged demon with yellowed fangs and small taloned hands. This was a *Narain!*

Brought into this world by the rent Zarek Yannis had torn in the fabric separating the dimensions, the wizard Lorennion had used the mind-warping demons as an advance guard to his castle keep in Agda's wood.

There Goran had first encountered the filthy creatures and seen the minds of his human companions enslaved by the Narain's mental powers. Like faithful hounds answering their master's every command, Davin, Lijena, and the others believed themselves worshipers of gods descended to earth, who dwelled in the gold and marble palace Mapalah.

Only the Challing had been unaffected by the Narain's hypnotic presence. Assuming the form of one of the hideous demons, he had penetrated their magic defenses, discovered that Mapalah was nothing more than a dung-heaped tree. After rescuing his human companions, Goran had set fire to their tree palace and killed the majority of the creatures. Only a scattered few had escaped into the sky.

It was one of those escaped demons that controlled the pirate crew, Goran realized. That explained the humans' curious ecstatic expressions. The pirates fought unknowingly for a demon, their minds bedazzled with golden images of winged celestial beings too pure and good to be mortal.

Goran saw them as they were: gray-skinned, leather-winged, and vicious.

The Narain gave two quick flaps of its wings as it peered around the deck with an arrogance that destroyed Goran's promise to himself not to attack until he knew success was assured. War cry ripping from his throat, the Challing launched himself forward.

The gray horror reacted with birdlike speed and leaped high. Its batlike veined wings furiously beat the air as it lifted from the deck.

"Kill him! Kill the blasphemer!" the Narain's high-pitched voice screeched in horror as the Challing's club with two pointed spikes whistled toward it.

"By Nyuria's burnt arse!" Goran roared in surprise and anger.

In obedience to the demon's unholy command, Arkko's arm snaked out, hand momentarily snaring the flame-haired giant's ankle.

Goran stumbled a half step to gather his balance. But the club missed his mark, the Narain's skull. The tip of one spike sank home, ripping the membrane of an outstretched wing.

Screaming in pain, the Narain wobbled wildly in the air. Its wings flapped in desperation while it righted itself and grabbed a cross spar with taloned hands.

"Stop! You can't kill a god!"

Davin jumped to his feet and clawed at Goran's right shoulder. With a grunt and a swing of his tree-limb thick arm, the Challing sent his friend sprawling backward. Ten other sailors and pirates shoved from the deck and closed ahead of the barrel-chested giant to block his path to the Narain.

Venting a roar that rose from the bottom of his lungs to push from his throat, Goran lowered neck and shoulders and charged. Gagno flew as if he had grown wings when the Challing plowed into the men. Arkko fell next, dragging down a half-dozen others as he tumbled backward, arms and legs flaying.

"Stop him! He defies a god!" the Narain screeched from its perch on the cross spar.

"Come here, birdman," Goran shouted, once more hefting the spiked club. "Come and fight if there's a drop of courage in your craven black heart!"

"Kill him!" The Narain's terrified cry rose an octave in pitch, obviously bewildered by its inability to rob this one defiant man of his senses. "Kill the human scum!"

Goran grinned. He was a Challing, not a human! And Challings were not confused by such diabolical magical mirages, an advantage the changeling played for all it was worth.

With another roaring battle cry, the red-bearded gargantuan swung the club in a circle above his head then sent it hurling upward. The missile missed its mark, spikes embedding themselves in the mast, but the heavy thud of steel to wood distracted the screeching Narain. In that instant Goran leaped for a dangling rope. With the speed and agility of man born to the sea, Goran climbed until he stood on the spar.

The wounded Narain cowered against the main mast.

"You are not like them," it spat in a rasping voice. "What are you?"

"Your death!" Goran carefully placed one foot in front of the other, inching closer to the Narain. Weaponless, he'd have to kill it with his bare hands, a situation that couldn't have suited him better.

Apparently recognizing the seriousness of its lofty position, the gray-skinned demon unfolded leathery wings and lifted into the air.

Like a madman Goran sprang. His arms encircled the Narain's slender waist and closed like a vise.

Together Challing and demon hovered in the air for a wobbling moment. Then they fell. Slowly at first, as the Narain's wings beat wildly to carry its crushing burden out to sea; then they plunged like a rock, their bodies disappearing in a spray of foam as they plummeted into the ocean.

Davin Anane blinked, a cry of horror dying half born in his throat. He shook his head and blinked again. Terrifying reality penetrated his cotton-packed brain. In the instant Goran and the god had struck the waves, the god had transformed into a hideous gray-winged demon—a creature he had first met in Agda's forest. *Narain!* In that moment of realization he understood all that the Challing had done, once more saving him from becoming a thrall of the fanged demons from a realm beyond Raemllyn.

"A rope! Throw him a rope!" Davin cried out when he saw Goran's head bob above the waves. "Get him a rope."

"Aye!" a voice answered from the Jyotian's right.

In the next moment coils of rope snaked outward into Goran's waiting arms.

# chapter

## 8

THE CHALLING PEERED blearily through his good eye and saw Davin Anane offering a hand to help him over the *Twisted Cross'* rail. Accepting the proffered aid, Goran hauled himself onto the deck, heaved a weary sign, then shook his head, sending a major shower of saltwater in all directions.

"You had us fearing you'd drowned," said Davin.

"A Challing can't drown. I don't think." Goran pondered the question for a few minutes, then shook it off as unimportant. Why not change his shape into that of a fish? A big one, to be sure, but fish. Perhaps a narwhal. Or he could have tried to emulate the Narain and sprouted wings to fly.

"The demon . . . I saw it flickering between god and hell creature, but I was helpless against its will"—this from Captain Iuonx, who pushed through crew and pirate to the changeling's side. "Ye killed the demon who enslaved us."

"Aye!" Goran's chest swelled, and he beamed a grin that ran from ear to ear. "Crushed the life from his foul body with these very hands. His bones snapped like the breaking of great limbs of a mighty oak. . . ."

"More likely you crushed the creature with your own bulk when you hit the water," Davin whispered under his breath.

"It was a fight few could have survived," Goran continued, ignoring his friend's sarcasm.

"With that I'll agree!" The captain slapped Goran's shoulder. "Below with ye. You've earned a well-deserved rest. I'll see that hot food and drink is brought to ye to remove the ice from your bones. Never let it be said Captain Haigex Iuonx doesn't reward those who serve him well."

The captain's gaze turned to those around him. "Nor let it be said that I do not punish those who would treacherously attempt to harm my ship. Take the sons-of-sea-slugs who would pirate us, men!"

The pirates no more than blinked and stared in a dumbfounded daze as the *Twisted Cross'* crew stripped them of their weapons and bound their hands. Davin watched in amazement before realizing the attackers had been under the Narain's spell for days, maybe weeks, and had yet to recover from the shock of having their mental chains removed.

"You." Arkko nudged Davin. "Take care of your friend. The Cap'n and I will deal with these bastards!"

Davin didn't argue, but followed Goran into the hold. The Challing found a blanket atop one bunk and used it to towel his dripping hair and face. Another blanket he bundled about shivering shoulders as he sat on the edge of a bunk.

"The water's like ice," Goran said through chattering teeth. "My muscles bundled like cords the instant I hit the sea. A man wouldn't last long in such cold . . . a human, that is."

"There was only the one Narain," said Davin, his thoughts elsewhere. "If there had been more, we would still be under their spell. The few that survived burning Mapalah must have separated."

"Or become separated," Goran said with a shiver. "The winter storms are still active along this coast."

"However, it happened to come here, it seized a crew of the pirate vessel. They worshipped their new captain—as I can well imagine!" Davin shuddered at the memory of his own imprisonment by the Narain. He had seen golden gods and fabulous palaces where there had been only ugly demons and putrescence and filth.

"Here," Arkko called from above. "Give this to your friend, then get topside."

Carefully Davin accepted a bucket the first mate handed down. Inside was a roasted hen and a mug of foaming ale. He passed the Challing his reward. "Not the gruel Arkko slopped out earlier."

Goran grinned as he ripped off a golden brown leg and stripped it of meat in one bite. "If there were more, I would offer you some, Davin. But this hen is far too small for one as large as myself. And . . ."

Davin left his friend muttering as he climbed back to the *Twisted Cross'* deck. A cold chill ran along his spine when he saw the harsh punishment Captain Iuonx had decreed for the Narain's pirate crew.

The pirates begged for mercy; some openly wept. For Captain Iuonx the matter was resolved. Coldly he watched as man after man was tossed into the rolling sea.

Only when the last had been banished to this watery exile did Captain Iuonx board the pirate ship. He ordered Arkko and a dozen trusted crewmen with him. Davin watched from the deck of the *Twisted Cross* while the captain unloaded what meager treasures there were to be found.

He seemed perplexed that a pirate ship carried so little gold. Davin didn't bother informing him that the Narain cared nothing for wordly riches. This scavenging mission was for slaves—human slaves to serve the Narain's every whim. Davin envisioned the pirate ship scouring the sea lanes and returning its hapless victims to land where the Narain built another "palace."

Stripped of its valuables, the captain ordered the pirate vessel sunk. Arkko complied by opening the ship's sea cocks.

As the merchanter's sails billowed and she once more slid northward, the pirate ship listed to one side, then filled with water and rapidly sank. So it was the *Twisted Cross* sailed away on the fresh breeze, captain and crew oblivious to the pleas for mercy from a full forty men still treading water.

Only when the cargo ship rounded an outjut of land did the wind drown the cries of the doomed men. Davin shivered again, his attention turning back to the *Twisted Cross* and her crew. Arkko supervised the sewing of ten bodies into hastily constructed canvas bags. Ten bodies—ten crew members who had resisted the Narain's damnable power long enough to be cut down by pirate blades.

"It'll cost us more than them men," old Gagno whispered as he slipped to Davin's side. "Cap'n work us to the bone. Still, what's left of us won't be enough. He'll have to put in at Faldin to hunt up more men."

"To hunt more men . . ." Davin's sarcasm faltered, washed away by an unexpected glimmering of hope. "Faldin, we'll put in at Faldin!"

Certain he went unwatched, Davin slipped into the hold to repeat what Gagno had said to the Challing while Goran finished the last of his mug.

"So?" Goran stared at his Jyotian friend and belched. "What means Faldin to us?"

*"So,"* Davin persisted, "this presents us an opportunity straight from Jajhana's generous palm. Iuonx will have to put in to Faldin. If we work well until then—"

"He'll trust us in port," finished Goran, grinning with understanding. "And we find our way to land and freedom."

"A good plan," Davin said, "since I have no desire to make seafaring my life."

"Land to the starboard!" the lookout's cry echoed to the deck below.

All the sailors rushed to the right side of the merchanter to gaze at the harbor that opened in the distance. Only Davin and Goran hung back, feigning disinterest at the prospect of nearing Faldin. As they'd anticipated, Arkko came by and used a short whip to drive the sailors back to their stations. The mate glowered at the two adventurers but said nothing.

Davin winked at Goran, who smiled broadly. They were as good as ashore. They put their backs to heaving on a rope that furled the sails. By the time the *Twisted Cross* swung into Faldin's shallow harbor, they were exhausted but pleased. Arkko and Captain Iuonx took them for loyal crew members now, hopefully forgetting that the two were purchased and impressed into duty.

"We've lost too many crewmen to continue," Davin heard the captain say to Arkko. "We've got to recruit more in Faldin or be forced to turn back."

"Crimps are expensive," the mate said.

"Damn the expense. We must get to Evara. The pirate ship put us a day behind schedule. If only we hadn't lost so many men in that battle." Captain Iuonx walked to the rail and peered inland at Faldin. "A miserable port, this one."

Davin edged closer to hear the captain's reason for thinking Faldin such a bad port.

"No honest crimps work here. Can't buy good seamen anywhere but in Weysh."

"We have a pair of workers in the red-bearded giant and his scrawny companion," said Arkko.

Davin silently cursed. He didn't want praise, he wanted to be ignored. If he and Goran were at the forefront of Iuonx's thoughts, the captain might order chains prepared to hold them until Faldin lay far behind. Davin wasn't sure of the ship's next port of call, but it would be many weeks distant. Of that he was certain.

"We'll need a dozen more like them to get past the whirlpool." Iuonx scratched at his beard.

"And the Cape Terror lighthouse," added Arkko.

The rest of their conversation was lost in the loud lapping of waves against the *Twisted Cross'* hull. Davin moved away, not wanting to be seen.

He hurried below decks to where Goran played dice with several of the crew. As usual the Challing won consistently. But he had tempered his zeal for gambling and his skill at winning with a modicum of common sense. If he'd won too much, the rest of the crew would have slit his throat and tossed him overboard.

"A fantasy brought on by poor food, nothing more," insisted Goran. "There's no wench aboard this ship. Why, where would one so lovely hide?"

Davin's pulse tripled. Three others knelt around the dice ring; the one shaking his head was the sailor the Jyotian had caught with Glylina.

The man shook his head. "I saw her, I tell ye. A lovely one she was, too. Like nothing of this world. Fair of face, and full of figure that promised the pleasures of a high-priced courtesan of Kavindra."

"What do ye know of the capital's courtesans? Ye've spent your entire life at sea. And what courtesan would have ye in her bed?" another sailor jibed, and winked at his companions.

"But I tell ye, I saw her. It was the wench that took me purse!" Glylina's would-be patron protested.

"Like as not it was that ugly redhead walrus in Weysh that seduced ye and took your purse," another of the men replied, laughing with delight.

The hoodwinked sailor protested, which only drew more laughter. Goran looked up and caught Davin's nod. Collecting his winnings, the Challing disengaged himself from the dice game and drifted off, apparently to find a hammock to sleep. He managed to pry loose a locked hatch and emerge on deck. Davin joined him seconds later. The sun had set and the *Twisted Cross'* running lights cast dancing shadows across the harbor.

"We can escape now. There's a longboat pulled up and waiting for Captain Iuonx and Arkko to go ashore. They're to meet with a crimp and buy new slaves for the crew."

"They'd best think of purchasing two additional ones—to replace us!" Goran chuckled, his eyes lifting to Faldin's harbor lights.

Davin pulled the Challing down behind a pile of ropes when

Captain Iuonx and Arkko stalked by. Their heavy footfalls told of anger in the officers. Davin whispered to Goran, "Do you think they've found us out?"

"More likely someone stole food from the locker. I heard Arkko complaining earlier. I think he steals it himself to maintain a hold over us," the changeling replied.

Quieter than shadows, the Jyotian and the Challing slipped over the rail and dropped into the boat. Before they could unlock the davits and begin lowering the small craft to the choppy water, they heard the officers returning.

". . . go in now and be back before midwatch," Arkko said. "That'll allow you time to meet with the crimp."

"They'll find us," muttered Davin, realizing their tenuous plan might shatter in the next heartbeat.

He and Goran needed minutes not seconds to make good their escape. The pair would be discovered before they managed to unknot the ropes.

Davin's eyes darted from side to side, alighting on an avenue of retreat. He tugged at Goran's crimson sleeve and pointed. The flame-haired Challing at first shook his head, then came to a quick decision and leaped to the tiny ledge running around the stern of the *Twisted Cross*. Fingers gripping at ornate carvings, Goran worked his way around to the other side and out of sight. Davin followed—just in time.

"What's that?" Captain Iuonx's voice came from behind the Jyotian. "I heard noises."

Arkko dropped heavily into the longboat and set it swaying. The mate quickly examined under the seats and looked up to his captain. "Nothing amiss, Cap'n."

"Humph." Captain Iuonx stepped into the boat and nodded for his first mate to lower the craft.

Pounding hearts lodged in dry throats, Davin and Goran watched as Arkko lifted the oars and rowed strongly for shore.

"We could swim for it," suggested Davin.

"In that murk? What fish might there be to nibble our toes?" Goran shook his head with disgust. "Besides, I've felt these icy waters, remember?"

Davin refused to let the matter drop. "You just don't want to expend the effort."

However, the Challing managed to convince himself that the swim into the city was their only means of escape. "Our other course is to remain on the *Twisted Cross* and work until we die or until some pirate vessel laden with Narain overwhelms us. Here, take part of this. I don't want to be weighed down too much."

Goran handed Davin a pouch with half of his gambling winnings. The leather purse tugged on Davin's belt as he tied it securely. Better to enter the water without an extra burden, but Davin knew gold and silver couldn't be left behind. They'd need this and a healthy portion of Goran's pouch to buy horses in Faldin. He had no desire to linger in a seaport and possibly be taken by another crimp.

"So we swim for it, eh, friend Davin?" Goran climbed to the rail, paused, then made a clean dive. He entered the inky water without a ripple.

Davin's dive produced more noise, but not enough to rouse the watch on deck. Most of the sailors drank heavily of the cheap ale Arkko had furnished; it served a dual purpose. It kept the seamen content and their minds off escape. And for those who tried escape, it became harder if they were drunk.

It wasn't hard drink that leeched at Davin's strength; it was the cold. The frigid water sucked at his body heat with each stroke of his arms. Like stone his legs kicked. Nor did the clothing he wore help. Saturated with saltwater, his clothes doubled the burden of moving through the choppy sea.

Still he struggled to swim. His wasn't a life to be spent in slavery. Davin Anane had to be free to live life to the fullest. There were too many realms yet to visit, too many fat gem merchants with treasures awaiting a man with sharp wits and quick fingers.

His arms and legs turned from stone to lead. Davin halted, treading water to regain his breath. It was a mistake. The instant he stopped his forward motion, his muscles corded in cramping knots! He sank!

Black water broke over his head. He sputtered and thrashed. Water from the vile harbor rushed into his mouth and down his throat. He fought hard against the sea—and it overwhelmed him. Dread Nalren, God of the Oceans, closed a clammy fist about him, claiming another life, another victim.

Davin Anane tried to call out to Goran for help. He failed. Towering waves rose above him then smashed down, driving him toward the bottom of the harbor. Too weak to fight, he sank into the icy, inky blackness, to drown, to die.

# chapter
## 9

BLACK QAR CALLED to him. "Davin, Davin Anane!"

The dying Jyotian sputtered and thrashed about, vainly trying to hold Death at bay. Hands with fingers like tempered steel seized his shoulders, wrenching and jerking him from side to side until he cried out in pain.

"Damn your eyes, man. You're wasting precious time! Come on, Davin! Come along, we must not tarry!" Black Qar boomed in a voice that was definitely masculine.

Irony touched the corners of Davin's mouth, bitter irony. Even in death he garnered bits of knowledge. The Dark One *was* male! In life the young adventurer had been as confused about Qar's gender as were Raemllyn's priests. Female, neuter, or male, none were certain. Now he knew! He frowned; the trade of sweet life for that tidbit of theological insight was lacking.

"Hurry, man!" Qar persisted, violently shaking him. "We can't waste the whole night!"

Davin coughed, spat, then wearily opened one eye. He blinked and blinked again in surprise. Qar's visage wasn't frightening: not in the least! If anything, he looked much like Goran One-Eye. Laughter rolled from his chest. Even as a shade he could not escape the damnable Challing.

His belly laugh transformed into a wracking cough that awoke a barrage of agony in every muscle of his body. To escape the pain, he doubled over and tightly drew himself into a fetal position.

Qar would not be denied. Demanding hands slowly straightened his limbs and rolled him to his back.

"Wake up, Davin. We must get away from the docks."

The last son of the Jyotis House of Anane opened his eyes again. The voice and face could not belong to the God of Death! "Goran? Have you died, too, friend Goran?"

"Who else would it be?" the gargantuan changeling replied
with lifted eyebrows. "And no one's dead, thanks to me!"

Davin shook his head and instantly regretted it. The simple
movement made it feel as if everything had come loose and
tumbled about inside his skull. He moaned when he pushed to
an unsteady sitting position. The spinning world gradually
quieted, but the pain refused to go away.

"What happened? I remember swimming. The water was
so cold. My muscles cramped and bound themselves. It was
impossible to keep afloat. Then everything turned black." Davin
frowned and peered at his friend. "I thought Qar had come for
me. I thought *you* were Black Qar."

"'Tis a role ill suited to a Challing." Goran spat in disgust.
"I prefer things of life, not of death. That's why I bothered to
fish your worthless carcass from the harbor."

Davin's arms and legs no longer refused to move. He flexed
toes and fingers, then got to his feet. Although his legs quaked
with each movement, he pronounced them capable of walking.
Shivering in the cold night breeze, he glanced around. They
stood along Faldin's waterfront. With Goran occasionally lending him a steadying arm, they began to walk toward the town's
lights.

"I know now why Captain Iuonx wasn't afraid the crew
would desert the *Twisted Cross* while he was in Faldin. Only
a pair of fools would try swimming for freedom in freezing
water." Davin shook his head, unable to believe he had attempted such a feat.

"I didn't notice," Goran replied offhandedly. "Although I
admit a cup or five of hot spiced wine would edge away the
chill that now seeps into my bones."

*"Did not notice the icy bite of the water?"* Davin stared
incredulously at his companion.

Goran shrugged broad shoulders. "I plunged into the water
and decided that my Goran form wasn't adequate. Therefore I
changed into something more . . . aquatic."

"What?"

"Not quite human, not quite piscine, but a combination of
both. I found swimming invigorating."

Davin studied Goran, uncertain how to reply. Although he
had no need of magicks, this shape changing *had* come at a
good time. Yet he could not shake the restless disquiet that

niggled at the back of his mind. Goran might become Glylina or a Faceless One or a fish at any moment—without warning! And it was the unpredictability of the Challing's power that frightened him.

"This is a pathetic city," Goran complained while they walked down ill-lighted streets. "Smell it? It's an open sewer. And look at the people! Not a handsome man in the lot. Not a winsome wench to idle away hours with. All are so ugly. This is a miserable port, and one we'll be well away from."

"Aye!" For once Davin agreed with his friend. Their misadventures in Weysh and aboard the *Twisted Cross* had diverted them from Lijena and the Sword of Kwerin Bloodhawk for far too long. Through chattering teeth he added, "I'm freezing. We'll find a stable and purchase mounts and a warm berth for the night."

"A stable? You jest, Davin! We deserve more. An inn! A good tavern with ample food and ale to quench thirst and stave off hunger." Goran shook his shaggy head. "A stable is for horses and mules!"

"Use your head," Davin snapped. The wetness of his clothing and the night's cold lowered his tolerance for the changeling's constant arguments. "Captain Iuonx contacts crimps in Faldin. The first ones they'd seek out to kidnap are travelers at inns. Who'd notice or care if a stranger vanished? And we'd stand out for any caring to look."

"They don't know we're gone." Goran refused to be swayed. "Captain Iuonx may be a tyrant, but he's not possessed of magicks that allow him to see across the harbor and back into the *Twisted Cross*. We can do as we please. Believe it, Davin. We are free!"

"A stable," Davin insisted. "We'll have plenty of time to find ale and companionship once we're away from Faldin. Perhaps in Nawat or Solana."

"Nawat! Solana! Those cities are months away to the south . . ." Goran's cry of outrage trailed to a sputtering end when the red-bearded Challing jerked his head around. His single eye flew wide and he roared. "Nawat and Solana are *southeast* of Faldin! No, Davin! No! No! No! I'll have no more of chasing that bony wench across the face of this mud ball you humans call a world! Let her take the accursed sword, and may her skinny arse be damned!"

"Goran, I can't let her go. You *know* that! Too much is at stake!" Davin gritted his teeth. He was in no mood to verbally spar with his companion.

"What of A'bre? What of your promise to aid me in finding the way back to my beloved world of Gohwohn? Have you forgotten that?"

The Jyotian winced as the Challing's words struck home. He indeed owed Goran a debt—his own life—one that had increased this night. But the sword must be placed in Prince Felrad's hands, and there was only one way to do that—find Lijena Farleigh.

"We'll seek A'bre, my friend. I have given my word on that," Davin said. "But first we must again journey to Bistonia and reclaim the Sword of Kwerin Bloodhawk."

"Bah! By Nyuria's flaming pitchfork, what care you of Raemllyn's petty politics?" Goran bellowed another protest. "How many times have I heard you say that you didn't care whose arse sat on the Velvet Throne?"

In truth Davin didn't, as long as it wasn't Zarek Yannis. His hate for the usurper was personal, not political. If the Sitala permitted, one day he would end Yannis' life at the end of his own sword!

"Can't you get it through your thick head, it's not politics that's caught me in its web, but the fate of this world?"

"No more than you can seem to grasp that this world isn't mine! It's Gohwohn's beauties I ache to see again! How long must I suffer the chains of this realm?" There Goran left the matter, dangling and undecided.

With ill grace the two adventurers trod through Faldin's streets to locate a stable near the edge of the coastal town. At least a paint-chipped sign hanging askew above open double doors proclaimed it to be a stable, one with the look of a poor owner. The wood sadly needed paint, the yard stood ankle deep in horse manure, and a stableboy sitting just inside the door had let the tack he'd been cleaning slip from his fingers as he'd nodded off. Loud snores greeted the two thieves when they slipped into the stable.

Davin pursed his lips in doubt while he studied the horses contained within. They were starved, ribs standing out in bold relief along their sides. All needed currying, and many showed open, festering sores that had gone untended for days.

"Hardly worth stealing." Goran shook his head in disgust.

The Challing's words woke the stableboy. He started, then stared at them with saucer-large brown eyes. "Good sirs, I didn't hear you enter."

"Are these sickly beasts for sale?" Davin asked.

"Aye, that they are. They are the best Master Pynsartti has."

"I'd hate to see how this Pynsartti lives," muttered Davin. Louder, he asked, "How much for a pair of the best?"

"I . . . I don't know. The master handles all sales."

"Where can we find this Pynsartti?" Goran questioned.

"At the inn down the lane. Not more'n a five-minute walk." For the first time the boy appeared to notice Davin's and Goran's drenched clothing.

"Fine!" cried Goran before Davin could stop him. "We'll find this Pynsartti and conduct our business over a cup of mulled wine."

"They have good wine there, or so I've heard," the youth said. "I don't have the money to often partake in such fine beverages."

"We'll return with a bill of sale for the steeds," vowed Goran.

The Challing set off down a cobblestoned road, as though he cared little whether Davin followed. The Jyotian thief *did* follow, wary of Captain Iuonx's scouting for unwilling recruits.

"A place I'd expect Pynsartti to frequent," Goran said when they reached their destination.

The inn was shabbier than the stable, a fact that gave the Challing no pause. Goran pushed through the door to enter the establishment's public room. Davin edged inside and hastily surveyed the room. He saw no sign of either Arkko or Captain Iuonx.

Uneasy, Davin dropped onto a bench in a dark corner of the room while Goran went to the broad, stained bar and flipped a coin in payment for two flagons of ale.

Goran placed a flagon in front of his friend. "Drink hearty. This is better than the swill aboard ship." Goran had finished his first tankard and had ordered a second before giving Davin another glance.

"Not so loud. Do you want everyone to know we've jumped ship?" Davin warned.

"You flee from shadows. Faldin is large enough to swallow us without a trace. Captain Iuonx will never find us. Trust the gods, Davin."

Davin Anane snorted in disgust. He *didn't* trust the gods. How could he when they allowed such misery to run unchecked through Raemllyn? Why should Zarek Yannis ascend the throne and depose the rightful heir? Why did the Faceless Ones again roam Raemllyn after so many years of banishment?

"Let's find Pynsartti and make our deal. We'll seek out a smith on the morn and buy weapons." Davin sipped at the bitter ale.

"You seek Pynsartti?" a man at the next table asked. "Excuse me, but I overheard. What is your business with Master Pynsartti?"

"Come, join us in a flagon," Goran invited.

The man, small and nervous, with twitching eyebrows and the look of a trapped beast, slid into the spot opposite Davin.

"You know Pynsartti?" the Jyotian asked. "We are in need of horses. We visited his stable and picked out two of the finest. We wish to purchase them."

"You are travelers?"

"We are only passing through Faldin," Davin cut in before Goran could launch into a detailed description of their entire sea voyage from Weysh. "Our horses died, one from a broken leg and one from exhaustion carrying his bulk." Davin tilted his head to the Challing and rolled his eyes.

"Aye, that could be. Where do you go?"

"Nawat," answered Goran, glowering at his companion.

Relief suffused Davin. In that one word the Challing had acquiesced to Davin's desire to once again begin the search for Lijena and the magic-forged sword she had stolen from them.

"My horses will serve you well." The man's eyebrows twitched even faster, reminding Davin of mating caterpillars. "I am Pynsartti."

"We need somewhat more than the horses. Alas, we left our tack with our fallen animals. We had no wish to be weighted with saddles in wilderness. Can you supply all we require?"

Pynsartti peered nearsightedly at Davin. "Been raining? You both look drenched."

"A waterfall," Goran answered. "We passed under a waterfall. Clumsy of us, wouldn't you agree?"

"What waterfall? I know of none near Faldin."

"The horses," pressed Davin. He diverted Pynsartti's attention before Goran's exuberant storytelling sunk them waist deep in trouble. "We will leave in the morn, after we find weapons to replace those lost along the trail. Unless blades can be found this night."

"Come along, then. I can outfit you, even with sword and dirk if that be your need. The city's smith works out of my stable," Pynsartti said. "But why you'd want to leave in the middle of the night and miss all Faldin has to offer is beyond me."

"We . . . we're under orders. Our mission is of the utmost importance," Davin said in a low conspiratorial tone.

Pynsartti's eyes turned to thin slits as he studied the Jyotian. "For whom do you ride? These are perilous times."

"It wouldn't be fitting to mention our master." The lie sat uneasy with Davin. The sooner they left Pynsartti and Faldin, the happier he would be.

"If we ride for Zarek Yannis, there is a special price on all the horses," Pynsartti said.

Something in his tone warned Davin. Before Goran could leap on the promise of a bargain, Davin spoke. "We ride for another."

"There can be no other save Prince Felrad."

"Draw your own conclusions," said Davin, the sternness in his voice calling an end to the questioning. "Our mission is important, and we must hurry."

"Well, let us not tarry. Come along, and I'll see the prince's men astride the best in my stable."

"Nothing would please us more," Goran curtly replied, obviously bored with the verbal maneuvering.

In less than twenty minutes fifty silver eagles changed hands. Davin and Goran owned the least scurvy of the horses, tack— although serviceable, that had seen better days—and two swords and dirks of a style not seen in Raemllyn for at least two decades, although each was well-balanced and honed to a razor's edge. For another five eagles the stable master tossed in two moth-eaten, cowled, woolen cloaks. Though they smelled of years of dust, they cut the night's bone-chilling bite.

"You ride for Nawat, eh?" Pynsartti said, scratching his chin while the two saddled their mounts. "Dangerous route along the cliffs out by the sea. You might tumble off in the dark, and nobody'd be the wiser. Then again, you might consider a slightly longer, but much gentler road through the forests."

"What dangers lie there?" asked Davin.

"Not many. A few animals, but they don't hunt after twilight. A pard has staked the territory for its own." Pynsartti shrugged. "But the route is longer."

"Thank you for the advice." Davin mounted.

Goran started to protest, to beg for another few flagons of ale at the inn. Davin's expression quieted such a demand.

"The cliff road splits to the left, the forest road to the right. Both join again about ten leagues down the coast." Pynsartti twitched and went back inside.

The last Davin saw of the stable owner, he counted and recounted the fifty-five silver coins. From his aspect this might be the loftiest profit he'd made in months.

"Which way?" Goran asked as they rode from the coastal town. "I'm for the cliff road. What difference does it make if it's the more dangerous, eh? Adds zest to the trip." Goran lowered his voice, but Davin still overheard: "By Nyuria's bald pate, it might be the only interesting portion of the trip."

"The forest." Davin decided the stable master had been right, it might be the safer—and if it took them inland, all the better.

At a fork in the road Goran raised a hand to halt Davin. The Challing tipped his head to one side, listening intently. Davin strained to hear what Goran's more sensitive ears had already discerned: the clop-clop-clop of a horse on the forest road ahead. The hoofbeats retreated from them.

"There's only the one rider." Goran One-Eye dropped to the ground and studied the tracks in the dirt. He looked up at Davin, the green witch-fire ablaze in his single eye telling his friend he saw by more than the light of Raemllyn's two moons. "No sign of another passing this point recently."

"We'll follow, but at a distance. If that pard decides to attack, let our unknowing scout be its victim." David nodded to the forest trail.

Goran mounted and reined after the Jyotian. Forest rose on either side, engulfing them with its bare-limbed late winter embrace. Of animals and other life Davin saw little, except night predators seeking foolish mice.

"Davin, ahead. Look at the notch cut through the hill." Goran pointed to a spot where a low hill had been gouged to permit the road to remain level. It seemed pointless. "It was cut with magicks. I *see* the spells still remaining."

*See* was the wrong term, Davin realized. Goran didn't actually *see* the magicks, but *sensed* where spells had been employed. If active sorcery or witchcraft threatened, the Challing, hopefully, would discern it clearly.

"Forward, with caution," Davin warned, trying to ignore the hairs prickling at the back of his neck.

Tapping the flanks of their mounts, they slowly entered the path of magic-hewn rock. A silence that cloaked even the sound of the night breeze settled about the pair.

"I like this not." Goran twisted in the saddle, head craning from side to side. "Spells have been worked here but a few hours ago. My flesh prickles with the power."

"Are you . . ."

Davin's words drowned in the sound of hoofbeats, approaching fast from the rear! A dozen armed men rode down on them hell-bent for leather.

"Something's amiss! But cold steel will set it right! Nothing like matching blades to fire the blood!" Goran roared with relish as he wrenched sword—

No sword, but a twisted, dried branch came free from his scabbard!

"Nyuria's arse! What kind of fools are we?" Goran flung the useless length of wood into the night.

"Ensorcelled ones!" Davin's own blade proved to be a gnarled stick, and his dirk a leafless twig. "Run, Goran, run for it!"

Davin spurred his mount. Or tried to!

An invisible fist closed about him to lift him from the saddle and hold him dangling in midair. A chorus of savage curses announced that the Challing found himself similarly trapped.

Below, riders drew to a halt in a circle and dismounted. Six ropes sailed upward, three looping over each chest of the two adventurers. Like an insect trapped in a spider web, Davin hung in midair. The spider's deadly jaws were five drawn bows aimed directly at him and the Challing.

"Take the forest road," Goran mocked. "It's safer!"

"Aye, it is," came a tremulous voice below. "For me." Pynsartti stepped forward and grinned as his companions hauled their captives to the ground. The man's nervous gestures had magnified. "This is a good night's work. With the other one we caught, we have three to sell to Captain Iuonx."

*"Iuonx!"* Davin and Goran chorused.

"A crimp sells to anyone in harbor. Haven't been many travelers coming to Faldin of late. Damn Zarek Yannis!" Pynsartti motioned. His men securely tied the two.

At arrow point Davin and Goran were forced into the back of a flatbed wagon hidden at the side of road. Another man, bound hand and foot, twisted about to glance at them.

"The rider who will act as our decoy," Goran said scornfully.

The man looked at them curiously. Goran went on to explain.

"Had I but known there were others on the road," the trussed-up man said, "we could have joined forces. Ambushing three might have been proven more difficult."

"We should have taken the cliff road," Goran grumbled.

Davin said nothing; Goran was right. The Jyotian's misery doubled when the wagon bounced to life, rolling back toward Faldin. Nor did its wooden wheels miss one bone-jarring pothole in the road. Davin found it almost a relief when they arrived at the Faldin docks. He hardly minded when Arkko planted a booted foot in his side, cursing him for a fool and a landlubber.

"Hates to pay our price for a second time," ventured Goran glumly.

And received a sharp blow from Captain Iuonx's swagger stick before he was tossed into the longboat for the return trip to the *Twisted Cross*. Only with the first light of morning did Arkko release the ropes that bound the three unwary sailors Pynsartti had provided. An hour later the merchanter slipped from Faldin's harbor, back onto the waters of the Oceans of Kumar.

## *chapter*
# *10*

DAVIN ANANE DESPERATELY clutched at the rail of the tossing ship, fighting the nausea that churned his stomach this way, that way, then inside out. He cursed Raemllyn's pantheon of gods, the five fates called the Sitala, and his own parents for giving him birth. The string of profanities brought no relief to his knotted gut. Neither did repeated attempts to force his belly to upchuck the burden it still carried from the morning meal.

The source of his distress—a raging gale that tossed the merchanter as wildly as the Jyotian's stomach turned somersaults. For seven days the *Twisted Cross* had sliced through the waves, racing on the winds of an approaching storm front. Two hours after rounding the aptly named Cape Terror, the ship's luck had run out—the storm overtook them.

Davin ineffectually wiped rain from his eyes and peered at the lightning-wracked sky. The young thief had drawn watch duty, but for what he watched, he couldn't say. The torrents of pounding rain limited vision to the bow of the cargo vessel.

Lightning and ear-splitting thunder cracked the sky directly overhead. Spidery legs of actinic light missed the *Twisted Cross'* masts, but ghost lights danced along the spars. The shimmering green cast a wan illumination that turned everything—including the two other unfortunates on deck—into a ghastly netherworld scene.

The booming strands of a bawdy ballad detailing the erotic abilities of Kavindra's women drew Davin's attention to the right. Goran One-Eye opened a wooden hatch and climbed onto the deck. A broad grin split his bearded face from ear to ear while he walked to his friend, his booted feet never faltering on the tossing deck.

"Ho, friend Davin, everything holding together well in the storm?"

"The *Twisted Cross* is; I'm not." Again Davin felt the urge to retch, but his stomach refused to accommodate him. He cursed and spat bitter bile from his mouth. The only bright spot of this miserable day was not having to pay Arkko for his meals. The Jyotian doubted he would want food for the rest of his life!

"All's well on this front, then." Goran slapped his companion on the shoulder. "But the other one captured with us. Have you heard him?"

"He seems surly, but why shouldn't he be? I'd be surly, too, if some crimp roped me, tied me, and then sold me to Captain Iuonx." Davin's mood ill-prepared him for the Challing's ceaseless chatter.

"Your bitterness at our fortune surprises me! You'd think you were the one choosing the forest route, the one believing Pynsartti, the one who—"

"You've made your point." Davin hung to the rail as another wave of nausea assailed him.

"No, I haven't." Goran spoke in a voice so low that Davin strained to hear over the whine of the wind and the crash of the sea against the ship's hull. "Tacllyn-lin-Bertam, or Bertam, as he calls himself, isn't the surly knave you make him out to be. He's a cunning one, but not surly."

"What do you mean?" Davin didn't really care, but he had learned long ago there was no method existed to waylay the changeling when he was of a mind to speak.

"That," said Goran, "is not clear, even in my mind. He talks to all, but listen to his tales!"

"He spreads dissension?"

"In his way. Quiet, here comes Bertam now. Ask him about the weather, but be prepared for quite a tale." Goran fell silent.

"You my replacement?" Davin asked as the man approached, struggling against the wind.

Bertam nodded. The man stood at a medium height, just a little under Davin's own six feet. Even the dancing green light and whipping rain could not disguise hair as black as a raven's wing. But it was the lanky man's pale blue eyes that held Davin. Those contained a flash of distant light that bespoke madness.

"Then relieve me," Davin said. "I've no desire to stand here longer than necessary."

"Tarry a few minutes," Bertam urged. "We have much in common, you and I. The three of us do," he added, glancing at the one-eyed giant. "We are all *doomed.*"

"I know, and I wish the Gods would grant us a quick end."
Davin attempted to make light of the man's comment.

"Not the seasickness," Bertam replied, his blue eyes narrowing. "The demons! They lurk in the storm, waiting for us
to wreck so that they may dine on our mortal souls. Black Qar
will never greet any of us—the demons won't let us have such
relief, even in death."

"He does go on, doesn't he?" Goran nudged the Jyotian and
winked.

"Scoff if you will, but I know. I *know!* They slither out of
impenetrable fog banks and snap men from the decks. They'll
drag the unsuspecting overboard. Then the true torture begins.
They aren't easy with sailors. Our lives will be forfeit, but
death will not be granted. Only suffering. Suffering unknown
to any of us!"

"I know suffering." Through the quavering veil of nausea,
Davin studied Bertam.

What Goran had hinted about the man seemed true. There
was more to him than met the eye. Bertam endured the pitching
deck well, too well for someone used to keeping both feet on
firm ground. He climbed rigging with an agility usually lacking
in landlubbers. And he learned each task assigned him with a
speed that spoke of a hidden sailor in Tacllyn-lin-Bertam.

The only thing that didn't seem to fit was his attitude.
Bertam constantly spread these wild tales of demons in the fog,
of titan mist monsters great enough to swallow the *Twisted
Cross* without a belch.

*Why?* Davin had no answer.

"You haven't seen any of them, have you?" Bertam abruptly
demanded, staring at the Jyotian.

"Of your monsters? No, nothing." Davin shook his head.

"They skulk along the coast near Cape Terror. They killed
all humans at the lighthouse. I know it." Bertam cast a sly
sidelong look at Davin and Goran, as though weighing their
reaction to his words.

The young thief's answer was forgotten in a lightning flash
that illuminated the tossing sea. He gaped, and thrust a finger
toward a heavy fog bank. "There! Look! By all the gods!
Look!"

The apparition flickered beneath another searing bolt.

"There! Do you see it?" Davin Anane strained, almost falling over the rail, in his attempt to discern—*what?*

"I see nothing." The Challing barely glanced in the direction of the apparition.

Davin turned to Bertam; the man's expression was not one of fear or vindication, as Davin would have expected. Only a quiet amusement danced on his lips. The set of his body showed no tension. It was as if he played a game well and now saw victory as his—or an audience applauding.

"I . . . I must have been mistaken. The rain. My sickness. Forgive me. Bertam, it's your watch now." Davin reached out and put his arm around Goran's broad shoulders. Queasy as his stomach was, he didn't need support, but acted out a small drama for Bertam's benefit.

Once below decks, beyond the man's ear, Davin asked, "You didn't see it?"

"I saw nothing. Bertam's stories have fired your imagination." Goran shrugged. "You constructed a beast out of the thunderclouds. He works his storytelling magicks well on everyone."

"I saw something," Davin answered, less certain than he had been a moment ago. He *thought* that he'd seen a ship with a serpentine sea monster coiled about its prow.

"I saw only you and Bertam," Goran said with another shrug.

"He doesn't believe the tales he spins, does he?" Davin asked. "His reaction to my . . . sighting wasn't what I'd have expected from someone terrified of mist creatures. He seemed amused rather than afraid."

"He's an odd one and up to no good, of that I'd lay odds. But it's nothing to do with the *Twisted Cross*." Goran's brow furrowed. "What manner of man allows himself to fall prey to a crimp? If he'd wanted aboard the ship, he could have merely volunteered."

"No, I don't think so." Davin pursed his lips thoughtfully. "How many of the *Twisted Cross'* crew volunteered? Not many. If Bertam had, he would have stood out as unusual."

"He's that, for all his being captured." Goran snorted.

Davin's stomach heaved in counter to the *Twisted Cross'* rocking. The ship lurched starboard, his belly rolled port. Waving an end to their conversation, the Jyotian found an empty hammock and dropped into it. When he kept his eyes tightly shut, he could endure his churning stomach. The swaying around him vanished, and the ship's motion lessened. Davin drifted

into a fitful sleep peopled with demons and creatures too bizarre
to describe.

"... rising up to devour all aboard the *Kavindra Crescent*.
It was an awful sight. The waters of the Kumar rolled red with
sailors' blood. And the *beast!* It lapped up the grisly feast!"

Davin turned to a side in the hammock, his eyes blinking
back the fuzzy haze of sleep.

"You tell a good story, Bertam," Goran's voice boomed.
"But how much of this have you witnessed with your own
eyes?"

"Enough, Red-Beard." Bertam paused dramatically. When
the pale blue-eyed man spoke again, his tone was low and
solemn. "Too much."

"You work to frighten us. Why?" This from a sailor whose
face Davin could not see.

"Not so." Bertam sucked at his teeth. "I only urge caution.
These are treacherous waters. We must be continually alert for
the beasts that prowl this coast. Upper Raemllyn is fraught with
them. We passed Cape Terror and escaped unscathed. Others
weren't on such good terms with Nalren, gracious God of the
Sea."

Davin rolled from the hammock. To his surprise the deck
felt almost steady beneath his feet. From topside came the
rhythm of gentle rain. While he slept, the brunt of the storm
had apparently passed. For that he gave thanks to Nalren, the
Sitala, and Jajhana.

Davin moved closer to the men circled about Bertam and
perched on a bale of cloth. He smiled at the thought of the
planchets buried within. None of the others in the crew appeared
to know that they were helping Captain Iuonx in a counterfeiting
scheme.

Of Bertam he asked, "What happened at Cape Terror? I
heard Arkko mention it several times."

"You know not of their deaths?" Bertam appeared shocked
that any could be this ignorant. "A full score of warriors controlled the Cape Terror lighthouse. Ask any sailor who plies
these waters and you'll hear tales of intense storms that last
for weeks. Without the lighthouse it is impossible to steer past
the jagged coast. Many's the ship that smashed to splinters on
those rocks."

"So? This is little different from other points along Raemllyn's coast," Davin said.

"Not so. The warriors pledged fealty to Prince Felrad. Their fees, as they called them, went in support of his attempt to regain the Velvet Throne."

"Some good came of it, then."

"A matter of interpretation." For an instant a darkness clouded Bertam's face.

Davin stiffened. Was that it? Did this man support the usurper Zarek Yannis? Did he spy for the whoreson?

Bertam glanced at those seated about him. A vague smile touched his lips when the other sailors clustered tighter. "A full twenty armed men controlled the lighthouse and the single road leading to it. Some might say they extorted money from the passing ships. Others might call it paying fees to a rightful High King of Raemllyn."

"What do you call it?" Davin Anane pressed.

Bertam's face betrayed not even a flicker of emotion, a reaction that only increased the Jyotian's suspicion.

Bertam turned back to the others. "They would collect their passage fee or turn off the lighthouse. Many had refused to pay and claimed that the lighthouse was sighted in a different position, one that caused them to wreck. At least the handful of *survivors* claimed this."

Gagno spoke up. "For my part, I doubt any of Prince Felrad's soldiers would purposefully wreck a ship at Cape Terror, although the reports of them looting the ships that did crash are well known throughout this portion of Raemllyn."

That Davin could believe. Why leave a wreck to the action of wind and wave? Salvage what was left and profit by the misfortune of others.

"The *Lady of Evara* was a coast hugger," Bertam continued, ignoring the old man. "Never did the ship go beyond the sight of land. And its captain, being a staunch supporter of Prince Felrad, always paid his fee. But when he sent a longboat ashore, the lighthouse agents were nowhere to be seen.

"Being a prudent man, he sailed on, but with full lookouts and extreme caution. He caught sight of the Cape Terror light at midday. Rather than tempt the Sitala by continuing on and hoping that the light would guide him past the treacherous coastline, he waited. And it was a good thing he did."

"No light in the lighthouse that night," guessed Goran.

"None. The lighthouse stayed cold and dark. The next morning the captain sent a full dozen of his most trusted sailors ashore. When none returned, he sent five more. They failed to return. The captain of the *Lady of Evara* began to worry. Sorely short of crew because of these ventures, he did what no captain should have."

"He left the *Lady of Evara* and went ashore himself." Gagno's eyes widened.

Bertam fell silent. The creaking of the *Twisted Cross* filled the hold.

When he spoke again, Bertam's voice dropped to a lower tone. "What the brave captain of the *Lady of Evara* found wasn't meant for human eyes."

"Everyone at the lighthouse had died," someone said.

"Dead?" asked Bertam, a quaver in his voice. "No, they had *died*. Horribly. Nowhere the captain stepped did he tread on dry rock or clean lighthouse floor. Blood. Everywhere! It sucked at his boot soles as he entered the lighthouse. Every step up the spiral staircase to the top, he found only severed limbs—and blood.

"Everywhere blood. When he reached the top of lighthouse, he saw a sight reserved only for those tortured in the lowest depths of Peyneeha by Black Qar himself. Three men had been in the light. Their bodies had vanished—but their outlines were burned into the lighthouse walls.

"One had died with arms outstretched—or so it appeared from the silhouette seared *into* the stone wall. Another had been caught in profile. His mouth is forever engraved in the wall, open and silently screaming." Bertam paused and shuddered. "Of the final one in that lighthouse, I can't even bring myself to speak. It was too gruesome to relate."

"A fine story." Goran made no attempt to hide the doubt in his voice. "How do you explain the Cape Terror light being on when we passed?"

Bertam smiled, and his eyes flashed their madness. "No human runs the light now. No one *human*."

"So demons help us along our way. We should consider ourselves lucky," Goran replied with a grunt of contempt.

"For that, perhaps. What of the other obstacles in our path to Evara?" Bertam shook his head.

"What other obstacles?" Gagno asked, nervously licking his lips.

Davin stared at the gathered sailors. Although he might concur with Goran's disbelief, the others believed, or accepted a kernel of truth in Bertam's tale. The Jyotian saw the fear on their faces.

"The destruction of all men at Cape Terror lighthouse is nothing," said Bertam. "Nothing when you consider the beasts lurking in coves and inlets along this coast. They slither forth and hide in fog banks waiting for unsuspecting ships—like the *Twisted Cross*—to come by."

"And then?" urged Gagno, hands atremble.

"Then their misty jaws open and close. Ships sink. Sailors are lucky if they drown. And unlucky if the demon creatures find them and . . . but there's no need to describe their hideous fate. The creatures do not allow them easy lives. Let's leave it at that."

With a shake of his shaggy red mane, Goran rose and motioned for Davin to follow him. Bundling himself in a dark brown slicker, the young thief climbed topside after the changeling. Behind them Bertam lavished with great care gory descriptions of the creatures lunging from the dark, from impenetrable fog banks, from curtains of gray mist hanging on the water, rising from the depths to destroy unsuspecting ships.

"I must agree with you. He'll have the crew in mutiny before we reach Rakell." Davin leaned against the railing and looked across the now calm water.

The storm had abated, and a new dawn threatened the east with its cold light. Of the crew, Davin saw nothing. Even the pilot seemed to have abandoned his post. Davin shrugged away the missing man. Often the pilot roped the wheel to maintain course while he went below to grab a quick nap.

"Mutiny doesn't seem to be what he wants. Listen to his tales. It's as though he works to frighten the crew to death." Goran scratched a hand through a soggy beard. "What the man is up to eludes me. But by all this world's gods, you can wager it is *something!*"

"To what end?" Davin wondered aloud. "Why bother? To prove that he can do so? That doesn't go along with your feeling that he wanted to be captured back in Faldin and brought aboard the *Twisted Cross*."

"Maybe it doesn't matter what ship," said Goran. "All I know is that no stretch of Raemllyn could have so many demons and not burn itself to the lowest depths of Peyneeha. After all, I know—great Nyuria!"

Davin saw Goran turn pale. In the six years he'd traveled with the Challing, never had he seen such an expression of stark terror. Goran One-Eye had endured torture and hardship and kept his courage. Now he backed from the *Twisted Cross'* rail and crashed into the main mast.

Davin swung about. "Father Yehseen's burning beard!" he exclaimed. Davin Anane backstepped. "It's Bertam's doing. He's put this thought in our minds. Goran! Tell me it's only a chance formation in the fog bank."

"It . . . burns with magic!" Awe filled the Challing's voice.

Davin turned; Goran's single eye danced ablaze with green witch-fire. Spinning about, the young Jyotian ran and leaped up the steps to the watch deck three at a time. Neither pilot nor officer stood watch. Snatching up the captain's spyglass, he hoisted it and peered through its black length.

"It *does* burn with magic!" Davin gasped.

He twisted the eyepiece in an attempt to sharpen the image. The shape drifted in and out of the fog. A vagrant breeze shifted the wall of mist to again reveal the ship Goran had first sighted.

"It glows as if it burns, but I see no flames," Davin said, squinting through the spyglass. "And there's no crew on its fore decks. Goran, what do you see?"

"I see nothing but the magicks powering it." Goran's eye blazed with almost the same intensity as the ship. "It's a ghost ship, crewed by spirits from the netherworld. Steer to avoid it, Davin. Do it!"

Davin turned to the wheel. The pilot hadn't abandoned his post—willingly. Both the man's severed hands remained about the wood!

Davin took an unconscious step forward and caught himself. The hands moved on the wheel, turning the *Twisted Cross* toward the fog bank where the phantom vessel sailed!

Hefting the spyglass high above his head, Davin smashed it down on the fingers of the left hand. He pulped the fingers, but other than to slow the trickle of blood and the white flash of sundered bone, he accomplished nothing. The hand held firmly, gliding the *Twisted Cross* toward . . . what?

Davin grabbed the wheel in an attempt to wrest it from the hands. He failed as surely as if he had fought a god.

"Help me, Goran. We've got to keep the ship from entering the fog." Horrified, Davin cast a glance forward.

The shimmering red-cloaked ghost ship emerged and came closer.

Again he threw his weight against the wheel, and again he failed to overcome the strength of those blood-dripping disembodied hands. Goran joined him in the task. The pair of them bent strong backs to the effort—and managed to break off a wheel spoke!

Still the merchanter sailed toward the ghost ship.

"Pry the fingers loose!" cried Goran.

Fearfully Davin touched one hand. The gods didn't strike him dead. Demons didn't spring forth from the decks. Davin's courage soared; he grabbed the left hand with both of his and yanked.

He had no more luck freeing the hand from the wheel than he had trying to turn the ship against the wishes of the bodiless hands.

Goran's immense strength proved equally useless. They fought against demon magicks, not human hands.

"We've entered the fog. The ghost ship! There it is! It intends to ram us!" The Challing thrust a finger toward the prow of the *Twisted Cross*.

The immense red-glowing ship loomed above them, twice the size of any vessel Davin had ever seen on Raemllyn's seas. Mounted under her prow was a figurehead, a wooden replica of a fanged serpent. It was this that he'd mistaken earlier for some writhing beast coiled about a ship!

But ramming was not the purpose of the titan vessel. Before its bow sliced through the *Twisted Cross'* the ship turned to draw alongside the merchanter, matching the smaller craft's pace.

"Captain Iuonx, the crew! We must warn them!" Davin shouted.

"This is not for them." Goran's voice was distant and hollow, almost as if enthralled. His single good eye stared at the ghost brigantine. "There's no crew on that ship. Look, Davin. See? No one crowds against the rails to peer at us."

The Challing abandoned all attempt to turn the *Twisted Cross'* wheel. Instead he went to the rail and climbed onto it.

"Goran, don't. You can't go aboard that ship," Davin shouted after him.

"It needs a crew. It *wants* a crew."

Goran reached up and grabbed a rope. With a leap, and great agility, he scrambled up into the *Twisted Cross'* rigging, making his way through the ropes like a brightly clad spider. Three quarters of the way up the main mast rigging he halted, found a line, and swung across to the ghost ship.

For all its shimmering appearance, Goran's boots slammed hard into its deck. Davin heard the impact and watched as his friend vanished aboard the demon ship.

"Damn his eye," the Jyotian cursed. "And may Iuonx and the *Twisted Cross* be damned!"

He couldn't allow the Challing to face the mysterious ship alone! Davin clambered up the rigging and glanced back to the deck. Still no one had emerged from the hold.

*Magicks!* He sensed them aswirl about him. Had they robbed the whole crew of their senses? If so, why was he unaffected?

Davin's chest heaved as he sucked in a steadying breath. Grabbing a rope, he pushed off with both feet to swing outward to the phantom vessel.

He cleared the ghost ship's rail and released the rope. His booted feet struck and skidded across the highly polished deck in a wobbly dance that ended when his shoulder collided with a thick mast. For all the ship's shimmery appearance, it proved painfully solid.

"Goran?" His voice seemed muffled, unreal.

The Challing did not answer.

Davin glanced around. The ship was immaculate. Everything appeared in place, the gear properly stowed, the ship a captain's dream. But of crew Davin saw nothing.

"Here, Davin. Down here." The Challing opened a door leading to the captain's cabin. He motioned for Davin. The Jyotian had to squint; Goran's eye burned with a witch-fire so intense it was painful to behold.

Davin yelped when he touched the door. A fat blue spark leaped forth to dance between his fingertips. Hesitantly he pressed through the entrance and down a short flight of steps. The scene that greeted his eyes left him breathless.

"Not even the High King's palace in Kavindra is so lavishly appointed." Everywhere he looked lay jewel-encrusted furniture, tables of the finest wood, gold and silver chasing on cut crystal goblets, small curtains of fine Huata lace. Davin knelt and touched the coverlet on a large bed.

"*Danne* work," he whispered.

This large cloth had been embroidered by forest spirits held in thrall by a sorceror. Davin stroked a palm over its weave; he felt the sprites' tears in the thread.

"Leave it, Davin," Goran called to him. "Look at this."

Davin blinked and pulled himself away from the cloth. The thought of stealing the *danne* work never entered his mind, even though it would bring a mountain of gold bists if sold to the right merchant. Nor did he consider stealing anything from this room. He had no desire to tempt the unknown powers that stalked these empty rooms, the deserted decks.

"This map is unlike any I've seen before. Do you recognize the terrain?"

Goran moved aside to allow Davin a clear view of a map burned with cruel force into a tabletop. Here and there tiny spires of smoke rose, as if the branding had occurred only seconds before they entered the cabin.

"It seems familiar. Yes, it is. Look, Goran. Here is Uhjayib. Pahl is misplaced. No, this must be Pahl." Davin tilted his head from left to right, then back again. The map was of Raemllyn, of that he was certain, but a Raemllyn unknown to him. The upper and lower realms were closer together, as though they had been shifted by some world-shaking force. "I don't know what this spot is. Not a city."

"The Tombs of A'bre," Goran said in a choked voice.

"What?" Davin's head jerked up.

"Remember what I was told? I must find A'bre if I want to return to Gohwohn?"

Davin remembered too well. Although Raemllyn hadn't treated him ill, Goran One-Eye desired to return to his own world, where he would be free of the flesh that now bound him. The legendary city of A'bre held the key for Goran's return.

"Here lie the Tombs of A'bre," Goran repeated.

The Challing's finger stabbed down to the point on the map of Lower Raemllyn that Davin didn't recognize. The Challing's entire body stiffened. Davin grabbed him, to pull him from the unseen danger.

His own body froze. Images blasted his brain. He rolled and soared and dived—and through it all he saw a cavalcade of evil, of sorcerous powers unknown to humans. Even Zarek Yannis' release of the Faceless Ones seemed gentle in comparison to what atrocities the mages of A'bre committed on themselves—and others.

Amid this pageant of horror, Davin saw a curious symbol, a pure gold replica of a broken tree leaf.

Goran yanked away, and Davin sank to his knees, panting. He looked up. The Challing's eye continued to dance with witch-fire. As if drawn by unseen arms, Goran stepped to a small cabinet mounted on the far wall.

"Goran, don't touch it!" Davin shouted in warning.

Too late! The Challing threw the double doors open and reached inside. When his hand withdrew, he held a piece of golden leaf in his palm—the leaf Davin had seen in his vision. Lifting it by an attached thread-slender chain, Goran dangled it before his eye for a moment, then hung it about his neck.

. "We can go now," Goran announced.

Davin Anane swallowed hard. The same shimmering red light that veiled the ghost ship now engulfed the Challing!

# chapter
## *11*

"You . . . you're part of the ship!" Davin Anane's gray eyes widened then narrowed. The hairs on the back of his neck prickled.

The Challing shimmered with the ship's magicks, as if the spells that controlled the phantom vessel wove the single-eyed giant into its fabric. The Jyotian trembled with the realization that what Goran had said earlier was true! This ship sailed the seas in search of a crew for its ghostly decks.

It had just recruited two thieves!

"We must go topside now." Goran's voice resonated and reverberated as if shouted from the bottom of a deep well.

Without further word or gesture the changeling brushed past Davin. The light touch of the Challing's hand sent the younger thief reeling back, the sting of a million fire ants jolting through his body.

Staggering on rubbery legs, Davin trailed his glowing friend from the sumptuous cabin and onto deck. Not to the rail to swing back to the *Twisted Cross,* but up to the captain's position near the wheel Goran strode. Arms locked behind his back, the Challing stood with eyes focused on far horizons, the master of this ensorcelled craft.

"We must return to the *Twisted Cross*. We can't stay here," Davin pleaded, fearing that it might be too late for either of them to take the return path. Too long had they remained aboard this phantom of the seas.

*No!* The heir to the House of Anane refused to accept such as fate—trapped, sailing the seas for eternity.

His chest heaving as he sucked down a determined breath, Davin moved to the rail and its crimson, veiling light. Twenty feet below, the *Twisted Cross* rode the gentle waves under full sail. The pilot's disembodied hands remained clutched in a death grip about the wheel; still neither officer or crew member trod the deck.

"Now, Goran! We must return now!" Davin shouted. "Return before this ship drifts back into the fog!"

"There are other worlds," Goran said in a curiously flat voice. "We can explore them in this fine vessel. We can live as kings while we sail."

"This demon boat's course is set for Peyneeha's depths!" Davin snapped. "Black Qar lures our souls to Hell!"

"This is *my* ship. No Challing has ever sailed such a marvelous vessel. We will rove the seas, plundering at will. Watch!" Goran lifted a hand and pointed upward.

The sails above unfurled from the monstrous ship's three masts.

Davin swallowed hard. The moment the wind caught the fabric it would be too late! He either returned to the *Twisted Cross* now, or never!

"Farewell, my friend. Our times together have been good—more than good. But our paths at last part." Davin climbed the rigging and snared a dangling rope in his hands. "I wish you only good fortune in your search for A'bre."

Like springs uncoiling, his powerful legs shoved outward; he swung over dark waters.

"The Oceans of Kumar are mine," Goran called, his voice lacking a hint of triumph.

The pendant—the broken gold tree leaf—hung around Goran's neck and bound him to the vessel. Davin was certain of that, just as he was sure that had he stolen any of the riches in the captain's cabin he, too, would have been swaddled in a shimmering cloak of red magic.

Davin was no master mage possessed with the counter spells to break the ship's control over his friend. The Jyotian saw but one avenue to free the Challing—brute force! He grimaced at the thought of pitting his strength against the glowing red giant's might. Only a fool would even consider such a contest.

*I've acted the fool more than once in my life!*

The young raven-haired thief now swung above the merchanter's deck. Yet his hands remained clutched tautly about the line. Davin Anane had no intention of abandoning a friend stranded aboard the glimmering deck of a hell-bound ghost ship, even a friend as garrulous as the Challing! Not while he still lived.

Reaching the end of his pendulous arc, Davin swung back toward the phantom vessel. His legs opened wide as he homed in on Goran, who stood staring at the filling sails. Without word or whisper the Jyotian descended like a hawk swooping down on unsuspecting prey. And he struck! Strong legs scissored closed about Goran's bulky, glowing red torso, wrenching the changeling from the spell-woven deck.

Bestial rage roared from Goran's throat; mighty hammerlike fists pounded the ensnaring calves and thighs about his writhing body. Still Davin locked his ankles, cursed with each jarring blow, and clung to the rope.

Arms threatening to dislocate from shoulder joints, palms burned raw on mist-slick hemp, the young thief cried in pain as he once more swept outward toward the *Twisted Cross*. The House of Anane's last son barely cleared the merchanter's battered wood railing on his return arc. Gratefully he released the rope.

Together human and Challing tumbled, spilling onto the cargo ship's deck. Davin groaned as the impact drove the wind from his lungs. Through a haze of numbing white-hot pain, he tightened his leg lock about his friend.

Goran struggled, cursing his friend's parentage and detailing a variety of dread poxes the gods would rain down on the Jyotian. Davin's strength was no match for the Challing, who twisted free, jumped to his feet, and stood, glaring down. "By the gods, Davin! Does insanity devour your brain? The middle of the night is no time for some childish wrestling match!"

"The ghost-ship . . . had to . . . get away. If we didn't . . ." Davin sputtered between gasps for air.

"The ghost . . ." Goran's expression transformed, as though a mask of wax melted from his features. The crimson light enveloping the changeling faded. "The ship of magicks! I remember it now. I . . . I took this pendant." He fingered the gold leaf chained around his thick neck. "After that, all is veiled to me."

"You became a part of the ship." Davin pushed to his feet and moaned. Although he detected no broken bones, every muscle in his body was strained and bruised. It didn't matter! Goran and he had escaped the ghost ship with their lives.

"I remember nothing after putting this around my neck." Goran held the sundered leaf between forefinger and thumb. "The ship possessed me?"

"It did. But we're well away from it now."

He glanced over a throbbing shoulder. His heart lodged in the middle of his throat. The phantom ship was gone! The Jyotian spun around. Nowhere was it to be seen! Vanished into ocean or air, Davin didn't know, but the ghostly vessel had disappeared as though it had never existed!

Save for the pendant Goran now wore, the glowing ship might have been no more than a misty memory left from a nightmare.

"The gods," Goran said, while he peered at the waters about the *Twisted Cross*. "They play with us as if we were nothing more than toys."

"But which gods?" His companion's words rang true in Davin's mind. "They might seem capricious in their dealings with mortals, but there must be some reason to intrude on our lives."

"The Sword of Kwerin?" Goran asked, then he shook his shaggy red head. "No, not that. It's out of our hands. Your wench has it."

"She's not my wench," Davin said quietly. "You were shown the way back to Gohwohn. What can that mean?"

"I can go home!" Goran turned to his friend. "What else could it mean, Davin?"

"It means the gods want rid of you," Davin answered sarcastically while he massaged his aching shoulders.

"Or that they favor me and have granted me this boon. What does it matter to a Challing what drives the gods of this mud ball in all they do? I can return. All I need do is find the Tombs of A'bre." Again Goran touched the pendant.

"But what does *that* mean?" Davin pointed to the broken leaf.

Goran shrugged. "Your human gods often speak in riddles. Perhaps the pendant is such."

Davin knew of no legend or fable concerning a broken leaf of gold. Nor could he make sense of the strangely shifted map they had seen aboard the phantom ship.

"The fog's dissipated," Goran's voice intruded on his ponderings.

About the *Twisted Cross* day blossomed clear and clean. Cloudless blue reigned overhead. The sun hung a finger's width above the horizon, but of the captain and crew they saw no sign.

Davin's attention returned to the still crewless merchanter. He looked at the motionless wheel and the charred black that marked the spots where the pilot's severed hands had grasped the wood spokes. "Something is still amiss. Where are the rest—"

Ere he could complete the question Captain Iuonx bellowed a command to take in a forward sail. Arkko's whip licked at the back of a crewman too slow in his movement to please the mate. Davin and Goran blinked, neither believing their eyes. The *Twisted Cross* came alive with men who hadn't been there but a heartbeat before.

"You two, get your lazy arses up into the topsail rigging. I want a lookout in place before we hit the whirlpool. It's less than a dozen leagues away." Captain Iuonx turned and shouted new orders at Arkko.

Davin started to ask after the pilot. Goran took his shoulder and squeezed. Davin winced. As he turned to complain, he saw the pilot at his post, idly moving the wheel.

"Where have you been?" Davin refused to believe that they had dreamed the red-shimmering ghost ship.

The pilot looked up sheepishly. "Don't tell Arkko. I tied the wheel after the storm and went to sleep."

"But—"

"Let it lie, Davin," the Challing whispered. "The ship was meant for us and not them, and we've the captain's orders to climb the topsail."

Davin saw the Challing tuck a hand beneath his filthy, tattered crimson tunic and reassure himself that the pendant was real. When one dealt with the Gods of Raemllyn, it became hard to separate reality from dream—from nightmare!

# *chapter*
## *12*

NEITHER CAPTAIN IUONX's dreaded whirlpool, which had never been sighted on the smooth blue-green ocean, nor the small pots Goran One-Eye raked in during a small, friendly game of dice, occupied Davin Anane's thoughts while he sat slung in a hammock, trying to down a rapidly cooling bowl of gruel. His mind concentrated on thievery. Not his own exploits, but crimes in which he had been the unsuspecting victim.

Lijena and Elozzi and Pynsartti . . . the list of names seemed endless as they repeated ceaselessly in his head. Since this journey had begun six months ago, Goran and he had continually fallen victim to thievery of one sort or the other. *And we are the master thieves of Raemllyn!*

His wooden spoon made a sickly plop as he shoved it into the bowl of gruel with disgust. Nor could Arkko be forgotten in the listing of those stealing from them. The first mate's meals would have been a crime even if no price were attached to them.

Placing the dregs of the meal aside, he lay back and closed his eyes. The enticing vision of a frosty-haired blonde flitted across his mind's eye. *Lijena!* A hollow ache born neither of hate nor anger suffused his chest. *Where is she now? How fares she with the burden she bears?* He would willingly risk facing her promise to kill him if they ever met again, to be at her side once more.

The Jyotian pursed his lips and quietly shook his head. How the world had somersaulted and then stood on its head since he had encountered Bistonia's fairest daughter! How distant their paths ever crossing again seemed with each passing day!

". . . ghost ship you say?" Bertam's irritating voice wedged inside and shattered Davin's self-pity. "Not that, though I wouldn't gainsay it. But the monsters! They dwell everywhere along this coast. Fierce jaws, incredible fangs, one quick bite can snap a small vessel like the *Twisted Cross* in twain!"

"Less children's tales, please. Roll the dice or pass them!" Goran complained. "Are you here to play or to frighten us with your sordid tales?"

"I seek not to frighten, only to inform—to warn! These are the most dangerous waters surrounding Raemllyn. The hell-spawned beasts are the product of evil magicks. Sorcerors cast out of Raemllyn once congregated along the northern shores and tried to outdo one another in their awful creations."

Davin heard Goran gust a heavy sigh that announced the dice game had drawn to an end through no fault of his own. The others were more intrigued listening to Bertam's tales than they were following the roll of the ivory cubes. In truth Davin didn't mind, although the lack of winnings would lighten their purses. He found himself increasingly interested in Tacllyn-lin-Bertam's motives.

What drove the man to spin such wild, gory tales? Surely Bertam realized he fired the crew's imagination, sending it soaring toward the point of uncontrollable panic. Soon every man jack of them would be seeing these mythical monsters lurking behind each foam-capped wave. Davin's thoughts wandered to a single conclusion—Bertam was an agent sent by Zarek Yannis to sow the seeds of discord aboard the ship.

If that were true, Bertam did a yeoman's work. And what of the gold-plated disks hidden in the cloth bales? Were they destined for Prince Felrad rather than the usurper, as he had first suspected?

"Teeth," Bertam continued in a breathless fervor, "bigger than knives! Swords! I've seen them. On my last voyage from Weysh to Rakell I saw the monsters with my own eyes!"

Davin sensed intrigue spinning here, but could not locate the thread of its weave. What use did Zarek Yannis have of such men, if it was true the usurper had war vessels patrolling this trade route? Why bother with individuals like Bertam?

A scream like the howl of a man bitten by a mad dog rang through the hold. Davin jerked upright, gaze shooting to the men encircling Bertam.

Gagno shoved to his feet as he screamed again. His right hand clawed a dirk from a scabbard hung at his waist. Sweat poured from the terrified man's face when he lifted the blade and waved it at Arkko. "Monsters! You and your Cap'n Iuonx won't be feeding me to no monsters!"

"Don't ever draw on me, Gagno. Not if you want to keep your worthless hide intact. I'll flay you a hundred times a day until we make port." Arkko met the challenge with a cold emotionless glare. He then turned to Bertam. "And you, if I hear you spreading your lies again, you'll chase the ship all the way to Evara."

The mate spun and stalked off. Gagno's trembling hand returned dirk to sheath. He wiped at his face and settled back in his bunk, his eyes nervously darting about the hold as though he expected the shadows hid unseen demons.

"He might threaten," said Bertam, "but the magical creatures birthed by vengeful mages threaten even more."

When Gagno stretched out on his bunk, Davin did likewise in the hammock. Lijena's image returned to taunt him when he closed his eyes.

Shrieks like those of a tormented soul in the fiery inferno of Peyneeha's lowest level shattered Davin's listless sleep. He rolled from the hammock and crouched, awaiting attack. It didn't come, but another scream wailed from topside.

*Gagno!* He recognized the old sailor's voice. A third wailing cry sent him running through the hold and up the ladder. There he peered into a night turned silver beneath Raemllyn's sister moons.

Frosty winged shapes darted and plunged across the deck. High-pitched squeals echoed through the night. *Sea bats!*

Davin breathed a sign of relief when he recognized the fluttering shapes. The avian creatures lived on rocks along the coast and often ventured far out to sea in their search for insects and small careless fish coming to the ocean surface to feed. Although they were disconcerting, the sea bats weren't dangerous.

Gagno's scream was that of a man beset by demons loosened from Nyuria's hellish cages!

"Gagno, they're harmless!" Davin called out. "There is nothing to fear."

The Jyotian's words did nothing to waylay Gagno's terror. The sailor ran wildly about the deck, slashing at the air with his dirk. The silvery forms easily avoided the recklessly jabbing blade.

"They're harmless," Davin repeated. "Merely bats."

Gagno raged. "They're monsters! They're everywhere. They

crawl into my ears and nose and suffocate me. I can't breathe! They come for me. No, Black Qar, I deny you! I won't go with you!"

"Gagno, he speaks the truth." This from the pilot, who lashed the ship's wheel in place and approached the raving sailor.

Davin motioned for the man to stay back. The pilot shook his head and grabbed for Gagno when the old man darted near. For his effort the pilot was rewarded with a deep slash across the belly that spewed forth dark blood. His cries joined Gagno's insane ranting.

Davin danced back when Gagno swung his way. He ducked and the older man's blade whistled over his head to sever three ropes behind him. Still Gagno ran about the deck, his blade slicing anything in its path. Line and ropes parted; the upper masts creaked. The sailor's screech was the heart of madness as his head jerked up to glare at the furled sails. In the blinking of an eye he darted to the rail, jumped atop it, and scrambled into the rigging. Behind him webbed rope fell to the deck as he cut away rigging to prevent easy pursuit.

"Stop the madman!" Captain Iuonx cried as he rushed from his cabin. "He'll ruin us. Damn the bastard's eyes! He's slicing our sails. Stop him."

"The monsters. In the ocean! The monsters rise up to devour us. Look at them coming for us!" Gagno screamed down on those who gathered below.

Davin cast a quick glance at the calm ocean surface. Like a liquid mirror it stretched featureless to the horizon. No demonic creature rose to devour the *Twisted Cross*. Whatever Gagno saw, it was the product of his own mind, stirred to life by Bertam's ghastly tales.

"Get him, damn you all!" roared Captain Iuonx.

Gango reached the lowest spar and hacked away the binding ropes. When one furled sail fell out, he ripped its length with his dirk. Upward he scampered, more quickly than any ape from distant Uhjayib jungles. He worked his way up the mast to reach the mainsail. His dagger flashed left and right, leaving destruction behind.

Davin stood on the farthest side of ship from the berserk sailor. With the rigging in front of him intact, he had a chance of reaching Gagno denied the others in the crew. Davin Anane climbed! His rope-blistered hands turned to fire. He ignored both pain and blood and moved faster.

Gango now started slashing the rigging holding the main cross spar. If he destroyed it, the *Twisted Cross* would require long days of repair, possibly in drydock. The merchanter might never reach a port unless Gagno stopped—or was stopped.

"The creatures. See their eyes? They burn with hatred for us. They'll eat us all!"

"Gagno," Davin said, trying to keep the panic from his own voice. "I'm here to help you. There are no monsters. You're imagining them. Bertam has planted the seed in your brain and now it's growing."

"Beasts of horrible aspect!" Gagno moaned. "They'll wreck the ship!"

"You'll do it for them if you don't stop." Davin sidestepped along the spar toward Gagno.

The madman deftly retreated farther out on the spar. Below him was the sea's mirrorlike surface. Davin silently thanked the gods. If they both tumbled from this precarious perch, he'd prefer that the ocean broke their fall than the ship's wooden deck.

"See?" demanded Gagno. "The monsters. See them?"

Davin knew better than to look down. Vertigo would destroy his balance and send him headlong into the water. He held out his hand to the man. "Give me the knife, Gagno. There's nothing to fear. Nothing."

"Bertam was right. The beasts rise from the mist and come for us."

"There's no mist for them to hide in," Davin said. Even as the words left his mouth he knew that logic meant nothing. Gagno had passed beyond common sense and fought from fear, from irrational panic.

"The monsters! They seek me out! They want me to die!"

"No, Gagno." Davin inched along the spar and grabbed the man's knife hand.

For a moment Davin sensed success. He held Gagno's arm at an angle, robbing the sailor of any leverage. But the blood on the Jyotian's hand betrayed him. His grip loosened and Gagno yanked his wrist free. The sailor's blade swiped out, missing Davin's chest by the thickness of a single strand of hair.

"You! You try to feed me to the sea monsters. I won't let you. I won't."

Gagno lunged for Davin's midriff. The Jyotian twisted aside to avoid being gutted. He slammed his fist down on the side of Gagno's head. The sailor lost his footing. Davin's right hand snaked out, dodging the knife and locking about the older man's wrist. Agony flared in the thief's right shoulder; the strain of the burden awoke muscles abused by his and Goran's escape from the ghost ship.

"My shoulder," he groaned. "Pull yourself up!"

The sailor only emitted tiny frightened squeaks, and swung, dangling in Davin's grip.

Far below, beneath the mirrored smoothness of the Oceans of Kumar, Davin saw two luminous yellow eyes staring up with unbridled malevolence. Eyes as large as a man's head even seen from the height of the ship's mast.

In the next instant the silvered mirror of water exploded. A monstrous serpentine head erupted amid foam and spray. A fanged mouth gaped wide and dark.

That moment of shock and disbelief combined with the slick blood that oozed from his wounded palms. Gagno's wrist was like glass as it slipped between Davin's grasping fingers.

Cartwheeling through the air, Gagno screamed all the way down. The monster deftly caught him in its mouth, swallowed, then slid beneath the surface of the sea.

Davin's head swirled; Gagno had been right! Shakily the Jyotian straightened. His foot slipped from beneath him. He fell, hands frantically seeking purchase.

He grabbed a rope—only to discover Gagno's blade had severed half its thickness. One by one the uncut strands popped under his weight. When the last one snapped, Davin Anane plunged toward the ocean and a hungry demonic beast that lurked beneath the waters!

# chapter
## *13*

DAVIN ANANE STRUCK the ocean shoulders first with arms and legs flailing. The impact and the shock of the icy water demanded and received an uncontrollable startled cry of pain. Saltwater filled the Jyotian's mouth and tried to gush down his throat to his lungs.

Thrusting aside the panic eating at his mind, Davin twisted and kicked out with both legs. Ignoring his throbbing shoulders and the fiery sting of brine bathing the raw wounds of his palms, he swam.

*Downward or up?* He didn't know. The fall left him stunned and disoriented, lost beneath the water's surface. Again panic flared, threatening to rob him of what remained of his senses. He didn't know up from down—and somewhere within these waters lurked the monstrous serpent that had devoured Gagno!

*I move!* He felt himself drifting in the frigid water. His natural buoyancy lifted him toward the ocean's surface. Arms reaching out in long, painful strokes, legs kicking with all their strength, he struggled through the inky water to the silvery forms of Raemllyn's two moons, Bak and Kea, liquidly glimmering above.

Davin's head popped above the surface. The air's ice breath slapped his face, opening mind and senses. Clearing mouth and nostrils, he sucked in; cold air rushed in to fill burning lungs.

"A line! Throw me a line!" he managed to call after another gulp of air.

Whether his voice was too weak to be heard or the crew had not noticed him, the young adventurer wasn't certain. He lifted an arm, waved it above his head—and slipped beneath the water. A scissored kick of his legs brought him to the surface again.

Sailors lined along the railing far above his head. He saw
them point, saw the waggling of their heads and the excited
movement of their mouths. But none made a move to aid him.

"Black Qar take you all, help me!" Davin shouted. "Throw
me a line!"

Still the crew did no more than point downward.

Before the thief could utter another curse, he understood
the reason for their reluctance. Some*thing* encircled his legs
and yanked him beneath the waves.

Twisting, writhing, the Jyotian struggled to break the tightening grip that bound ankles and calves. His efforts were for
naught. Down toward the frigid depths of the Oceans of Kumar
*it* dragged him.

Flowing with the overwhelming force that tugged him downward, Davin doubled over in an attempt to dive. The command
for his muscles to move never left his brain. The sight of the
dark mass that moved within the murky waters momentarily
robbed him of sense and reason.

About his legs a monstrous tentacle serpentinely coiled upward toward his thighs. But it was the sea serpent attached to
that binding appendage that paralyzed the Jyotian with terror.
In the watery darkness he was unable to see more than a vague
image of the beast's massive, bloblike proportions. Like a quav-
ery shadow it was. Within the center of that darkness a mouth
the breadth of a man gaped wide to expose a mouth ringed
with recurved teeth. A huge green eye blinked balefully above
the round mouth, as though the nightmare-escaped creature
appraised the morsel of food it had snared.

Ever closer to that cavernous maw the heir to the House of
Anane was tugged. Like a tormented man who had passed
beyond the veils of pain, it was as if he were an observer
watching another being devoured. He no longer fought, but
simply stared, accepting death's inevitable journey.

Again the creature blinked its single orb; a reaction that
Davin imitated. Something swam directly for the monster's
eye. Then he saw nothing. Currents of swirling blackness gushed
out to envelop the creature. At the same moment the tentacle
entrapping his legs loosened and slipped away. Life returned
to flaccid muscles, and Davin kicked away.

More unconscious than aware, the Jyotian broke the surface,
gulping down lungfuls of cold winter air. Less than an arm's

length from him the ocean erupted, and Goran One-Eye rose gasping for breath.

"A line, damn your pox-eaten hides! Throw us a line," the Challing bellowed.

From the *Twisted Cross* Arkko shouted an angry order. A thin rope flew over the merchanter's rail to slap into the water.

"Goran!" Davin stared at his friend, uncertain whether to believe his eyes.

"Who else would it be?" The Challing swam to the rope and waited for the Jyotian. "You've got to stop trying to save fools who tempt fate. Gagno wasn't worth it."

"Thank the gods you don't listen to your own words," Davin said as he took the rope and began to climb.

"The gods had naught to do with it." Goran snorted, then added, "It was a matter of habit! A bad habit in all likelihood, saving your life over all these years."

"They'll live," Captain Iuonx's gruff voice greeted the two as they crawled onto the ship's deck. "Get them and the rest of the scum back to their bunks, Arkko. We've the sails to repair and a whirlpool to face on the morrow. Damn Gagno! Would that the bastard were still alive so that I could strip his hide from his miserable body!"

"Up you go." Goran reached down and helped Davin to his feet.

"You risked revealing yourself," Davin whispered while they moved toward the hole. "Even though my life was at stake, you should have been more careful."

"What are you talking about?" asked Goran.

"Why, you shape-changed and then plunged in to fight the sea creature."

"I did?"

"How else could you have killed such a powerful monster?"

"But I didn't change shape," Goran said, sounding surprised. "I never thought about it until this moment. I could have changed into a narwhal. Or perhaps something truly vicious, and frightened off the beast. But it never occurred to me!"

"You fought that *thing* while still in your human form?" Davin's eyes widened.

The dripping giant shrugged and grinned. "I am a Challing after all. Besides I didn't kill the slimy beast . . . merely blinded it. Now below with you. I've wasted enough of a good night's rest."

Davin didn't answer, merely climbed into the hold in awe of his companion's strength and bravery.

"That's the last of the sails. Gagno was sloppy even as a madman. A few pitiful rents, nothing more." The Challing lounged back, feet propped up on a bundle of cloth.

"He was too much out of his mind to be systematic about his efforts," Davin answered. However, his thoughts were on the creatures he had seen last night. "Maybe Bertam's tales aren't so farfetched. Did we encounter the monsters he warns us about last night?"

"Hardly," scoffed Goran. "An oversized sea squid was after you, nothing more."

"It wasn't a squid that devoured Gagno." Davin shook his head. "It was like a sea serpent, only twice as large as any I've sighted before."

"'Twas the night playing tricks on your eyes, my friend. A squid got old Gagno and nearly had you for desert. And who should know giant squids better than I? I've seen dozens of them, most larger than this one."

"When?" Davin cocked an eyebrow suspiciously. Within weeks after Goran had killed the mage Roan-Jafar, they had joined forces to rove across the stretches of Upper Raemllyn. There had been no time for Goran to have encountered even one of these gigantic squids, much less the dozens he claimed. "Or do you mean there are such in Gohwohn?"

"My precious homeland? Hardly. Nothing is static of form in Gohwohn. No, I first saw one of those creatures off Meakham, in the Sea of Qatera. And it was that beast that robbed me of my precious eye."

"What are you saying?" Davin tried to roll over in his hammock and entangled a foot in the webbing. He groaned. Fate trapped him into listening to another lie spun around Goran's missing orb.

Before Goran could launch the tale, Bertam came over and hunkered down by Davin's hammock. A twisted little smile of amusement curled his thin lips when he looked at Jyotian and Challing before his gaze settled on Davin.

"You were lucky," the man said, eyes dancing with merriment. "The demons residing within the veiling mists seldom allow a mortal to escape their clutches."

"That was no demon," said Davin. "It was a sea squid. Goran saw it closely."

"It was a beast from the mist, one spawned by the renegade mages of Raemllyn," insisted Bertam.

"A squid," Goran bellowed. "Do you call me a liar?"

"No, no," Bertam said hastily, falling back against a bale and holding out his hands to fend off the angered Challing. "I only meant that you might have been mistaken. You dived so deep; you fought for your friend's life. Did you see the beast *that* closely?"

"I saw it," Goran grumbled.

"Ah, but you weren't able to examine it. How could you? You were courageously rescuing Davin. Tell me, isn't it possible this was a beast of magical origins?"

"Flesh and blood," said Goran, but the tone he used showed some doubt existed.

"A magical beast might show itself as being of flesh and blood," argued Bertam. "Sorcerors are wickedly crafty with their spells. This might be just the first of many such creatures."

"I'll grant that I may be wrong, but it had none of the feel of evil magicks about it."

"What does a wanderer such as yourself know of forbidden magicks?" Bertam arched an eyebrow.

Before Goran could open his mouth and reveal the exact extent of his knowledge of mystical lore, Davin cut in. "Why are you so intent on proving this more than a natural sea creature?"

"I only wish for all aboard the *Twisted Cross* to know the danger Captain Iuonx sails toward. To be warned is to be ready for . . . anything."

"After being so intimately embraced by the squid's tentacles, I'm on guard." Davin grunted, although he was less than convinced that his eyes had mistaken a squid for a serpent.

"That's all I want," Bertam said without a trace of sincerity in his words. The man quickly left. Minutes later Davin heard Bertam muttering to others in the crew how Goran had branded the squid a creature of magical origin.

"But I never made such a claim," Goran protested, hand balling to hammerlike fists. "It's time someone closed the whoreson's foul mouth!"

Davin restrained his companion with a firm hand on the

changeling's broad shoulder. "Bertam is correct in one respect, though. If we are warned, we can be on guard."

"I'll watch him for the slightest mistake," vowed Goran.

"There's no need. What's he to do? Sink the ship? If the *Twisted Cross* sinks, so does he."

In truth Davin had no glimmering of Bertam's secret motives. It made no sense to drive men mad, as Bertam's fanciful tales had done with Gagno. The *Twisted Cross* might have been seriously crippled, or even left adrift by Gagno's wild actions. How would any man have benefited by that?

"Topside, all ye scurvy rats!" Arkko's voice called down into the hold. "We set sail, and Captain Iuonx wants every man jack of ye on the decks!"

With Goran mumbling about having just worked his fingers to the bone mending the sails, Jyotian and Challing left their bunks to climb the ladder to the deck.

There Arkko tapped their shoulders and pointed to the main mast. "Lookouts again. And keep your eyes open. The whirlpool's no place for a man or ship to end a life!"

Reaching his high perch, Davin wrapped a rope about his middle and hung from the uppermost rigging like an insect caught in a spider's web. He slowly spun from one side to the other, eyes scanning the water for signs of rock or other obstacle to the *Twisted Cross*' smooth passage. When he scanned the horizon, his jaw sagged.

Beside him Goran gasped. "I see why Captain Iuonx fears it so!" Goran's good eye focused on the maelstrom aswirl in the distance.

The raging vortex of water churned, a full league separating side from side. At the periphery only small currents were visible. With every full rotation around the core, the water became more turbulent, foam and spray spewing into the air, the force more intense, the likelihood of escape less a possibility. If the *Twisted Cross* became trapped in that swirling oceanic equivalent of quicksand, it would be broken into splinters.

What of the center? Neither Goran nor Davin saw into the core. How many ships had been sucked into that point and pulled down . . . to what? To the lowest levels of Peyneeha?

"Might this be Bertam's beast?" asked Goran. "At the center of that whirlpool?"

Davin considered. Although some magical beast might crouch in the maelstrom's heart, he didn't see how such a large vortex could be maintained year after year by some mage's magicks. The spell would require continual tending—and what mage possessed that much power? Even the dreaded Lorennion had been too feeble to affect the ocean on such a scale. No man or woman since the days of Kwerin Bloodhawk and his mage Edan had wielded such power. The magicks that once bound Raemllyn had been in steady decline for those thousands of years—until Zarek Yannis revived the Faceless Ones.

Davin swallowed hard and shifted position to get a better look at the whirlpool. Could this be Yannis' doing? It was said that his war vessels patrolled the northern coasts of Upper Raemllyn to interdict shipments to Prince Felrad's fortress at Rakell.

Davin shook off such suspicion. Captain Iuonx had traveled this route for years, long before Zarek Yannis had ascended the Velvet Throne. The whirlpool wasn't of magical origin, or if it was, it couldn't be Yannis' doing.

Goran bellowed down that the whirlpool had been sighted. Davin saw Captain Iuonx's immediate response. The man ordered the pilot to steer northerly, well clear of even the most remote current from the vortex.

"We'll miss it by five leagues and more," said Goran. "I, for one, have no desire to skirt closer. In this Captain Iuonx has made the right decision."

Davin said nothing. He frowned as he studied a storm cloud the vortex seemed to suck from the sky. *No!* He shook his head. The cloud bank was beyond the maelstrom and appeared to be laying atop the water. The surface of the ocean stretched peacefully to that point, marred only by the whirlpool now to their starboard. Above both cloud and whirlpool, the sky grayed with the coming evening.

"I don't like the look of that." Davin pointed toward the dark storm front they approached.

"What's a little wind and rain when we've skirted past a monster like that?" Goran peered over a shoulder, still staring at the maelstrom.

Disquiet suffused the young Jyotian adventurer. There was something—something different—about the approaching clouds, something he could not put into words, but sensed. He called down a warning.

Below Captain Iuonx lowered a spyglass he used so intently to study the circular ripples marking the whirlpool's boundary.

"I see the storm. Nothing but a winter gale. Keep your eyes peeled for real danger!"

"But Captain, there's something amiss. Those aren't ordinary storm clouds. They . . . they seem to have a life of their own. They move wrong for clouds."

Captain Iuonx glared up to the top of the mast. "I'll have none of that talk from you. I've ordered Bertam to stow his wild stories. I'll not have it! From ye or Bertam! Attend to your duties or I'll have ye given fifty of the best across your back!"

Davin did as ordered, his attention focused on the cloud bank. Could the storm drive the *Twisted Cross* back into the swirling death waters of the maelstrom? He tried to discard the notion, but couldn't.

"Davin, look at the storm. It takes the shape of a beast with mouth wide." Goran's voice intruded on Davin's dark thoughts. "It is truly a strange formation, one unlike any I've seen before."

"The captain's not going to swerve to avoid the storm," said Davin. "I think he's gong out of his way to steer around the whirlpool and doesn't want to lose more time."

"There's been enough lost already," Goran agreed. "Gagno put us a full day behind schedule with his insanity."

"What does lost time matter?" asked Davin. "We're not in this crew of our own free will. Or have you forgotten that we were twice sold into slavery?"

"Captain Iuonx's not a bad master," said Goran.

"Any master is."

"On that point I will not argue. But I have become used to bondage—the bondage of this human form." Goran stared down at his immense, powerfully muscled frame. "In Gohwohn we shifted shapes whenever it amused us, which was often. That is denied me here."

"Not often enough is it denied you," Davin grumbled out of habit, but his mind was elsewhere.

The aspect of the cloud bank into which the merchanter sailed grew more ominous. Black, as if laden with heavy rains, the clouds clung to the ocean like a shroud. As the *Twisted Cross* left behind the whirlpool and slipped toward the storm, Davin saw no indication of rain falling. Only the mockery of jaws opening—and the *Twisted Cross* sailing squarely down the storm beast's gullet.

The cargo ship slid forward easily, gliding along the glass-smooth ocean. Davin looked up and saw the long tendrils of misty cloud descend as if the insubstantial beast closed its jaws. He shuddered. Only imagination, he told himself. Morbid imagination.

A scream ripped through the stillness. Davin spun and faced the stern. One sailor stood with his back arched, his face a mask of agony. At first Davin saw no reason for the odd behavior. Then it became horrifyingly obvious.

A thin, wispy tendril of fog slithered up and over the railing to stroke across the sailor's throat. Like a garrote the wet fog closed around the man's throat. The sailor's face turned livid as air was cut off from lungs. The more he struggled, the redder his face became.

"He's being strangled!" Davin cried, untying himself and scrambling down the rigging. He hit the deck in a run for the stern, with Goran at his heels. Neither officer or crew moved toward the dying man as the Jyotian darted past the wheel where the pilot and Captain Iuonx stood transfixed. Davin grabbed the sailor's arm and tried to pull him free of the imprisoning mist fingers.

He failed. The sailor might as well have been locked in place with iron chains. Davin watched in helpless horror as the lacy tendrils of fog tightened and life fled the man's body in twitching muscle spasms. Only when the crewman hung limply did the fog fingers release its victim.

The fog swirled, retreated, then took on substance again, this time reaching for Davin. He backed away, stepping over the sailor's corpse.

"Goran! The mist takes on a life of its own."

"A malevolent life, at that," said Goran. The Challing interposed himself between Davin and the mist.

For a moment the mist appeared to be confused, to not understand this ploy. Davin saw Goran's eye burning with witchfire. The magicks astir in this storm were potent enough to awaken Goran's latent talents and bring forth . . . what?

The fog thickened, surged, and smashed against Goran's barrel chest. The red-haired giant bellowed even as his eye blazed an emerald green.

Then it was over. As quickly as the attack had come, it ended. The fog dissipated as if in the presence of syrupy spring sunlight.

"It's gone," Goran said, rubbing his chest. He acted as if he'd been stung by insects.

"Gone," Davin repeated dully. He turned and saw Captain Iuonx's horrified expression. Another of his sailors had perished, not to some night-preying sea serpent or squid, but living mist!

Beyond the captain of the *Twisted Cross* stood Tacllyn-lin-Bertam. His expression wasn't one of horror but of . . . amusement!

# chapter
## 14

"HOW ARE WE supposed to see living fog at night?" Goran spat in disgust. "Iuonx says keep the *Twisted Cross* clear? How, I ask you? How?"

Raemllyn's moons more than adequately lit the ocean with a sheening mantle of reflected silver. For leagues in all directions the night was clear and calm, a situation for which Davin Anane silently thanked Great Yehseen. Since the brief encounter with the living mist, nary a man aboard the merchanter had seen sight of fog bank or monster lurking beneath the water.

"I can see all right," Davin said, grateful for the peace of their early morning watch. "Just keep me awake and I'll keep the watch."

The Jyotian's request was a mistake. In not specifying the manner in which Goran was to disperse the veils of sleep, Davin left himself wide open. For the next half hour the Challing systematically cursed every member of Raemllyn's pantheon of dieties. When he had profaned the name of even the most minor god, he began anew itemizing their personal habits and failings. The changeling ended by casting aspersion on their heredity and generally berating everyone and everything in Raemllyn.

"I grow weary, friend Davin. This ball of mud you call a world drains me with each passing second." Goran heaved a pathetic sigh, and his single eye drooped forlornly, like that of an old hound. "How I ache to forgo this human body and return to Gohwohn. There we know how to live. Without form!"

Davin hid his amusement by glancing out to sea. Ever since he'd known the Challing, Goran had vehemently protested his imprisonment in human flesh. Yet let them enter a city and the changeling's mood changed drastically—as drastically as his body did on occasion.

Davin snorted. Nor did a male body seem enough to sate

his friend's appetite. Now that he regained some measure of his Challing powers, he shifted to female shapes to more fully examine the human condition from every side—and position!

With a bewildered shake of his head, Davin scanned the eastern horizon. He could do without such explorations of human sexuality on Goran's—or Glylina's—part. The world was a strange enough place with magicks thought long dead being reborn.

Davin did a double take, his eyes narrowing as he peered eastward.

*Nothing.* He reassured himself that he hadn't seen a flash of phosphorescent green near the line where night met the sea. *Merely moonlight dancing off a wave in the distance.* The sea squid, the fog, and Bertam's tables had left his thoughts scrambled. He was as bad as the rest of the crew, seeing writhing things out of the corners of his eyes.

"At least there are stars here," Goran said, punctuating his sentence with another ponderous sigh. "Though these heavens pale in comparison with the jewels that fill Gohwohn's sky."

Davin's head lifted to the wheeling constellations above. The Wardog, a winter constellation, dipped low over the horizon and made way for the star patterns more appropriate to spring. The Throne was visible along with the most complex of the constellations, the Chained Maiden. Davin traced along the broken links to the Maiden's starry wrists, to the necklace of bright red and green stars, past that to the gauzy starfall of her hair.

A warm, comforting sensation filled the young freebooter as memories of his youth in Jyotis edged aside thoughts of fog and monstrous serpents. How many nights had he spent lying atop grassy hills and staring at the sky, tracing out the Maiden, learning and sharing the secrets of youth? Had there been a better time or place in which to be alive?

Davin's thoughts darkened. All that had been before Berenicis, known as the Blackheart. Lord Berenicis safely seated atop the throne of Jyotis had destroyed the House of Anane and Davin's mother. He then falsely labeled Anane's last son a murderer, forcing Davin to flee his homeland before the executioner's blade found his neck.

"Good night to be asail," said Goran, easing Davin from his remembrances. The Challing nudged his friend. "Isn't that Tacllyn-lin-Bertam below?"

Davin shifted his position in the ropes and stared down to the deck. Bertam walked from the hold to the *Twisted Cross*' prow, to stand near the railing, staring eastward.

"I wonder what stirs him in the middle of the night?" Davin watched the man lean on the rail. "There's no one about to frighten with his tales."

"Forget him, Davin. Enjoy the night. Both moons are bright like silver coins in the sky," Goran said, apparently not wishing to be bothered with thoughts of the lean Bertam and his pale-blue eyes afire with sparks of madness. "It is a good night. No storms, no clouds."

"Does it matter? The fog bank today was no natural storm. That demonic mist might appear anywhere—and I'm certain Bertam knows more about it than he's told us." Davin blinked when his head jerked around to face Goran. For an instant he imagined green flames of witch-fire adance in the Challing's single eye. But when he looked again, there was nothing.

"He's done his best to frighten everyone out of their skins."

"That he has," Davin answered, still unable to fathom Bertam's motives, but equally unable to believe the man an innocent spinner of wild tales.

"Dawn will be upon us within the hour." Goran once again changed the subject.

Davin glanced back to the eastern horizon. Just above the glass-smooth water the night's blackness faded to the grays and purples of predawn. He shivered and hugged his cloak tightly about chest and shoulder. Spring might nip at winter's heels, but its warming breath had yet to touch the air.

Again he did a double take. Nothing! He blinked and rubbed his sleep-weary eyes. It was there again, neither a trick of mind or eye. "There, see it? Underwater?"

"Aye! Nyuria's scorched arse! What is it?"

A shining vee of phosphorescent green water trailed behind a monstrous black object. The burning trail homed on a course that would intersect the *Twisted Cross* in a matter of minutes.

"Danger! All hands to their posts! Prepare for boarding!" Davin yelled down to the ship.

Below, the somnolent pilot jerked awake. Other voices picked up the Jyotian's warning cry. Arkko stumbled on deck, followed by a line of crewmen. From out of his cabin Captain Iuonx hastened to his position by the wheel. The bearded man thrust a finger toward the glowing green that rushed toward the ship.

"We're of no use up here." Goran disentangled arms and legs from the rigging. "I have no desire to watch the *Twisted Cross* sink beneath me. I'd rather go out fighting."

"A serpent," Davin said, studying the green-glowing trail more carefully. "And a big one!"

"If a serpent bleeds, it can die." Goran kicked free and fell toward the deck.

At the last possible instant he grabbed a rope. Davin saw the mighty muscles stand out on the Challing's shoulders as he broke his fall to land lightly on deck. Scarcely had he brushed off his hands than Arkko shoved a war club at him. Goran took it and grinned so broadly Davin could see it from halfway up the main mast.

Davin alighted in time to pick up a rusty cutlass. He spun awkwardly, bumped into Arkko and said, "Sorry." When he turned back from the cursing mate, he had a sharp, shiny dagger to supplement the sword.

Goran's grin widened when he glimpsed Davin's pilfered booty. A grin that shattered when a man's scream rent the darkness.

Davin pivoted, sword and dirk raised to meet attack. Not the head of the monstrous serpent he had sighted from above, but the leathery tentacle of a titanic squid lashed the air to dip over the side of the cargo ship. Angry red suckers on the underside sought and found human flesh. A sailor frozen in fear died when the tentacle coiled about his midriff, hoisted him from the deck, then dragged beneath the Oceans of Kumar.

"Davin! Behind you!" Goran roared a warning.

Again the Jyotian thief spun. A second dark tentacle mottled with patches of phosphorescent green lifted above the *Twisted Cross*' rail. Davin's cutlass found the groping appendage. Curved steel bit into leather-tough flesh. Halfway through the thigh-thick tentacle the blade sliced. Yellow blood boiled from the wound, but the tentacle did not retreat as the Jyotian had expected.

Instead it whipped up like a striking cobra, suckers attaching themselves to his sword arm. Three swipes of Arkko's stolen dagger and Davin severed hungry flesh and danced away from the monstrous arm that would have swept him overboard.

A loud *whish* came from his left. Goran brought down the war club with every ounce of strength in his mountainous body. Pulped flesh rather than clean cut left the tentacle sundered in twain. While the still-living portion of the hellish appendage slithered back into the sea, the remnants of tentacle writhed its death throes on the deck.

"No sea squid this!" Goran pointed to a dozen or more of the tentacles as they rose from the depths and lashed about the ship.

Above those flesh-seeking whips of living leather arched a scaled neck fully as thick as the largest of Agda's massive trees. And atop that neck, the head of a gigantic serpent. Unblinking slitted eyes of yellow and green glared their malevolence down on the ship's decks.

"What manner of beast is it?"

Goran's question went unanswered. Davin darted across the water-slick boards of the deck to aid a sailor entrapped in a tentacle that coiled about his legs.

Too late was the Jyotian's cutlass. Before he took two strides the monster hefted the hapless wight over the rail and wrenched him beneath the foaming water.

In the next pounding beat of Davin's heart, the massive neck of green-glowing scales arched and the serpent's head plunged into the water.

Then there was nothing, except for gentling ripples that spread upon a quiet sea.

"It's taken its meal and left us be," someone whispered behind Davin as the *Twisted Cross*' crew stood staring about in cautious disbelief. Another voice answered, "Aye, but when will it return?"

Davin turned to his friend. "What is this thing? You're the world traveler, the sailor without peer."

Goran glanced at the still tentacle he had severed, and scratched his thick beard. "A changeling creature mayhaps. One able to take the form of squid or serpent . . . or both in the same instant?"

Davin shook his head; he had no answers either. Whatever the monstrous beast was, he was certain it had not been born of this realm.

The Jyotian's gaze slowly traveled about the ship, searching, and found Tacllyn-lin-Bertam. The man still stood at the merchanter's prow. An expression of ecstasy twisted his features in a grotesque mockery of human pleasure.

• • •

Davin winced when Arkko's whip bit its tenth lash into the sailor's bared back. The sweat-glistening man sagged against the mast while the *Twisted Cross'* first mate coiled his whip and tucked it into his brass-buckled belt.

"Cut him loose and douse his hide with seawater!" Captain Iuonx called out. "Twenty lashes for the next man who even whispers that the *Twisted Cross* should seek refuge along the coast. My ship's a merchant vessel, and I'll see that she makes her port of call—*on time*—if I have to throw each and every one of ye to sea serpents to do it!"

With that the captain pivoted smartly and strode back into his cabin. Every eye remained on his back until the door to the cabin slammed shut.

"Ye heard our cap'n." This from Arkko, whose voice could not disguise a hint of terror. "Back to your duties, and be quick about it."

Davin sensed an undercurrent of dangerously mounting tension in the crew as they silently returned to their posts. There was more than last night's attack at work here. Death was common to those who sailed Raemllyn's seas, even though hell-spawned monsters from the ocean's depth weren't.

"Bertam is right," two sailors whispered when they stepped past the Jyotian. "We should put in to land before the beasts devour all of us!"

*Bertam!* Davin should have known the man was at the root of the insanity that had possessed the ship this day. The whipping he had just witnessed was the second within hours. Both men had demanded that Captain Iuonx seek safe harbor along the coast.

And there had been fights! Five times before the noon sun shone on the merchanter's decks, men in the crew had gone at each other's throats. Iuonx's armed guerrillas once more stood guard along the rail, a measure that had been unnecessary since the ship had left Faldin.

"Bertam works them well." Goran nudged his companion and nodded to the lanky man who slipped from sailor to sailor. "See how he moves from one to another, whispering a word here and an encouragement there?"

Davin nodded as he started up the rigging to once more take his position as lookout.

"We could eliminate many of our problems by tossing him overboard," suggested Goran.

"Are you of mind to do so?" Davin paused and looked over a shoulder at his friend.

"Of course not, but it's tempting. We have to keep him alive. How else are we going to learn what the man's about?" Goran smiled wickedly. "That's another thing that intrigues me about being in human form—curiosity."

"It may not matter." A wave of icy cold worked its way up Davin's spine. He pointed toward the eastern horizon, where another fog bank formed. "Is it natural or magical?"

Goran shrugged. "Who can say?"

"We'll be able to," said Davin, uneasiness rising even more within him. "We're sailing directly for it. I wonder if Captain Iuonx knows."

Goran collared Arkko as the mate passed by. The man swung on Goran, and the Challing released him. Without a word Goran indicated the fog.

"The cap'n knows what he's doing," said Arkko.

"It might be another like the other we encountered. Can't we steer around it, just to be safe?"

"Too much time's been lost by the likes of ye standing around and spinning your wild fancies. Get back to your posts and pray I don't make an example of ye."

Once again Davin noted the terror the first mate carried in his heart as he stalked away. A hint of hysteria quavered in his words; the whites showed around his eyes. Arkko's muscles were tautly bundled like a man about to explode.

When the mate was out of earshot, Davin said, "The *Twisted Cross* isn't going to survive much longer. I wish we were close enough to land to try swimming for shore."

"Remember what happened last time?" Goran posed. "The water's still cold. And all I know is that Raemllyn is somewhere in that direction." He waved his arm, indicating the south.

"We wouldn't have the time to swim," said Davin. "The fog's too close. And it looks ominously similar to the bank we encountered yesterday."

Course unfaltering, the *Twisted Cross* sailed directly for the fog bank. Again Davin had the premonition of a mouth opening, of the fog swallowing them whole. He looked above and saw thin ridges of mist dropping down: teeth. Ahead he saw dull red: throat.

When the *Twisted Cross* passed through the mouth, Davin looked to the stern. The mouth closed, the teeth meshing like prison bars, shutting off their escape.

"To your posts," Arkko bellowed when he noticed the crew's attention centered on the mists that enveloped the ship. "This is only fog. I'll tolerate no more malingering!"

The first mate's command drowned in a shriek of pain and horror—a terrified cry from the pilot which abruptly ended in a strangled gurgle.

A misty tendril formed above the man's head and dropped to loop around his neck. It constricted! So swift and so powerful, it closed like the snapping of a thread-thin garrote. The pilot's head leaped from his shoulders in a spray of crimson.

The door to the captain's cabin flew open. Seeing headless pilot toppled to the deck, Iuonx darted toward the wheel. His first step on the blood-drenched boards sent his legs out from under him. He fell, head popping loudly against wood. Nor did he rise.

The *Twisted Cross* sailed on, out of control!

Neither Davin nor Goran noticed as they scrambled from the mast. About them the mist took on solidity; slavering beasts of pale gray formed to loom above them, pouncing beasts of prey intent on devouring all aboard the *Twisted Cross*.

Goran cursed at the top of his lungs when he swung war club into a crablike creature the size of a dog that came scrambling across the deck toward his legs. The beast vanished into a smokey haze the instant the spiked club touched it.

Three feet away a wolf with three heads materialized in the fog and leaped for the Challing!

"How do you kill such? Look!" Goran demanded while swinging his club again.

The creature's skulls should have exploded like ripe gourds under the club's impact. Instead they evaporated into mist. The weighty weapon passed through them, leaving only eddies in the fog.

"By Father Yehseen's gnarled knuckles, don't stop fighting them!" Davin called to Goran as his cutlass impaled a gray tricorn that darted from the churning clouds. "We can't kill them, but they can rob our lives!"

The Challing gazed about the merchanter's deck. None in the crew, no matter what manner of weapon they wielded, had any more luck than he—and yet the tendrils found legs and arms and necks and squeezed the life from the sailors.

The battle went against those aboard the *Twisted Cross*. They couldn't fight beasts who turned to mist when attacked but proved all too solid when the battle flowed in the other direction.

Davin saw that Goran's eye danced with the witch-fire. The Challing proved an accurate indicator of the diabolical magicks weaving around the ship, for all the good that did. Davin slashed repeatedly at a toadlike beast. A quick dagger stab forced it to vanish into a wet puff of fog; Davin had scant opportunity to rest. The creature reappeared a few feet distant and launched itself at him anew.

Davin backed away until he bumped into Goran. Together they fought back to back, cutlass and club constantly slicing at the ceaseless barrage of nameless horrors that pushed from the mists. A human-headed bat disappeared when Goran's club struck it in a powerful swing; a lizard the size of a man vanished on the backswing.

Likewise Davin split a Narainlike demon from head to tail and ripped open the misty belly of a beetle that walked on human legs. However, he raged in pain when one beast of the mist penetrated his defense and raked a misty talon along his right leg.

The appendage, mist though it was, cut like steel. Davin lost his footing and collapsed to a knee. Still the mist came for him—in the form of a striking cobra. The Jyotian's wrist flicked, and the tip of the cutlass sent the deadly serpent back into the fog that had given it birth.

Struggling to his feet, leg burning as if on fire, he faced a raging great cat and another of the toadlike creatures. Both sword and dagger leaped out, dispatching the misty demons.

"We can't fight much longer," Davin panted. "We're tiring, and there seems an inexhaustible supply of them."

"Can't fight longer anyway," Goran said. "Look. Above, to the sides, all around."

"Black Qar be damned!" Davin gasped in unbridled horror.

A circular band of mist formed on each side of the *Twisted Cross*. It arched into the air to join above the mast. The band tightened, squeezing inward. The ship lurched; boards moaned as if a human in pain. Timbers gave way and the mast warped to starboard, threatening to shatter. Still the band of mist closed on them.

"It will cut us in twain," Arkko cried. "Stop it!"

Neither Davin Anane nor Goran One-Eye moved. How could either defeat fog?

The *Twisted Cross* lurched harder. The band squeezed downward, driven by magicks intent on splitting the merchanter and sinking her in the living mist.

# chapter
## 15

"SHE'S BREAKING UP! We're going down!" A frightened cry tore from the lips of a sailor. Like a virulent disease his fear swept through the imperiled ship until the throats of the crew burned with their terrified howls. "We're sinking! We're splitting in half."

The timbers of the *Twisted Cross* creaked and groaned between the ever-increasing pressure of the descending band of mist.

Only two aboard the merchanter, an exiled Jyotian and a changeling from another dimension trapped in human form, broke through the numbing horror of their plight and rushed midship. With weapons lashing they battled the crushing band in the same manner as they had fended away the myriad of creatures the fog unleashed on the deck.

All in vain! Goran One-Eye's doubly spiked war club passed harmlessly through the misty band. Davin Anane fared no better; his ill-balanced cutlass raked the fog with no effect.

"Back!" Goran shoved his companion backward as he made a hasty retreat from the tightening gray arch. "She's going to give way!"

Claw-torn thigh throbbing, Davin stumbled across the deck, trying to maintain his balance. His back slammed heavily into a mast, reawakening the pain of still healing shoulders.

A crack thundered like the ear-deafening splitting of a gigantic tree snapped at its base in tornado winds. A side member of the *Twisted Cross* broke and shattered under the mist's demonic force. Splinters the length of a man's forearm showered the air like a barrage of miniature arrows. Davin threw himself to the deck and protectively shielded his head with hands and arms as the deadly missiles whistled above to embed themselves in the mainmast.

"The ship's doomed! And we with it, I fear, friend Davin!"

Goran shouted while he agilely rode the deck buckling beneath his feet. Futility filled his voice and glum expression.

Davin pushed to his knees. Still the unrelenting mist squeezed down around the merchanter like some unholy snake coiled about its helpless prey. Sailors screamed their terror, cursed the cruel fate the Sitala had dealt them, and prayed to deaf gods for salvation.

Except for Tacllyn-lin-Bertam!

The mast lending support to his pain-wracked body, Davin pulled to his feet and stared at the man. Bertam struggled to retain purchase on the quaking wooden deck. He desperately clung to the ladder that led up to the wheel deck where Iuonx fought vainly to turn the ship away from danger. However, neither terror nor fear etched their deep lines on Bertam's face; instead Davin saw an expression he could only describe as triumph.

Bertam's pale-blue eyes lifted to the mist. His mouth jerked wide and he screamed into the face of the clouds.

Lightning! An actinic bolt seared through the mist like a grotesquely twisted blade wrenched from some sky giant's forge. Thunder rolled with the anger of Mount Tenhine erupting, its reverberating force throwing Davin against the mast.

"Magicks." Goran staggered as though reeling beneath a mighty blow. "I feel it! It knots my gut! It burns my eye!"

Davin stretched out an arm and snagged Goran's wide leather belt. Shoulders protesting with flaring pain, he yanked the stumbling Challing to the security of the mast.

Lightning and thunder split the sky once more. Then the wind roared. Born in the single throb of a heart, a howling gale rose, tossing the *Twisted Cross* from side to side. Timber and board groaned as though in agony. Davin and Goran locked arms about the shaking mast and held on for their lives.

Others were not so lucky. Davin saw two sailors lifted from the deck and hurled over the rail as though some unseen hand caught them in invisible fingers and flung them into the ocean.

"The mist!" Davin shouted into the yowling wind. "The fog is torn away!"

Goran's single eye burned like a living jewel as witch-fire flared. But whether he saw the living mist ripped apart until only smoky threads wove about the ship, Davin couldn't tell. As the last of those misty wisps dissipated, the wind's scream fell to the whisper of a gentle breeze.

"Gone!" Davin gasped, unable to comprehend the preter-
natural forces that had battled for the merchanter. However, he
thanked Yehseen and Nalren and any other god or goddess who
protected the ship this day.

Beside him Goran groaned and sank to his knees. "Nyuria's
arse! I've felt nothing like this since moments before we encountered the *kehdeen*." Goran's eye, still aglow with flames
of green, lifted to a clear sky. "Is another of those damnable
creatures about?"

Davin searched the cloudless blue for the twin-tailed winged
dragon of Gohwohn. Neither dragon nor gull could be seen.

"By the gentle gods, it passes." The Challing's eye returned
to its normal jade with golden flecks. He shoved from the deck
and stood shakily. "Whew! The magicks are gone and left me
as weak as a babe in its mother's arms."

"Rest on the deck." Davin could not disguise his concern.
It was a rarity to see his friend so shaken.

"Nay!" Goran waved the young Jyotian away. "I need but
a moment or two to regain my breath."

"Are you certain? You may . . ."

Captain Iuonx's railing voice blanketed Davin's words. The
captain shouted orders, his arms pointing here and there at his
ship and crew in an attempt to regain a semblance of order
aboard the *Twisted Cross*. The blighted vessel listed heavily
to the port side. The mainmast had escaped damage, but the
foresail had been snapped off by the constricting bands of the
preternaturally solid mist. Captain Iuonx leaned far out over
the side and studied the ship's tortured hull.

"Bad!" the officer growled. "See, Arkko? The keel hasn't
been broken, but the hull is leaking there and there and there.
We're shipping water badly. Get a crew into the hold to work
the pumps. We'll sink straight to the bottom unless ye put their
backs into it."

Arkko hurried off to get a half-dozen sailors working the
hand pumps. Large hoses were draped over the side and the
pumps began, amid much groaning and complaining from
the four men operating them. The other two sank waist deep
in the filthy bilge-laden water already shipped, and made certain
that the hoses stayed clear of debris that might foul the pumps.
Every ten minutes two of the pumpers exchanged places with
those in the hold.

Others were put to work buttressing the crippled ship's struc-

ture above decks. Goran and Davin helped force a brace against
the port side under Captain Iuonx's direction. Wiping sweat
from his forehead, Goran rested and studied the damage done
to the ship.

"We'll never be able to sail to Evara," the Challing said.
"Look? See the splits in the hull? If we all manned the pumps,
the *Twisted Cross* would still take water and eventually sink.
We'll have to put in to land for repair."

"That won't please Iuonx," Davin replied, "but he's the
only one. However, there's one among us who may be more
pleased than the rest of us."

"Bertam?" Goran glanced around and saw the amused, almost mocking smile twisting Bertam's lips. "He has the look
of a man who single-handedly defeated Qar's own demons!
Wonder what the whoreson is up to now?"

The Challing's comment sent a shivery chill racing up
Davin's spine. Was Bertam somehow responsible for the gale
that destroyed the mist? Or had both fog and wind come at his
beckoning?

The young freebooter shoved the ridiculous thoughts aside.
He had not witnessed Bertam weave a single magical gesture
with hands or fingers. Like every man aboard the *Twisted Cross*
Bertam had clung for his life and screamed his curses against
both wind and fog.

"Land ho! Ten leagues to the port, by five points. Clear seas
all the waaaay!" The joyous cry edged aside Davin's dark
ponderings.

Iuonx rushed to the port, hoisted his spyglass, and spent the
next five minutes peering at the find.

"An island," the captain said, his voice curiously flat. "Not
one I've ever seen, and I've sailed this route for thirty years."

"What difference does it make?" Arkko asked anxiously.
"We need a safe harbor to repair the hull. We're sinking, Cap'n.
Without a considerable amount of work, we'll vanish beneath
the waves."

"What's the difference, ye ask. This is no island I've ever
seen, either with my own eyes or on a chart. Never heard talk
of it in any tavern, from any other captain or sailor. Where has
it come from?"

A smile still twisting his lips, Bertam turned and descended
through a hatch to work with the crew in the hold.

"A fair island, Cap'n," said Arkko. The mate leaned over the rail and alternated between keeping a close watch on the leaking hull and the way the *Twisted Cross* eased into the peaceful island harbor. "The green blanketing that mountain speaks of a dense forest."

"We can use the peaceful water," said Captain Iuonx. He shouted orders, the sails were furled, and the *Twisted Cross* slowed.

Davin stared across the natural port. If some magnanimous deity had cut this harbor for the *Twisted Cross*, they couldn't have found a better anchorage. Thin coral reefs formed a natural barrier, breaking waves and robbing any but the most virulent storm of its impact. Less than five minutes swim separated ship from white sandy beach. Beyond that rose a gentle sloped mountain with a cloak of forest green.

"Ample trees for repairing the hull," said Captain Iuonx. "They will do us well until we reach Evara. There's no time to properly cure the wood, but we can't linger here long. There's cargo to be delivered, and we're sorely behind schedule."

"Why not linger?" Bertam suggested. "This promises to be a fair island. We can use the rest, especially after such . . . horror."

"There's been no horror, Bertam," snapped Captain Iuonx, obviously fearing any reminder of past woes would reignite the crew's fear. "We survived this far because of my skill and the staunchness of the *Twisted Cross*. We'll make it on into port. Evara's not a week's sailing from here, if we're blessed with good wind and sound hull."

"Closer to two weeks," Davin whispered to Goran. "Even with a repaired ship and those winds he spoke of."

"In this I agree with Bertam," said Goran. "I've grown bored with the *Twisted Cross*' sameness. This island offers diversion. The chance for real food instead of the pitiful thin gruel Arkko dishes out. We'd not have to pay hard-earned coin for it either."

"It might offer more than simple change of scenery." Davin considered all that spread before him. Something was strangely out of place about the port and island. He could even sense it in the breeze's tender caress. *The breeze!* Davin's head jerked up. "What's the temperature, Goran?"

"Pleasant. Warm. Reminds me of an intimate interlude spent with a buxom wench in Kressia. Hot summer winds erased any sweat we happened to work up in our passion." The Challing grinned.

"It's warm, isn't it?" Davin pressed.

"Quite. Yes, of course it is. . . ." Goran's voice trailed off as though Davin's point penetrated his erotic memories. "Unusual. The winds have been bone-chilling till now."

"Until we reached this island. I'd sooner expect such a clime off the coast of Lower Raemllyn."

"Magicks?" Goran glanced at his fellow thief. "I sense no spell woven here."

Nor did Davin see a trace of witch-fire in the changeling's eye. Yet there could be no other explanation. He'd heard Captain Iuonx declare that this island had been on no chart, had been unknown to a sailor all his life at sea. The beasts in the mist were definitely of a mage's creation. If a sorceror conjured up such creatures, why not also magically produce an island?

"It's too convenient." Goran shook his shaggy head.

"Both you! Down into the hold and work the pumps," Arkko shouted at the two adventurers.

With a mutual groan Davin and Goran complied, emerging two hours later, weary in both body and spirit.

"Who's not been ashore for the carpentry detail?" Arkko questioned. His sharp eyes worked up and down the ranks of assembled sailors.

Neither Davin nor Goran had; both raised their hands.

Arkko took one look at Davin's injured leg and the way he favored his right shoulder and passed him by. To Goran he said, "You. Ashore. Help with planing the boards. We'll need at least another dozen that size." He indicated a stack stretching half the length of the deck.

"I'll go, too," Davin volunteered.

Arkko ignored him and moved on to other concerns.

"Don't worry, friend Davin," said the Challing. "I'll not get lost. And if I do, I promise not to forget you while I bask in this warm sun."

Davin pulled the Challing aside. In a low voice he said, "Keep alert. I've counted the number who have gone ashore to work. Less than half have returned. There's eight sailors unaccounted for."

Goran shrugged. "So they stayed ashore. Perhaps they are better carpenters or swing a harder ax than the others."

"Perhaps," Davin replied. "But look at Iuonx and Arkko. They have the look of men hiding something. Is that fear in their eyes?"

"Who wouldn't be frightened after all we've been through? Delayed reaction. I've seen it often," Goran boasted. "A human in authority performs well, then crumbles after the danger has passed. Not like Challings, who are definitely superior beings. We never collapse during danger—or after."

"If nothing has happened, you'll find at least eleven of the crew ashore. Count carefully," Davin cautioned.

"Don't use the hammer on your own thumb again," chided Goran.

With a laugh the Challing slipped over the side of the *Twisted Cross* and began swimming for shore. Davin watched his friend reach the white beach, shake himself like some brilliantly plumed bird, wave, then turn and stalk off for the small grove of trees beyond the sandy beach.

Goran One-Eye pulled himself out of the water and shook all over, reveling in the sensations. Water drying on his skin, the warm sun burning at his flesh, the light wind against his face, the way his muscles thrived on the exercise, it all excited the Challing.

In Gohwohn bodily shapes were a matter of whim. Sometimes a form might change from second to second. Whatever appealed to the Challing, or whatever stimulus touched the body, dictated form.

Not so with a human body. Frozen within a single shape forced Goran to appreciate each subtle nuance, the play of bone and muscle, of nerve and flesh. Even the occasional aches and pains he endured thrilled him as new and different experiences.

Goran stretched and yawned mightily, heard sawing coming over a low sand dune, and started toward it. He topped the dune and peered down into a dish-shaped depression where the sailors toiled. He started forward, then halted abruptly. Davin's warning resounded in his head.

"Eight unaccounted for, as he said," Goran muttered to himself. He saw only three at work.

Goran slowly walked down the sandy slope and hailed the men sawing at a large tree trunk.

"Glad to have another hand," said the closest sailor. "How're repairs going on the ship?"

"We'll be leaving within a week," Goran said, then probed for information on the missing men. "But the captain's upset that you're not working harder."

"Harder!" roared a burly sailor. He tossed down his saw and bellowed a wordless cry of anger at a pure blue, fleecy cloud-dotted sky. When he quieted, he demanded, "How dare Iuonx ask us to work harder? The three of us do all the work. We cut, we drag, we section and plane. We're doing the work of ten!"

"So I see," said Goran, trying to quiet the sailor, but thinking, *Eleven. You do the work of eleven men!* "There's supposed to be, uh, one or two others. Where might they be? Resting?"

"We're all that've stayed ashore," said the burly sailor. "And we're getting tired of it, too, even if this be a fine place."

Goran hid sudden doubts behind a broad smile. Davin had been right, or so it seemed. Sailors sent ashore had vanished.

*Aye, and there's a sense to it!* Goran brightened. Why shouldn't men suddenly disappear? This island promised to be a fine liberty port. Why should others, impressed into servitude as he and Davin had been, choose to work when they might wander off and curl up in the sun for a short nap?

Goran decided that sounded more appealing to him than bending his back to a saw. Experiencing what little pleasures the island afforded drew him toward the forest.

"Here now! Don't you go off to leave us this work. Carry those boards to the shore. The cap'n sends the longboat in twice a day to fetch them," a sailor called to him.

Goran stopped and stared at the pile of boards without any enthusiasm. But he bent his back, heaved, and lifted the heavy, splintery boards to his shoulders. Wobbling slightly under the awkward load, he started back up the dunes. He paused for a rest at the summit.

Goran slowly turned, studying the island. "A fair place," he mused. "One I ought to examine more closely." He considered dropping the boards and immediately seeking out any secrets hidden from the sight of his single eye. After all, he thought, such a place hidden from usual traffic would be an excellent spot for pirates to conceal untold treasures.

The possibility sobered the Challing. If such booty did exist here, it would be less than wise to call attention to himself.

Later, when he was unwatched, would be the right time to
wander away, he decided as he teetered down the inlet side of
the dune and found the spot where the boards would be picked
up by the longboat. He dropped the lumber with a loud clatter,
rested for a moment, then started to return to where the carpenters worked.

Atop the dune once more he saw the three sailors hewing
the wood below and another sailor diving over the side of the
*Twisted Cross*. "Ah, an additional recruit for this laborious
chore!"

Goran watched the swimming sailor veer from where the
lumber had been stacked. The sailor had no intention of gaining
the beach anywhere near him and the others. His strong stokes
steadily carried him at greater angle away from the work area.

Goran squinted into the sun, but failed to make out the
man's destination. The sailor pulled himself onto the beach,
stood, and held out his arms.

Goran let out a low whistle. His single eye might not be as
sharp as Davin Anane's pair, but little went by unseen. What
Goran saw—what the sailor did once ashore—drew him as
surely as a whirlpool drew a ship!

Thoughts of felling trees and planing boards blinked from
his mind, totally forgotten. The Challing hit the beach in a full
run.

Such luck as that man has should be shared, Goran declared
to himself. The Challing grinned broadly. And there is no one
more deserving than I to help him share such bounty!

# chapter

# *16*

GORAN ONE-EYE CHUCKLED with delight while he trailed the distinct footprints from white sand beach into forest. It was easy to imagine Davin raging for weeks over this missed opportunity.

Goran smirked smugly. Little wonder that eight sailors had vanished on this balmy isle. If those aboard the *Twisted Cross* had glimpsed the treasure he had seen, all hands would abandon ship.

Nine! Goran corrected the count of missing seamen, adding to the tally the sailor he'd seen swimming ashore. He laughed heartily. No, make that ten! Why return to such a miserable existence when promise of a better life was dangled in front of his nose?

The sailor's tracks led into a thicket of tangled vines and brushes. The Challing slowed his pace, although his heart continued to pound like myriad hammers on a single steel anvil. The spoor was harder to follow here. A torn leaf or a broken twig added to his excited quest. However, occasionally the muscular giant resorted to dropping on hands and knees to peer at the disturbed dirt, his good eye only inches from the ground.

"Yes, yes!" he said aloud with the joy of a child facing a mountain of presents on his nameday. "Three of them! The sailor's boots—with holes in the soles and two nails protruding for grip on slick decks—and two other sets of oh-so-delicate bare footprints. By all the beauties of Gohwohn, they were such comely wenches. Aye, and with enough meat on their bones to make them interesting!"

Goran One-Eye shoved to his feet and trotted deeper into the wood, his mind focused on two things—the women he had seen lure the swimming sailor from the beach into the woods. Two particularly well-endowed women!

The beguiled sailor Goran had spotted had no other choice

134

but to abandon maritime duties. If the man hadn't, the Challing would have questioned the possibility of serious injury to head and other portions of the sailor's anatomy.

Graceful and spritelike the two were! Goran savored the mental image the two nymphs left in his mind's eye, one with hair like spun gold and one with tresses as fire-kissed as his own flaming mane. They had waved enticingly at the sailor then danced into the wood the moment he gained the beach. The man had needed no further beckoning. Nor had Goran!

Goran halted again to stoop and study the blurred imprints in the soft dirt. The women were too fine for the sailor to claim all for himself. The scurvy-ridden son of a sea slug was far too greedy for his own good. Two women were apt to place a strain on his physical abilities—aye, and even endanger his heart!

He, Goran One-Eye, would remedy the situation by lightening the man's burden. The blonde especially sparked the changeling's interest. He was only too willing to show her all she needed to know about the crew of the *Twisted Cross*.

If the foolish sailor protested? Then the worse for him. For Goran would steal the redhead away as well.

After all, wasn't he Challing? Hadn't he seen all Raemllyn? What woman wouldn't desire his company to that of a smelly sailor whose idea of fine cuisine was rotted fish! And whose courtship rituals might entail nothing more than catching her with a grappling hook?

A hissing snarl of a large animal set a wall of bushes ahead of the Challing to trembling.

Goran dropped onto his belly and wiggled forward, pushing beneath the veil of leaves. His heart tripled its pounding beat, not in lusty anticipation, but in awed surprise!

Beyond the barrier of shrubs opened a small clearing, in the center of which reared a writhing yellow-maned wyvern. On the first joint of viciously horned wings it supported a body as thick as the torsos of two stout men. While its flat triangular-shaped head snapped and spat, it twisted about to use rear legs of rippling muscles and spurred hindfeet to rake at a frightened sailor pressed against the bole of an oak to escape the living nightmare.

There was no escape. Those curved spurs impaled the seaman's chest and wrenched forward. In the blink of an eye horned wings spread to pummel the screaming man. When the flapping appendages closed, the poor wight was no more. A shredded mass of blood-oozing pulp marked what once had been human.

The yellow-maned serpent writhed again. For a moment unblinking green eyes studied the mound of gore. Then the great head dipped and the creature dined.

A woman, the temptress with spun gold for hair, stood on the opposite side of the clearing. She clenched hands to her mouth in horror. Tears streamed down her cheeks.

Goran frowned. The tears were inconsistent with his immediate conclusion that the blonde and the now missing redhead had lured the sailor to his brutal death. Why weep for a man one trapped?

"Back! By all that is holy, away with you!" The woman took a bold step forward and waved her arms in the air as though she attempted to shoo crows from a freshly sowed field. "Away! Damn you! Let him be!"

The serpent's thick neck arched, multihued scales the size of small shields sparkling in dappled sunlight. Its ugly head shifted toward the blonde and it stared at her, although the creature did not advance.

The woman retreated, shuddering as a new flood of tears poured from her eyes.

The lovely woman was not some woodland siren luring unwary men to their deaths. Goran would have willingly wagered the weight of his and Davin's purses on that. Just as he would have gambled the maned serpent would turn on her the moment it finished its grisly meal.

More than lust stirred the Challing's breast when his attention returned to the monstrous winged snake and its blood-smeared maw, although he would have denied any other motivation, even to Davin. He estimated his chances against the creature and decided it would be suicide to face it without sword, ax, or club.

"But I am Challing," he said softly. "Haven't I fought even worse beasts than this? Haven't I fought the thrice-dreaded and Nyuria-cursed *kehdeen* and lived to boast of it?"

Goran's resolve faltered at the thought of the twin-tailed dragon of his homeland. Challings might not hold permanent form, but the same couldn't be said of the *kehdeen,* which preyed on all other creatures in Gohwohn and had a special relish for Challings. Because of this Goran harbored an instinctive fear of the flying serpentine beasts.

However, this was no *kehdeen*. It was only a vicious worm. It had killed one of Goran's shipmates and would soon turn on the woman.

A lack of weapons, save for those provided by his human body, didn't slow the Challing. Pulling legs and feet beneath him, he attacked!

The wyvern swirled about. It lashed out with powerful rear legs and wickedly curved spurs as the mountainous giant burst through the veil of undergrowth.

Fluidly Goran launched from the ground. With neck bowed and shoulders hunched forward, he flew above talons meant to rip open his chest and smashed full weight into the creature's spine. An angry hiss of shock and pain rent the air as the Challing felt the monster collapse beneath him, sending his own body rolling in the dirt.

"Don't!" the woman cried as Goran lumbered to his feet. "It'll kill you, too. Flee while you can!"

No thought of flight fluttered in the Challing's brain. The beast hissed and whipped an altogether too mobile head about to snap at Goran's face with a mouth lined with two rows of sharklike teeth.

Goran used the only weapon he had—his fists. Balled to hammers of flesh and bone, he struck first with the right and then the left, connecting solidly with the wyvern's jaw! Spitting in confusion rather than pain, the winged creature jerked back, head arching high.

It provided Goran an unexpected opening!

For a second time the Challing launched himself at the yellow-maned nightmare. Mighty arms closed and legs wrapped about the serpent's neck. Writhing, twisting, the monstrous demon struggled to dislodge the warrior who inched up its scaled spine. To no avail. Goran climbed ever upward along the quaking neck until he sat firmly behind the reptilian horror's head. He locked his legs with crossed ankles and reached down to grasp the serpent's jaw.

An impossible position! His intent had been to wrench the creature's head around and snap its spine. The serpent's head refused to budge. Though he strained to the limits of his might, the massive, triangular head remained immobile.

"By the gods' cold hearts!" Goran's spirits plummeted. He was defeated here, and should he give up his precarious seat, he would be the next course in the serpent's meal.

His eyes darted about in search of some low hanging branch. If he were to escape, it would have to be upward.

The world spun in a blur of colors. It turned over on its head and stood there while the Challing's stomach twisted and knotted itself. *Magicks!* The same muscle-mauling force he had felt aboard the *Twisted Cross* tore at his gut and head.

Like a man atop an untamed stallion he clung to the serpent's mane while the monster twisted and writhed. He held on for his life until the strength-draining wave of magicks subsided and the world once again righted itself. And still his arms could not budge that massive head or jaw.

*I am a Challing!* Goran refused defeat. *I will not die thusly!*

Power surged from deep within his core, as though his thoughts tapped a wellspring of unknown energy. It sizzled through him to focus in arms and hands. His single eye went saucer round. Beginning at his fingertips and spreading upward sparked the green light of witch-fire.

Only once before in his years trapped in the realm of Raemllyn, had he felt magic weaving through muscle and flesh as it now did. That was when he faced and defeated the demon guard of the sorceror Masur-Kell in Leticia.

From green to crimson his arms and hands burned. Slowly, ever so slowly, the winged serpent's head gave way, twisting backward until bone could no longer bear the pressure and snapped!

A death shudder quaked through the creature's length; its horned wings opened and flapped violently. Giving the triangular head one final twist, Goran leaped free and hit the ground in a roll that brought him to his feet ready to face new attack.

There was no need. The body flopped to the ground and lay twitching while the last of life leeched from muscle and nerve. As the Challing watched, the glow about his hands and arms faded back to green, then winked out.

"You . . . you killed it!" the golden-haired woman behind him gasped. She approached slowly, eyes fixed on the vanquished creature. "You slew it with magic!"

"No!" Goran started to protest, but realized there was no denying the witch-fire he had generated, although how he had awakened the magicks within his human body eluded him.

"How did you do that?" the woman asked, awe in her voice.

She looked at Goran with adoration blazing in her cornflower-blue eyes.

"I . . ." Goran stammered, collecting his chaotic thoughts. "A simple enough task, when you're trained for it. I am Goran One-Eye." The red-bearded giant performed what he considered to be a courtly bow. "If you should ever have need of rescuing again, please do not hesitate to call upon me."

"You faced a guardian serpent," she said, as though uncertain whether to believe what she had witnessed. "Of all the sailors, you're the first to defeat one. A hero come to rescue me!"

In the next instant the woman threw her arms around Goran's neck and buried her face in his shoulder. Her body shuddered as tears rained from her eyes.

"Come, come, lass, don't carry on so. Lift your head so that I might gaze upon your beauty." He lifted her chin with a fingertip.

"You have come to save me . . . save us, haven't you? Please O mighty mage, save us all!" the blue-eyed woman sobbed.

"All?" Goran's brow lifted above his good eye.

"The village—it has no name. We dared not name it lest we believe we were doomed to stay here all our days. A village of slaves," she answered, still clinging about his neck.

"If even one other is a quarter as beautiful as you," Goran said gallantly, "it will be my honor to but try."

"Th-they're all much prettier. They reckon me as the ugly one in the village."

"Surely there's a man or two who is hairier and uglier." Goran wiped away her tears with a fingertip.

"No," she said with a shake of her head. "There are only women in the village. Beautiful women. Doing h-h-his awful bidding!"

Goran blinked. What fortune! He'd searched for one voluptuous beauty to dally away the hours with and had stumbled upon a whole village of women! If the others in this village were a quarter as lovely as this delightful blossom, they'd be the pinnacle of feminine pulchritude. Though he found it impossible to believe the woman hugged about his neck counted as the ugly one—anywhere—in any group!

"Is the red-haired lass I first saw with you on the beach a part of the village?" Goran still wasn't sure whether to believe such good luck after endless months of misfortune.

"Awendala? Yes, of course. She fled when the serpent appeared." The woman nodded, gazing at her rescuer through liquid blue eyes. "She is *his* prisoner, like the rest of us."

"Who is it that keeps you prisoner?" asked Goran. "Some pirate or warrior?"

"A sorceror. We've tried to escape this Yu-Vatruk damned island, but we've failed repeatedly. His ward spells alert him of any attempt. And h-h-his monsters kill any who are brave enough to try to rescue us."

"That's why you lured the sailor from the *Twisted Cross?*"

"The *Twisted Cross?* The ship in harbor? Yes, we've tried again and again for help. Only one or two of us at a time can slip past the serpents. . . ."

"There are more like this one?" Goran kicked the creature's body with the toe of his boot.

"Many more. No one knows their number. I've seen as many as five fighting among themselves. Denorri has seen seven, but no one believes her. She's such a liar. Why, she claims she's seen the wizard holding us on this vile island!"

"You haven't?" Goran's brow furrowed. He'd hoped to be able to identify the mage responsible for all this misery and quickly dispatch him into Black Quar's deadly arms. But if this lovely woman couldn't identify her captor, what chance did he have?

"He waylays ships sailing along the coast of Upper Raemllyn and brings their crews to this island. The men die quickly, the most beautiful of the women are imprisoned. Of the o-others I can't say. I think he feeds them to the serpents."

"How do you know this mage is a man? Might it not be one of your rank, someone in your village? What better place to keep a watch on prisoners than among them?" Goran suggested.

"I've considered this, but new ships come all the time. No one leaves the village. How could the mage capture ships and never leave this island? We would detect the use of such potent magicks. We would!"

"I'm sure," Goran said dubiously. Brightening, Goran asked, "I have been such a churlish knave. I have introduced myself but neglected to allow you the opportunity to introduce your own lovely self."

"I am Kulonna, daughter of Duke Tun, liege of Litonya and

Melisa," she answered, still warmly clinging to him.

Goran blinked in surprise. If true, Kulonna had to be the most sought-for woman in all Raemllyn. Even more would be expended in finding her than he and Davin had put into trailing that skinny wench, Lijena Farleigh. And for the man returning this beauty to her father, there would be a shower of Raemllyn's finest riches. By Jajhana, Goddess of Fortune, could he have asked for no more!

"No," Kulonna said, as though sensing his thoughts, "my father has been unable to find me. Whether he has sent ships from Litonya seeking me out I cannot say. I hope that he has not." Tears again welled in her clear blue eyes. "The sorceror ruling this island would only destroy any such warship. H-he is too s-strong!"

"I make a rule of defeating pompous, overblown sorcerors." Goran's muscular arms gently closed around Kulonna's slender waist. The feel of her was good. "My friend Davin Anane and I have only recently defeated a pack of demons calling themselves the Narain. And after that we vanquished Lorennion."

Kulonna pulled back and stared at him. The tears vanished, replaced with doubt. "Do not toy with me. In all Raemllyn, Lorennion is the strongest mage. None bests him. I know. I've heard my father's mage speak of Lorennion in hushed tones, in tones of abject *fear!*"

Goran shrugged. "It's true. Believe it or not, as you see fit. But believe this. If any can free you and the others, it is my friend Davin Anane and I."

"You are mages?"

Goran laughed. "Better. We eat mages for breakfast." He turned his head in the direction of the fallen serpent, as if holding its magical death out as an example of all he might accomplish, given the chance. Goran didn't bother to burden Kulonna with the fact that he had no real control over his powers. It was just as likely that the serpent might have killed him as the other way around.

"I'll take you to the village. The others will be so excited. Only the thought of one day returning to our homes and families has sustained us. Now . . ." Kulonna's voice brimmed with hope and joy, "we'll all be eternally grateful."

A flame that suddenly flared in Kulonna's eyes told Goran what might be the full extent of a noble lady's gratitude. He approved wholeheartedly.

Kulonna took his meaty hand and pulled him toward a narrow trail cut through a small stand of trees. Goran held her back, studying the route to the island's interior.

"A moment. It might be best not to alert the others. Not yet. I need to communicate with my friend aboard the *Twisted Cross.*"

"You fear traitors in the village?" Kulonna bit a lower lip that was as red as wine.

"No, not at all," Goran said hastily.

"You're right to be cautious," Kulonna said. "It is unfortunately true that there might be those who, for misguided concern over their own safety, would inform the mage of your rescue plans. And I have no idea which of the prisoners it might be. We are all miserable. Anything might be seen as improving our life."

"You fear so for me?" he asked.

"I do," Kulonna answered. "The mage who imprisoned us is cunning. Two ships have been wrecked in the harbor since I've been here—and that has been only a month. My father sent me to Rakell as emissary." Kulonna bit back her words and looked fearfully at Goran.

"As Duke Tun's emissary to Prince Felrad?" Goran finished for her.

The woman nodded, her golden hair falling in delightful waves about her face. She peered up at the flame-haired giant, apparently fearing he would metamorphose into Zarek Yannis and condemn her for this treason against the High King.

"I care little for Raemllyn politics," Goran said, "but my friend is a staunch supporter of Felrad. Perhaps you and Davin might be able to come to terms."

And, he added mentally, take Davin's mind off that sickly wench who so obsessed his every thought. Goran would gladly give up any claim on such a lovely woman's heart for his friend if it'd make him forget Lijena. Goran smiled even more broadly as he thought of Kulonna's words: the others in the village are even lovelier.

His loss might be a small one.

"Listen!" Kulonna motioned toward the densest portion of the forest. "Another serpent. We must hurry and return to the village. Once there, it won't bother us."

Goran hesitated. The thundering sounds of a huge beast's

approach was ample cause for alarm, but to remain with Kulonna might mean death at the sorceror's hands.

"Go on, Kulonna. Run for the village, but say nothing about my presence. I'll join you there later."

"Goran?" She hesitated, her eyes pleading.

"Do it," he said, his deep voice hiding his uncertainty.

Kulonna impulsively kissed him, then rushed off.

"Yes, my lovely one, I'll join you in the village," Goran said to Kulonna's retreating figure. When she vanished around a bend in the trail, Goran looked for a spot to make his stand against another serpent.

Goran leaped into the low-hanging branches of an oak and waited there, ready to drop down on the serpent when it roared past. Every muscle tensed for action, he waited. And waited and waited. No serpent came, nor a monster of any kind appeared.

Goran peered through the tree limbs and still saw no approaching winged serpent. He swung from branch to branch into three other trees to search for another of the isle's reptilian guardians, before climbing back to the ground.

Walking softly, Goran explored in ever-widening circles. He found no trace of the beast that had made such horrendous noises. Puzzled, he turned and started toward the village, not following the dirt trail Kulonna had taken but walking parallel to it.

He emerged from the forest and stared down at the small village. Everywhere he looked Goran saw only long-limbed women of ample proportions, beauty at every turn, a veritable hedonist's paradise.

"Ah, Davin, you'll never know what you're missing. But be certain I will tell you—in great detail!"

Laughing, Goran One-Eye took one lumbering step downhill toward the village. A deafening roar froze the Challing in midstride!

# chapter
## 17

TWO LONGBOATS MADE their way from the isle's white beach to the *Twisted Cross*. Davin Anane's expression was as grim as the scene he watched. A full thirty men had sailed to the island this day; only three returned. Goran One-Eye was not among that number.

Around the Jyotian sailors spoke in guarded whispers, speculating on the fate of their fellow crewmen. Not so with Haigex Iuonx. The merchanter's captain raged. He cursed the gods and the fate that had driven his vessel to this accursed harbor. It did no good. The men who climbed from the two boats did not multiply.

"Demons, Cap'n," one of the men of the carpentry crew explained with body atremble and eyes wide. "Monsters, by Nalren. Ye can hear them moving in yon wood. Hear their unholy screams and the rustle of their scaly bodies as they move."

"Aye," another nodded, then added, "men venture into the forest to seek trees large enough for our needs ... and they never return. It's the beasts who get 'em. Ye can hear their cries—then the roar of the beasts."

"Bah! Slackers all! The poxied lot has wandered off and hidden to escape the work that needs doing!" Iuonx's hand tightened about his swagger stick as though he intended to strike the three. Instead he glared at the isle as the sun set behind it. "Arkko and his crew have still to report. The man will have the answers I need. Bring him to my cabin the moment he returns to ship!"

Iuonx pivoted and stiffly strode to his cabin. Immediately the remainder of the crew crowded around the three sailors. It took little urging for the three to detail all they had seen and heard, although none of the men had actually seen the creatures that supposedly inhabited the island.

"It seems your red-bearded friend is among the missing," a voice said softly behind the Jyotian.

Davin turned to find Tacllyn-lin-Bertam leaning against the ship's rail. The man's pale-blue eyes occasionally darted toward the island as though he waited for something to happen.

"That's quite a tale they told," Davin said, indicating the three sailors. His tone hid the concern twisting his gut. "More monsters, ones like those we encountered in the fog banks, if we're to believe them."

Bertam's eyes narrowed suspiciously for a moment, then that damnable amused smile uplifted the corners of his thin lips. "Aye, there's trouble here. It's as I warned. As you and the one-eyed one should well know."

"This island..." Davin stammered, taken off guard by Bertam's comment. He glared at the lanky man. "What did you mean by that?"

"If not by your own tongue, then time will reveal all." Bertam's amusement faded as his jaw set granite hard. "The sands run through your glass, Jyotian. When the last grain has dropped, then you will have Tacllyn-lin-Bertam with which to contend. That I promise you, you and the red-beard one!"

"You threaten us?" Davin's confusion grew. This wasn't a spinner of wild tales, but Bertam that had gone unglimpsed until now. He sensed an inner strength within the man that had been carefully hidden until this moment.

"I make no threats...now." Bertam laughed. "I'll wait until Arkko's return. Then, if need be, we shall talk again." Still laughing, Bertam stalked off, leaving Davin with mouth agape.

For an instant Davin considered following the man, to demand an explanation for his strange words. Instead he merely cursed and turned back to stare at the dark island. His thoughts centered on Goran, as did the prayers on his lips.

An ear-shattering roar and the beat of leathery wings sent Goran One-Eye sprawling on his belly.

A serpent twice the size of the one the Challing had slain launched itself from the trees to the right of his position.

On elbows and knees Goran wormed back into the woods to hide behind a fallen log. For all the boasting he had done to impress Kulonna, he was no fool intent on facing one of the creatures again. After all, he had no guarantees his fickle magicks would surface a second time this day.

Glancing up, Goran gasped. "It can't be!"

No airborne serpent this! The forked tail writhing behind the winged creature marked it as the most feared beast in the changeling's home realm of Gohwohn—a flying dragon, a *kehdeen*. It swooped low, talons brushing the treetops as it searched for prey to fill its great beak.

Goran had no doubt the prey it sought was a certain Challing entrapped in the body of a man. In the past he had successfully fought *kehdeen*, both in Raemllyn and in Gohwohn. But these were creatures native only to Gohwohn. The one Goran had encountered in the search for Lorennion's keep had entered Raemllyn through a rent in the fabric of space, just as Goran had. The difference seemed to be one of intent. A mage had purposefully drawn Goran to this dimension; the *kehdeen* came through untended—and unwanted—tears in the elastic boundaries between dimensions.

Yet the *kehdeen* passed overhead and flew on.

Goran saw why when he cautiously rose. The beast's attention lay elsewhere. A fog bank moved across a section of the forest; within the mist moved *things* too mind-numbing for even Goran's brain to accept as existing other than in the darkest of nightmares. Things that transformed as they hurled out from the misty clouds.

The *kehdeen* did not hunt, Goran realized; it fled! From the mist boiled monsters that dwarfed the *kehdeen*, until it appeared no larger than a small child's gentle pet. Talons cut viciously; teeth the length of sabers clashed; razor-edged wings sliced through the air. For the twin-tailed dragon of Gohwohn there was no escape. The beasts of the mist enveloped it.

Goran attempted to focus his good eye on the creatures and failed. They shifted bodily shapes even as he stared at them. Like creatures of Gohwohn they were, but they had not been born of the Challing's home realm.

In the blinking of an eye mist creatures and *kehdeen* were gone. Peaceful forest stretched before him. The fog bank evaporated to leave a bright, almost tropical sun sinking toward the western horizon.

Goran shivered. The magicks aplay on this island were more dangerous than those employed by Lorennion to maintain his Blood Fountain. But who controlled them? Who was the mage responsible for the *kehdeen* and the mist beasts—and the village overflowing with lovely women?

*Women!* The word rolled in the Challing's mind. What cared he of mists, dragons, and magicks. His purpose was to rescue a village inhabited by Raemllyn's most desirable beauties. Let no mere mage stand between him and the treasure he sought!

"Ah, Kulonna," Goran sighed aloud like some lovesick youth.

He gave his clothes a hasty once over and dusted off dry leaves clinging to blouse and trousers. It wouldn't do to appear in the village looking like some vagabond fresh from the road, with all those winsome young lasses just waiting to be rescued.

Whistling off-key, Goran set off to explore the village. Not openly, he told himself. It wouldn't do to excite so many women with his august appearance. He'd begin quietly, learning what he could from Kulonna, daughter of Duke Tun. After he'd satisfied himself that all she'd said was true, *then* he would venture farther afield and interrogate the others.

A task that might take days, he mused. Perhaps weeks. He hoped Davin didn't mind the wait.

"Blood!" The sailor held up a hand with fingers splayed wide. Crimson ran dripping from his palm. "Blood covers everything in pools!"

"By the gods, no!" This from Captain Iuonx, who stood staring over the rail at the empty longboat that had drifted on gentle waves from the island to the *Twisted Cross.* "It can't be. Arkko and his crew of ten were in that boat! Black Qar, it can't be!"

"It was to be expected, Captain. I tried to warn you, but my words fell on deaf ear." Bertam approached Iuonx and glanced at the boat. "There is nothing that can be done for those already lost to the beasts of the mist. However, there may be time to save the ship and the remnants of its crew."

"Damn ye!" Iuonx pivoted and glared at the lanky man. "I promised I'd flay your hide if ye ever spoke of the beasts again!"

"Examine this." Bertam eased an oiled pouch from beneath his shirt and handed it to Iounx. "If you still desire my hide after you've read what's within, then its yours."

"Wha—" Bewildered, the *Twisted Cross'* captain snatched the pouch from the man and opened it. His rage faded the moment he glimpsed the parchment within. "Why wasn't I shown this earlier?"

"In light of all that's occurred, I believe that should be obvious, Captain." Bertam glanced at the crew that gathered

to stare at the blood-drenched boat floating alongside. "Nor do
I believe this is the place to discuss, uh, business. Perhaps
your cabin would be more appropriate."

Iuonx nodded, turned, and led Bertam into his cabin. Davin
Anane heard a lock click securely in its niche when the door
closed behind the two men. While the empty longboat held the
others' morbid attention, the young thief stepped to the barred
door and pressed an ear to the wood.

*Damn!* His eyes darted about. Bertam's and Iuonx's voices
were indiscernible muffled whispers. If he were to learn why
a simple parchment transformed Iuonx from a raging lion to a
meek lamb, there was but one way.

Quickly crossing to the starboard rail, Davin climbed over,
his feet finding the narrow ledgelike rim of wood that encircled
the vessel. Cautiously he inched to the bow, then used the
ornate carving there for handholds to climb around and peer
into the window to the captain's cabin.

"You know of the false coins I carry for Prince Felrad?"
Iuonx stared up at Bertam.

"Aye, and the dies with which Zarek Yannis' face will be
impressed into their thin coat of gold. It was I who first suggested the subterfuge to Felrad. The false coins are to be distributed in the coastal cities the usurper controls. When they
are discovered, they will undermine his finances," Bertam answered as he stood before the captain's desk.

"That much I knew." Iuonx nodded. "But none made mention of a mage being sent to guard my cargo!"

*Felrad? Bertam works for Raemllyn's rightful heir?* Davin
blinked, trying to comprehend what he heard. *And a mage!*

"The prince believed it better that I traveled in secrecy."
Bertam shrugged.

"But why? And why aboard the *Twisted Cross?*"

"Captain, that is more than obvious. The cargo you carry
is too important to allow it to fall into the hands of a sorceror
believed to be in Yannis' service! Prince Felrad sent me to find
and defeat this demon man who controls the fog and its monsters. We've lost far too many ships in this area. He must be
destroyed! And the sooner the better. I hope I have your full
cooperation in this." Bertam fixed the captain with an icy stare.

"Yes, yes of course." Iuonx heaved a sigh. "My brain reels
with the intrigue of it all. Why didn't ye just book passage
aboard my ship? Why allow yourself to fall into the hands of

a crimp? And why, by the gods, did ye spread the tales of the sea monsters?"

"The necessity of deceit, I fear," Bertam began, and explained that survivors of other ships destroyed by the mage had mentioned one thing their vessels shared—they stopped in either Salnal, Weysh, or Faldin to take on crimp-purchased crew members. "It is in one of these northwestern cities we believed the sorceror boards a ship and begins to weave his spells."

Bertam then outlined how he arranged to have himself captured and brought aboard the *Twisted Cross* in Faldin to avoid suspicion. "My tales of the monsters in the mists were meant to force the mage to show his hand and confront me prior to an attack on the *Twisted Cross*. On that point I'm afraid I failed."

Iunox nodded. "Salnal, Weysh, or Faldin—it could have been any of the three cities, for we stopped at all the ports along the western coast." The captain shuddered and a name came in anguish from his lips. "Arkko! May this blackhearted mage suffer the damnation of Peyneeha's lowest levels for Arkko's murder! Privately Arkko urged me to find safe harbor, but I wouldn't listen."

"He sailed long with you?"

"Not for many years." Tears misted Iuonx's eyes. "We grew up together in Litonya on the Isle of Prillae. As youths we sailed together aboard our first ship. Friends all our lives, although our paths eventually separated. It was in Salnal I hired Arkko, after my first mate fell ill with the red lung. No better man could a captain desire to have at his side. I will miss him dearly."

"Arkko is beyond our help now, Captain Iuonx," Bertam said. "There is another who should be the focus of our full attention."

"The mage?" Iuonx glanced up. "Ye know his identity?"

"Aye!" Bertam stood straight and pursed his lips. "It is the one called Goran One-Eye. Twice while this ship was under attack by serpent and mist, I've seen the red-bearded one's single orb ablaze with magicks!"

"Goran?" The captain sat straight in his chair.

"Goran," Bertam confirmed. "And I believe the Jyotian Davin Anane is the mage's apprentice!"

*No!* Davin's mind reeled dizzily. Until now he had accepted

Bertam's tale. Now he knew the man for what he was—the sorceror who controlled both mist and the beasts it spawned! The whoreson cast an intricate web to ensare Iuonx and the *Twisted Cross*.

Whether Bertam worked for Zarek Yannis or for his own ends, Davin didn't know, nor did it matter. All that was important was that he get to a longboat and make his way ashore to find Goran—if the Challing still lived!

The young adventurer refused to consider the possibility Goran's soul now rested in the embrace of Black Qar. As Goran was often wont to say, he was Challing not human!

Carefully Davin began to pick his way back along the ornate carvings adorning the *Twisted Cross*' bow. He securely grasped the open mouth of a silver-lacquered whale and stretched his left leg to find purchase on the snout of a leaping porpoise—and slipped. Both legs fell from under him and he banged clumsily into the side of the ship, dangling by fingertips that grew less secure with each heartbeat.

"What!" The cabin's window flew open and Iuonx's head poked out. "It's the bastard Anane!"

Too late to make a graceful exit, Davin shoved away from the merchanter and fell toward the inky waters below.

Waters he never touched!

A glowing globe of blue enveloped his body. He hovered in the air, then began to rise. Through the cabin's open window he drifted and slammed down in a chair. The bubble of blue collapsed to bands that snapped about wrists and ankles. Struggle as he did, he was unable to break the magicks that bound him to the chair.

"Rope, Captain Iuonx. Tie our spy well!" Bertam's eyes blazed with triumph as he stared down at the Jyotian. His fingers constantly danced, firing the spell that had ensnared Davin. "It's time this swine spilled his gut!"

"Aye!" From a chest Iuonx produced a heavy rope and hastily but securely lashed Davin to the chair. The captain then flung open another chest—one filled with an assortment of knives and swords. He selected a double-edged blade the length of two hands and grinned at the treacherous mage. "In Nayati such a knife is used to dress a camel for a feast. I believe it will serve well to loosen this knave's tongue!"

"Nay, Captain." Bertam interposed himself between Davin and Iuonx. "The one-eyed sorceror may use spells to stay in contact with his apprentice. I don't want the Jyotian harmed. Goran may return if he believes that he can save his acolyte."

"Captain, he lies like a Chavali trader. Neither Goran nor I are mages. The man who would destroy your ship and crew stands before you now!" Davin shouted, while throwing his weight against the ropes.

Neither words nor actions prevailed. Captain Iuonx tried to sidestep Bertam, the gleaming blade raised for the kill. Only the lanky mage's quick hand saved the young thief. Bertam's arm snaked out, knocking the blade from Iuonx's grasp.

"Captain, we have need of this man and all he knows!" Bertam shouted.

"He must pay for all that was done to good Arkko." Iuonx spat through clenched teeth. "Must pay with his life!"

"That he will." Bertam's tone was like a gentle surcease. "I promise you that when we have the red-bearded one, you may do as you please with both of them. Until then this one must be mine. I have ways of making him sing like a bird!"

Tacllyn-lin-Bertam turned; his hands lifted and his fingers weaved mystical signs in the air. A shimmering globe of blue materialized from nothingness and drifted across the cabin to surround Davin's head.

"Now Jyotian swine, tell where hides your master, the mage Goran One-Eye!" Bertam demanded.

Davin spat in the mage's face, then cursed the man and woman who had given birth to such a craven.

Both spittle and curse were mistakes. In the blink of an eye the blue transformed to scarlet and flames devoured Davin's head!

# chapter
## *18*

GORAN ONE-EYE LIFTED the golden-brown hindquarter of his second roasted hare and devoured its succulent meat in one bite. He tossed the bare bone through the hut's open door, into the night. He then lifted a fistful of red *yutu* berries from a wooden bowl, tilted his head back, and let the berries trickle from hand to mouth.

"More rabbit?" The red-tressed, green-eyed Awendala edged a platter toward the Challing while she scooted around the crudely hewn table to settle her chair beside the flaming-bearded titan.

"Or perhaps another helping of *yalt* fruit?" Kulonna cast the redhead a reprimanding glare, then wiggled closer to the mountainous warrior. "Your cup is empty. Do you desire more of this weak Meakham wine? It is all that *he* allows us."

The changeling noticed Awendala wince at Kulonna's mention of their mage captor. In that almost indiscernible flicker of pain rested the agony of a year's imprisonment on the island. Of the thirty women held captive, Awendala had been here the longest.

For a full cycle of the heaven's houses the sorceror had used and abused her body. Although others came and went, ransomed to family and loved ones or sold into the chains of slavery, Awendala remained, the mage refusing to release her while she still served to sate his vile desires.

"Aye! All!" Goran devoured every scrap of food the two beauties placed before him, then washed down all with three brimming cups of wine. To be certain, the meal was a simple fare, but after a diet of Arkko's thin gruel for longer than the Challing wanted to consider, rabbit, berries, fruit, and wine were like the finest of feasts on his palate.

A truly satisfied sigh escaped his lips when he leaned back on a three-legged stool that barely contained his bulk and lazily stretched. "My lovelies, a man could ask for no more. It has been months since I have tasted a meal so delicious! My companion of the sword Davin Anane knows not what he has missed."

"When will you bring this Davin from the ship in the harbor and kill the sorceror who binds us?" Awendala pressed.

"On the morrow, as I promised." Goran lowered his arms, draping them about the shoulders of the two shapely women. A smile uplifted the corners of his mouth when neither moved away. "But first I must learn all you know of the man holding you on this isle."

"I've told you all I know." Kulonna shrugged. The movement brought her snugly into the hollow of his shoulder. Triumph sparked her blue eyes when she glanced at Awendala.

The fiery-haired woman bit at her lower lip. "I know nothing else to add to what I've already said. My mother and father and I were passengers on a ship bound from Yaryne to Orji. We were off the coast of Norgg when a mist enveloped the ship. When the mist finally parted, a demon gale blew us northwest for days, until we came to this island. My mother and father were among the first to go ashore; I never saw either again."

Awendala stiffened and fought back tears that welled in her eyes. When she looked up again, she drew a steadying breath and continued. "The swine calls himself Ah-Banh-Cee, mage of the seas. When he appears, it's amid swirling fog. He then summons one of us to the hut at the center of the village and uses the unlucky one until his lusts are sated. Since Kulonna's ship was destroyed a month ago, the triple-cursed pig has not visited himself upon us."

"Every few months a ship arrives and the village's women are marched aboard?" Goran asked.

"Most are sold into slavery," Awendala said with a nod.

Goran pursed his lips. Whoever this Ah-Banh-Cee was, he sounded more like a pirate plundering the sea lanes than a sorceror. Why would one who controlled the beasts in the mist be content with such petty crimes, when his power rivaled that of Zarek Yannis? Raemllyn might be his, yet he hid away luring merchant vessels to this deceptively treacherous island.

"And you can identify this Ah-Banh-Cee for Davin and me?" Goran asked.

"Every ugly feature of his face is etched into my brain."
Awendala spat on the floor. "Would that my own hand might
glide the blade that skewers his black heart!"

"Mayhap we can arrange . . ." Goran stammered and groaned.
The world around the Challing spun like a crazy top. Colors
rushed by, blurring into one another. His gut wrenched, knotting
itself into crochets. In a heartbeat strength fled his giant body,
leaving muscles liquid and flaccid. Goran collapsed atop the
table; a string of curses moaned from his lips.

And as had occurred twice before, the gut-wrenching spell
passed as rapidly as it had descended upon him.

"Magicks! The whoreson's spells are not to be taken lightly."
Weakly, his arms still shaking, Goran eased from the table.
His eyes lifted.

No longer nestled in his arms, Kulonna and Awendala stood
on the opposite side of the wooden table. Expressions of sheer
horror masked the beauty of their faces!

Davin Anane retained no sense of time or dimension. His
world consisted of two things—the curtain of leaping crimson
flames devouring his head, and agony!

"Where is the mage Goran One-Eye?" Tacllyn-lin-Bertam's
question reverberated within the Jyotian's skull for the thou-
sandth time.

Like all the times that had gone before, Davin did the only
thing Bertam's spell allowed him to do, he spoke the truth. "I
know not. Goran was sent ashore for carpentry duty and never
returned."

"Bah!" Captain Iuonx's disgust penetrated the barrier of pain
consuming Davin's brain. "You do no good with him."

"Aye." Weary resignation nestled in Bertam's single word.
"The dawn is near and still I have been unable to break the
spell that binds the Jyotian's tongue. The one-eyed sorceror's
power is greater than I expected. Few can resist the Hair of
Flame, even when so ensorcelled as this one."

The veil of licking crimson receded, and with it vanished
the mind-twisting pain. Through bleary eyes Davin saw the
blurred forms of the captain and the treacherous sorceror. He
remained in the *Twisted Cross*' cabin and not in the depths of
hell.

"Not a mark on his face!" Awe welled in Iuonx's voice.

"As I promised," Bertam replied with a touch of pride.

"We've wasted enough time on this one. Goran One-Eye is the real prize. We should be about our preparations for searching the isle."

"And him? Is he mine yet? He should pay for what was done to Arkko."

Davin's vision cleared enough for him to see the shake of Bertam's head. "Nay. We'll leave him here under guard as bait for the red-bearded bastard. If this smelly cheese doesn't draw the rat by this eve, he's yours."

A throaty chuckle that contained no trace of humor pushed from Iuonx's throat as captain and sorceror left the cabin, slamming the door behind him. Outside he heard Iuonx order two guards by the door.

With a shake of his head to clear his mind of a night filled with torturous magicks, Davin peered through eyes that shifted in and out of focus. Across the cabin Iuonx's weapons trunk lay open.

*Might as well be in Lower Raemllyn!* He jerked his arms against the ropes binding him to the chair in frustration. His heart doubled its beat. His wrists slipped beneath the coils. A smile touched his trembling lips as he tugged again, and once more his wrists inched closer to freedom.

His ceaseless struggle to escape the spell Bertam named the Hair of Fire had loosened the rope, and neither the sorceror nor the hoodwinked captain had remembered to check his restraints before leaving! Two more quick tugs and Davin's left hand slid beneath the coils without so much as skinning a knuckle. An instant later his right hand joined the left. Trembling fingers found the knots about his ankles and worked them free.

Standing, the Jyotian thief drew three steadying breaths before he risked his first shaky step. Three more breaths quelled the pounding in his temples, and he chanced walking across the cabin to the open trunk. From within he selected a scabbarded broadsword and razor-honed dirk, which he strapped to his waist.

While the crew outside prepared the longboats for the row to the island, a dazed Davin Anane managed to weave to the cabin's window, open it, then fall through to the ocean below. Shouts of alarm followed him in the night as he swam toward the white sand beach.

• • •

"Damn Iuonx! And may Bertam be double damned!" A growling voice drifted through the forest.

Davin froze where he crouched beside a clear running stream three strides across and as deep as a man's waist. His head cocked from side to side, listening.

"There's no chance here," another man's voice answered from beyond an entwined thicket of brambles at Davin's back. "We're not woodsmen meant to track through the forest. We're seamen! How can Bertam expect us to find the Jyotian and the one-eyed wizard?"

"As I said, may Iuonx be damned and Bertam doubly so," the first voice repeated as Davin turned and crept to peer through the brambles.

Five of Captain Iuonx's whip-carrying gorillas stood scanning the forest. Ten of the impressed crew members were with them; all carried sword or cutlass.

"Wonder where the cap'n, Bertam, and the others are?" one of the sailors gave voice to Davin's thoughts.

"Probably back on the ship while we're out here doing all the dirty work. Never trust a sorceror, 'specially one who passes himself off as a sailor, lads!"

"Arly!" A sailor grabbed the talking man by the shoulder and spun him around. "Look!"

Davin saw it, too. A fine mist shifted through the forest canopy. Overhead the sun was blotted out by a descending bank of fog.

"Back, lads." Arly motioned for his companions to retreat. "Bertam didn't say nothing about no fog. I don't like the—"

The man's sentence ended in an abrupt death cry. Beasts, creatures, *things* leapt from the mist. A bear with the head of a jackass raked a claw across Arly's neck, opening his throat from ear to ear. A tentacled serpent whipped out five arms, ensnaring and crushing just as many men. Beasts that defied description boiled over the company of sailors. Flesh was rent and devoured in the space of a single heartbeat. Then the men from the *Twisted Cross* were no more.

The same could not be said for the fog. With the myriad beasts it spawned each second, the gray veil drifted through the wood toward the brambles hiding Davin Anane.

The young freebooter shoved to his feet—and stumbled backward into the stream. Air, in a shower of rising bubbles, burst from his lungs when he gasped in surprise—an accident that saved his life.

To the bottom of the shallow stream he sank. Above, the fog and its ravaging creatures passed over the surface without causing a ripple. When the sun once more gleamed in the sky, Davin thrust above the water.

The living mist had departed, and the sound of songbirds awoke within the wood.

# *chapter*
# *19*

A SPITTING REPTILIAN hiss snapped Davin Anane from a half
sleep. His gaze shot to the end of the hollow log in which he
hid. His eyes went wide and round, and his temple pounded.

Twenty feet from where he lay, two gigantic serpent creatures moved through the wood. On muscular hind legs and with
horned wings folded and thrust forward so that the first joints
of those appendages served as forelegs, they walked-crawled.
Yellow-maned triangular heads and thick necks craned from
one side to the other, scanning the forest for prey.

With a prayer of gratitude to Jajhana, Goddess of Chance
and Fortune, and Pliaton, God of Thieves, for placing him
downwind of the creatures, the Jyotian watched the beasts plod
into the forest without a pause to glance in his direction. He
released an overly held breath in a trembling sigh, then wiggled
from the log and stood.

He never intended to sleep, only rest a few minutes in the
log's relative security. A night of Tacllyn-lin-Bertam's spell-
woven torture and a morning of dodging the *Twisted Cross*'
search parties, which scoured the woods, had left him exhausted, mentally and physically.

*Goran.* His friend's name echoed hollow in his mind. Could
he truly hope to find the Challing alive on this accursed island
with its beast-wrought living fog and monstrous winged serpents? Davin pushed away the doubt that wedged into his
thoughts. He had to believe Goran still lived!

Craning his head back, the adventurer brushed aside raven-
black hair and peered at the sun through the canopy of leaves
overhead. An hour, no more than two, passed while he slept.

He turned right, took a bearing on the crest of the small
mountain that rose from the island's center, and started toward
it. No rationale guided his strides, except that he felt the need
of a plan. To scan the isle from atop the mountain seemed the

place to begin. An overview of the island would give him a
sense of what he faced, a hint to places the Challing might
conceal himself, all the while avoiding the deadly beasts and
hellish mist that served as Bertam's guardians of this unholy
isle!

Davin stumbled to a halt. Lost in his thoughts, he had failed
to notice the forest abruptly opening before. He stood atop a
steep incline that dropped into a grassy valley at the foot of
the mountain. In the middle of that valley—a village!

He counted twenty well-kept huts below as he found a line
of bushes and saplings to hide his descent. What he didn't see
were people. No man, woman, or child moved among the huts.
He made his way down into the valley. Still the village remained
quiet.

Too quiet.

In a crouch Davin moved from the bole of one scattered
*morda* tree to the next as he crept to the village's edge. With
no one in sight, he shot to the back of the nearest hut.

"It's about time you got here, Davin Anane," a reprimanding
feminine voice chided.

Steel on leather whispered when the young thief eased sword
from sheath and lifted the blade ready to attack.

"Is that the way you greet an old and dear friend?" the
woman asked in a voice that rang vaguely familiar. "Lay aside
your blade. We've a village to move aboard the *Twisted Cross*."

With that a woman dressed in outrageous oranges and green
stepped around the hut. She stood in a defiant stance with hands
planted firmly on hips. The wind stirred the raven tresses fram-
ing her face as she grinned widely, her gold-flecked jade eyes
sparking with impish light.

"Glylina!" Davin's jaw dropped. He stared at Goran's feminine persona!

"Bertam has convinced Captain Iuonx that I am the sorceror
controlling this isle?" Glylina's eyes fired with anger when
Davin completed recounting his last night aboard the merchanter. "I'll have his tongue for those lies! And I'll have his
heart for what he's done here! Me, merely a lowly human
sorceror! The swine's a sly one! One who deserves all that is
coming to him!"

Davin licked the last crumbs of gorp—a mixture of grain,
berries, and honey—from his fingers, and glanced around the

small hut, eyes alighting on the red-headed Awendala who sat silently across the room. He then looked at Glylina and Kulonna, who nestled against the Challing's side.

Thirty women waited in the village's huts, ready to be led to freedom. Davin pursed his lips and shook his head. "I would feel far more secure were Goran at my side."

Glylina shrugged. "I no longer control my shaping, Davin. It's as I said, the magicks here are too strong. The undercurrents and eddies of spells affect me from one instant to the next."

"It's amazing to see!" This from Kulonna, who squeezed the Challing's arm with obvious delight. "He . . . she changes like that, even while we make . . . in the middle of . . . even when . . ."

"Never mind, my lovely." Glylina patted the blonde's hand. "Davin's not interested in hearing the details of our time alone together."

"Oh? Is he . . ."

Davin hid a smile of amusement behind a cup of watery wine. "A rent in the fabric separating the dimensions, you say?" Davin asked.

"Aye," Glylina nodded. "It's the same as I felt in Agda's wood."

"And Bertam is not responsible for the tear?" Davin covered ground already trod, but he needed time to fit the fragments of an evasive thought together.

"It has the feel of age to it," Glylina answered. "One of the rips Zarek Yannis created when he brought the Faceless Ones into Raemllyn would be my guess."

"And you think Bertam, who calls himself Ah-Banh-Cee, has merely woven a spell to bind the mist—the rent—to this island. That it is beyond his powers to create one?" Davin pressed, sensing the pieces fall into their horrible places.

"Yes, exactly. None except Yannis has possessed the spells required to bridge the dimensions since the legendary time of Edan, Kwerin Bloodhawk's long dead sorceror ally," Glylina replied. "However, even a minor mage, one holding only the knowledge of the outer rings of power, might possess spells needed to bind the rent to this island. Although such a feat would tax him greatly."

"A lesser sorceror," Davin rephrased Glylina's description. A humorless smile twisted his lips. "Gor . . . Glylina, sometimes your thoughts border on genius!"

"All the time, Davin." Glylina's well-endowed chest expanded with Challing pride. "Uh, what did I say?"

"Minor mage," Davin answered. "It fits with something that's been niggling at the back of my mind since I escaped the *Twisted Cross*. As spectacular and as painful as Bertam's Hair of Fire spell was, I've wondered why he simply didn't cast the Light of Truth."

"Aye!" Glylina sat straight. "That spell is known to all but the greenest acolytes!"

"What does it matter?" Awendala slumped in her chair, her emerald eyes shifting between Challing and Jyotian. "Ah-Banh-Cee may be a minor wizard, but he still controls this isle. Now he controls the ship Goran promised would free us."

Davin didn't answer. The young captive from Yaryne was right. Tacllyn-lin-Bertam controlled the mist, a power that could not be ignored. And as unwitting allies he had recruited Captain Iuonx and what remained of the *Twisted Cross'* crew. Or did he simply lure captain and crew onto the island to butcher them one by one?

"You say the rest of the mage's captives are ready to move?" Davin looked back at Glylina. A seed of an idea formed in his mind.

"I was preparing to lead them to the ship when you were sighted in the forest," Glylina answered with a nod. "Does it matter anymore? Bertam controls the ship."

"Not if he and the others search the forest for us!" Davin's heart pounded. His plan bordered on sheer insanity, but at least it was a chance! More than they had if they remained on the island. "If we could get the women aboard and set sail, we could leave Bertam and his accursed beasts and mist behind."

"We need a crew to do that," Glylina protested.

"There's the two of us," Davin answered hastily. "We could get the *Twisted Cross* under sail. And we have thirty hands to train as sailors. It won't be easy. Might even be impossible, but it's all we have."

"True . . ."

Glylina's words drowned in a thunderous explosion that quaked the ground beneath the hut!

Davin leaped from his chair and ran to the open door. Outside, the village came alive as screaming women abandoned their huts. Near the village's edge a smoking crater lay torn in the ground.

"Magicks!" Glylina pressed to Davin's side. Both of her eyes glowed with witch-fire. "I feel them weaving in the air."

From atop the forest ridge a ball of flaming crimson hurled screaming through the air. It slammed into the ground ten feet closer to the huts. Grass, dirt, and rock showered upward as it exploded in a consuming nova of actinic white.

"Ah-Banh-Cee!" Kulonna hugged close to Glylina. "He overheard our plans to escape and comes to punish us!"

A voice drifted into the valley from the forest. "I seek the mage Goran One-Eye and his apprentice. Surrender the two and no one will be harmed. Refuse and die!"

"Bertam!" Davin hissed. "The whoreson's found us!"

Another ball of flame shot from the forest and arced high above the valley. Downward it hailed atop a hut on the edge of the village. Again consuming light exploded. When the blinding glare faded the hut was gone and a smoking crater remained.

"I think we've underestimated Bertam's power, friend Davin," Glylina said with a weak smile of chagrin. "It's time we made a hasty retreat to reevaluate our position."

"Is there a way out of here?" Davin turned to Kulonna and Awendala. "Is there somewhere we can hide?"

"Only the mountain's caverns," Awendala answered.

"No, not the mountain!" Kulonna shook her head. "The mist hangs heavy around it most of the time. None of us have dared explore it." Kulonna shook on the verge of frightened tears. "None who remain, that is. All who had tried failed to return."

A fourth ball of flame exploded outside, and another hut vanished in exploding light.

"Mist or not, the mountain it is. Come, Gor . . . Glylina, there's no time to tarry. The madman intends to destroy the village!" Davin stepped outside, ready to dash for the mountain.

A hand locked about his arm, stopping him. He swung around and faced Awendala.

"You'll not leave without me. For a year I've endured this isle and its master. No more. Even death would be better than feeling his touch another time." The redhead's expression was set as firm as her words.

"Nor will I leave you!" Kulonna stared at Glylina.

The Challing shrugged when she turned to Davin. "I think the four of us had best hurry."

A fifth ball of fire tore into another hut as they ran from the village toward the mountain. Bertam's screaming rage rose above the fading din of the explosion.

"The mist." Awendala nudged the Jyotian's side. "It forms above the trees."

Davin glanced up and shook his head. "It's only natural fog forming as evening approaches." He left an *I hope* unspoken.

"Where are these Nyuria-cursed caverns you mentioned? It seems we've been walking all day!" the Challing protested behind the young thief.

Davin glanced over a shoulder and eyed his friend. The changeling once more wore Glylina's voluptuous form. Since their escape from the village, the undercurrents of the magicks aplay on the island had transformed her-him from Glylina to Goran and back again twice.

Davin drew a deep breath. The massive tree-limb club Goran had ripped from an oak during the last transformation weighted Glylina's arms like a millstone. If it came to a fight, he had only his blade and the knife he had given Awendala to depend on. He cursed. By all the gods, he hated magic and all it entailed!

"'Tis no natural fog," Awendala said as they climbed a treeless hillock on the mountain's side. "Beasts writhe within. Look!"

Fanged maws, glaring eyes, and taloned claws materialized and dissipated in the boiling clouds overhead. Yet the misty fog did not descend, but remained well above them.

"It's as though some force holds it back, keeping it from us." Davin shook his head, trying to ignore the prickle as the hairs on the back of his neck stood on end.

"Or is keeping it from this place." Glylina's eyes flickered with witch-fire when she pointed to a well-trod path leading to the leftmost of three caves in the mountain's side. "The wizard's lair is near."

"Bertam's lair?" Davin stared at the cave. "Are you certain?"

"Of course I'm certain," Glylina replied. "I feel his guardian spells acrawl on my skin like beetles!"

Davin's heart raced and his breath came quick and shallow. If they could penetrate Bertam's mountain keep, they might discover the means to defeat the wizard. Or at least unmask his treachery before Captain Iuonx and the *Twisted Cross'* crew.

"With care," Davin cautioned as he started for the cave. "Retreat at the first sign of danger."

"Such a hero," Glylina scoffed.

"Black Qar take you and your poxy eye . . . eyes!" Davin cursed without glancing over his shoulder "We've seen most of the *Twisted Cross* crew die. How many ships has Bertam successfully pirated? We are not pitted against a tyro. Bertam is dangerous!"

"He gets so emotional." Glylina winked at Kulonna.

"It becomes him," Awendala answered, a smile shooting to Davin.

A smile that received no reply as Davin halted at the cave's entrance. He saw nothing within except rock. He motioned Glylina forward. "Do you sense the presence of spells?"

Glylina stepped into the cave, halted, took two more cautious strides, then turned and walked outside again. She tilted her head to the roiling cloud of mist creatures above.

"The guardian spells are here, Davin. Not in the cave." She looked back at the cavern. "The spells are meant to keep the beasts of the mist at bay. I feel nothing inside."

With a final glance at the swirling creatures within the fog, Davin unsheathed his sword and entered the cave. His head turned right and left, scanning the cavern's walls, floor, and ceiling for any hint of a trap that had been laid for the unwary. Only rock met his gaze.

"You spend too much time fighting phantoms," Glylina said. "Save your energy for the real battle. When Bertam comes and finds us rummaging through his dreary hole in the ground—"

"Bertam? Bertam? We know of no Bertam, do we my lovely?" A male voice cackled from out of the cave's dimness ahead of the four.

"No, no, my love. We know no Bertam, only Ah-Banh-Cee, our most generous master," a feminine voice answered with a throaty chuckle. "It was he who sent us to greet his lovely visitors."

A clank like the sound of bones striking together echoed within the cave. The dimness took form.

At Davin's side Awendala gasped, a piteous sound lost in Kulonna's terrified scream. The Jyotian's heart leaped and lodged itself in his throat, which was suddenly as dry as the Great Desert of Nayati.

Two creatures with bodies and heads of humans scuttled over the cave's floor on the jointed legs of spiders. Hideous grins twisted the lips of both male and female as they gnashed their teeth and snapped giant mandibles before them.

# *chapter*

## *20*

DAVIN ANANE LEAPED to the side, then took three hasty back-steps to avoid the serrated mandible that lashed out in an attempt to open his belly. And nearly walked into the spider creature's other gaping claw! Glylina shouted a warning; Davin ducked. The mandible snapped closed the length of a finger's joint above his head.

"A dancer!" the male spider thing cackled, his green human eyes asparkle beneath a matted mass of red hair that fell across his forehead. "I love dancers. Used to be a dancer myself, I did!" The man-spider grinned at the Jyotian and winked. "Shall we dance?"

Both mandibles thrust toward Davin. He reacted rather than thought. His sword arm jerked up to whip his blade before him in a double parry of the seeking claws. In a single fluid circle his sword twisted in a tight arc, and he lunged, blade tip skewering for the groteseque beast's throat.

Before the sword sank home, the right serrated pincher leaped up and brushed away the blade. Davin jumped back to avoid the sweep of the creature's left arm.

"Yes, yes, my love," the female spider thing chuckled with glee. "Both are dancers. See how this lovely one glides across our ballroom! The blood of Ayame, Goddess of Dance, is like a fire in her veins!"

The she-demon's hideous laughter rolled through the cave when her mandibles struck like twin cobras!

Glylina leaped above the left claw that snapped at her ankles. In a maneuver that would have shamed Raemllyn's most famed acrobats, she drew herself into a tight ball to dodge the snap of right mandible when it sought to sever her head from her body.

Nor did the Challing's startling gymnastics stop there. Glylina somersaulted through the air and landed astride the spider woman's back. Her legs locked about the creature's belly; a Goran-imitating battle cry tore from her lips. Both hands clutching the massive tree limb, she hefted it above her head intent on crushing the beast's skull.

*"No!"* Awendala screamed. "Glylina no! The creature is my *mother!* Don't kill her. Please, don't kill her!"

*"Mother?"* Davin's and Glylina's voices sounded in single chorus. Their weapons hovered in midair.

"Mother?" This from the ghastly mating of woman and arachnid. The creature's mandibles clicked closed and its head cocked from side to side while blue eyes peered at the flaming-tressed young woman.

"And that's my *father!*" Awendala pointed to the arachnidian whose pinchers trembled but an inch from Davin's unguarded throat.

"No," a weak protest quavered from the spider-man's lips. A tear trickled from a green eye to roll down a dirt-caked cheek. "Awendala?"

"Yes, yes." The young woman cast aside her knife and opened her arms to the spidery horror. "Father, it's me. It's Awendala, your daughter!"

The creature retreated as the young woman stepped toward him. Tears flowed from both his eyes now.

"Away, child, away, away." This from the female spider, who also wept. "Neither my love nor I can control the bestial urges of our bodies. Away, child! You and your friends away, before the hunger grows too great within our bodies. Away, away, away!"

"Away, away, away," echoed the male. "Away, away, away."

Glylina lowered her club and she scampered from the back of the monster she rode. With an arm about Awendala's waist, she eased the young woman away from the trembling spiders.

"Away! You heard me, you did!" The female shouted. "There is nothing within but my love and I. Flee."

"No!" Awendala's head twisted from side to side in denial. She struggled to escape Glylina's hold. "I won't leave you. I won't!"

"Leave, yes. You must," the weeping male said. "There is no hope here for us, no hope. Save yourself, save yourself. Away, away, away."

Awendala collapsed against Glylina, her slender body wracking with sobs. "By the gods, how? How could this be?"

"Not the gods. No, not the gods." The female spider wagged her head. "It was *he* who did this. He who lives in the heart of the mountain. The heart of the mountain, yes."

"Jealous, he was," the creature's mate spoke. "Jealous, jealous, jealous. Had my lovely, I did. Yes. He had nothing, no one. Punished us, he did. Made us and placed us here."

The woman thing chuckled. "Fooled him, we did. We still have each other, we have. And he still has nothing. Nothing, nothing, nothing."

Davin's mind reeled. These things had once been Awendala's mother and father. Bertam's accursed spells had transformed them into grotesque mockeries of the man and woman they had once been, into creatures that rivaled the horrors that dwelled in the mist outside.

Davin found his tongue and spoke. "We seek the one who did this. The one who holds your daughter captive. We must pass and enter his lair."

"Not here, not here, not here." The thing that had once been Awendala's father scuttled forward a step, six spidery legs pumping and two mandibles held in the air. "Only my lovely and me here."

"The middle cave, yes. Take the middle cave." The still weeping woman spider added. "To the heart of the mountain. To the heart of the mountain."

"Go, go, go. Hungry we are. So very hungry." The male moved a step closer. "Flee, flee, flee."

Davin didn't argue. Both creatures inched forward. A bestial gleam replaced the sorrow in their human eyes. Taking Awendala from Glylina, he wrapped an arm about her waist and hastened from the cave, leaving the arachnidian remnants of her parents alone with their love and hunger.

"The heart of the mountain." The phrase her parents had used trembled from Awendala's lips. "This is *his* place!"

The cave opened before the four. At the mountain's heart lay an expansive crater. Above the jagged open rim that rose two hundred feet over their heads pressed boiling gray clouds. Beasts born in nightmares or the fever of madmen lunged and clawed as though trying to escape bondage.

"An ancient volcano," Davin mumbled, filled with a restless awe of this place—*his* place. "Bertam found himself quite a cubbyhole in which to hide."

"The creatures look like they're trying to break free, to descend on us." Kulonna hugged closer to Glylina.

"They are." Green sparks danced within the Challing's eyes. "I feel mounting magicks here. It's as though the spells that contain the beasts of the mist are being renewed even as we stand here."

"Pray they hold while we're within." Davin shuddered, diverting his gaze from the rolling fog above. He had seen what the creatures within did to a man—to fifteen men! A fate to be avoided if possible.

"What's that?" Awendala pointed to a structure rising from the crater's center.

Davin shook his head as he peered at four massive boulders twice a man's height. Each stood on its broad end to form a pillar that supported a flat slab of roughly hewn stone. Beneath the stone roof stood a square-cut block.

"An altar?" Glylina asked.

"Perhaps." With sword leveled before him, Davin started across the floor of the crater toward the structure. "But to what God?"

"The one Bertam worships, of course. What other deity could it be?" Glylina replied, exasperation in her tone. "Are humans unable to grasp the obvious?"

Davin ignored the changeling and cautiously stepped beneath the slab balanced on the boulders. Atop the altar lay two leather-bound books. "Bertam's grimoires?"

"What else could they be?" Glylina pushed past Davin, who probed the air about the tomes with his sword for spells that might bind the volumes. "You are far too wary when magicks are involved, Davin. Besides, I feel nothing other than the guardian spell that keeps the mist at bay."

Before the last son of the House of Anane uttered a warning, the Challing lifted the smaller of the books and tossed it at him. The young thief caught the tome and juggled it in his hand as though it were a hot coal.

"It's only paper and ink. It won't hurt you," Glylina said in disgust as she flipped the cover of the large volume. "Open it and read. Pay heed to any spell that we might use against Bertam."

Fingers atremble and breath quickening, Davin sheathed his sword and opened the book as the Challing suggested. The handwriting within flowed in bold strokes across the page. A

fact that surprised him; he expected to find indecipherable runes
or a jumbled code. He scanned the first page, then the next.

"This is interesting." Glylina jabbed a forefinger at the larger
tome's first page. "Neither the name Tacllyn-lin-Bertam nor
Ah-Banh-Cee is written here. This is the grimoire of a Kavindra
mage named Hel-k'lil." Glylina flipped through several pages
and shook her head. "The spells within are simple enough.
Love potions, sleeping chants—"

"Hel-k'lil's name is here, too." Davin glanced at the Challing. "Though this volume is no grimoire. It's a journal. It begins
with Hel-k'lil's days as an apprentice in the Acyt School in
Kavindra." He thumbed through the pages of the mage's diary.
Halfway through, the handwriting abruptly changed to an awkward scrawl. "What's this?"

"Mmmmm." Glylina's eyes brightened. "It seems this
Hel-k'lil knew more than how to brew love potions. Here's a
chant for summoning Nahtahl, the demon called Plague. And
this is a spell for binding storms. It appears well used, if the
finger smudges on the page are any indication."

Davin half listened while he flipped back through the journal, finding the place where the handwriting of the entries
changed. Back two pages beyond that point he started reading.
His pulse quickened with each word revealed.

"Listen to this! Hel-k'lil writes: 'Today I employed the ship
of the pirate Captain Kebatian, who is only too willing to serve
Zarek Yannis' cause as long as I supply him a steady stream
of ships to plunder.'"

"Zarek Yannis!" Awendala moved to Davin's side and peered
over his shoulder.

"Aye, the mage served the usurper," Davin said, then continued reading aloud from the journal.

As his companions listened, the Jyotian unfolded the tale
of a wizard whose duty was to terrorize the northern trade
routes of the Oceans of Kumar. The pirate Kebatian assigned
his second mate to aid the sorceror during the long journey
from Kavindra to the waters along Upper Raemllyn's north
coast. Surprised by the seaman's quick mind and willingness
to learn, the mage took the sailor underwing and began his
training as an apprentice.

"Here are the recountings of the sinking of twenty merchanters," Davin said. "It seems Hel-k'lil held the ability to

summon giant squids from the ocean floor. With the great creatures he learned to herd sea serpents."

"Of course!" Glylina's head snapped up. "That explains the tentacled sea monsters that attacked the *Twisted Cross*. Squid and serpent are natural enemies. A squid, maybe two or three, under a mage's magicks would drive a serpent mad with fear. It would attack anything in its path to escape!"

"And here is mention of this isle," Davin said. "It seems that Kebatian used the caves in this mountain to hide his booty. With holds abrim with riches, the pirate captain sailed for his hidden harbor . . . and there first encountered the mist!"

"Treasures! In these caves!" Glylina's expression brightened.

Davin hastily read Hel-k'lil's account of how the mist and its horde of demon creatures destroyed half the ship's crew before he found that he could control it with a storm-binding spell.

"It's as you thought." Davin looked up at Glylina. "Hel-k'lil recognized the mist as a physical manifestation of a rent between the dimensions. The creatures within are trapped between worlds. Only on occasion is one able to wiggle through to this realm of existence. Hel-k'lil thought to bind the mist and use it for Yannis' cause. However, he abandoned the task after a week. He writes that maintaining the spell 'drains a man of my many years. And I fear would even test the strength of one decades younger than I.'"

Davin paused, his attention returning to the journal. "Here the handwriting changes. The first words written are: 'Today Hel-k'lil died and Ah-Banh-Cee is born. Tomorrow the rest of the fools will follow the old mage. Then the northern waters will be mine!'"

Davin flipped through the remainder of the diary, scanning the pages. "The rest is an account of how Bertam lured ships to the island and pillaged them. When rumors of the horror lurking in these waters began to spread, his conquests stopped and he was trapped here. A storm drove a merchanter to the isle and he gained passage, claiming to be a survivor of a cargo vessel wrecked three years before."

Davin scanned several more pages before continuing to detail how Ah-Banh-Cee renewed his contact with pirates in the city of Salnal: "In return for a quarter of Bertam's booty, a

pirate captain sails to this island four times a year and returns
the bastard to the mainland."

"And there he finds his way onto another unsuspecting ship,"
Glylina added.

"The rest of the journal is nothing more than a log of the
ships he's destroyed and the riches he's amassed." Davin snapped
the book closed. "And there're the names of those he's sold
into slavery or ransomed."

"And my parents?" Awendala's emerald eyes misted with
tears when they lifted to Davin. "Are they mentioned within?"

The Jyotian nodded and drew a deep breath. "Aye. It seems
that Bertam considers you his greatest prize. He fell in love
with you during the journey from Yaryne. He approached your
parents and asked for your hand. They refused him. For that
he transformed them into the creatures we saw. He never intended to let you off this island."

Awendala shuddered as sobs quaked through her body. "Better my mother and father were dead than to live forever as
those ghastly *things!* If the gods knew mercy, they would spare
them from Ah-Banh-Cee's magicks."

Davin gathered her into his arms and held her. "He'll pay
for this. That I promise you. Bertam will pay the dearest price
of all—his life."

"Aye!" This from Glylina. "No empty words those. For
here is the key to destroying the whoreson!"

Davin's gaze lifted, but never reached the Challing. His
head jerked around as a man's voice echoed across the crater.
"The chase is ended. Prepare to greet Black Qar!"

There at the cave's mouth stood Tacllyn-lin-Bertam and
Captain Iuonx!

# chapter
## *21*

"BERTAM!" GLYLINA'S JADE-GREEN eyes darted around the crater, seeking an avenue of retreat.

None existed; Davin had already ascertained the helplessness of their vulnerable position.

"I have destroyed the spiders you left for us in the other cave," Bertam shouted. "Now I will destroy you!"

Davin saw Awendala stiffen and shudder. But no tears rolled from her eyes. Her wish that a merciful death be granted her parents had been fulfilled—not by the gods, but by the man who had so ensorcelled them!

"Back away slowly." Glylina motioned Kulonna and Awendala. "It's Davin and I Ah-Banh-Cee wants."

"Go with them, Glylina." Davin watched Bertam cautiously advance. The mage's hands drew mystical signs in the air with each step. "Bertam wants Goran One-Eye, not you. There's a chance you'll escape."

"Bertam . . . Ah-Banh-Cee?" Awendala took one stride and abruptly stopped. She looked at the two advancing men and then at Davin. "Neither of those men is Ah-Banh-Cee."

*"What?"* Davin's jaw sagged.

There was no time for the redhead to reply. Bertam's arms thrust board stiff before him. A red glow covered his palms and grew, swirling out until a ball of flame danced in the air. The wizard's wrists flicked; the burning orb arced across the crater.

Davin leaped, snagging Awendala about the waist. Glylina was on his heels with Kulonna tucked under an arm. The women's startled cries drowned in a thunderous explosion. White-hot light flared, and boulders groaned as they collapsed. Smoke writhed up toward the mouth of the crater from the shattered pile of rubble that had been an altar but a heartbeat before.

Awendala wiggled from the Jyotian's grip. Waving both arms above her head, she started toward Bertam and Iuonx. "These aren't the ones you want. Neither is the sorceror Ah-Banh-Cee. These aren't the ones you want!"

Before she took two strides, Davin once again caught her by the waist and dragged her aside.

For her efforts, a second crimson ball of flame shot from Bertam's palms and slammed into the ground where she had stood.

"To the crater's wall," Davin cried out. "Keep moving. Don't give him an easy target."

"Davin, we can fight him!" Glylina hefted the grimoire she clutched in her left hand. "I've Hel-k'lil's spells."

The Jyotian ignored the Challing as he led a zigzagging retreat for the crater's far wall. There was no time to weave spells, even if they were known. The thought of stopping, reading a page from the tome, then trying to cast an unknown spell was ridiculous!

A third exploding ball tore into the crater's floor at the four's heels. Thunder blasted, rebounding back atop them from the high walls.

Davin immediately changed course, swinging back in the direction from which they had just come. The maneuver saved them from a fourth orb of fire that ripped into the ground near the crater's wall.

"By Yehseen's staff, Bertam learns to lead his shots!" Davin halted and turned to the mage, waiting until another sizzling ball of death leaped from his palms before sprinting to the left.

"Davin," Glylina shouted as they dodged yet another of the exploding balls of fire, "I tell you I can defeat the whoreson! Divert him for a few moments!"

"Divert him. How in—"

The diversion came from high on the crater's rim. A ball of green flame screamed downward toward Bertam. The lanky mage's hands shot up. A flaming ball of red danced from his palms and leaped to meet the comet of green.

There was no thunder, no explosion when the flaming orbs collided. The magic of one cancelled the magic of the other. Red and green, the balls of flame winked into the nothingness that had given them birth.

"Who dares challenge the might of Ah-Banh-Cee!" A man's voice echoed down into the crater floor.

Davin's head jerked up. His mouth dropped open. Even with two hundred feet separating him from the wizard who ruled this isle, there was no way for him to mistake the familiar figure who stood defiantly on the crater's edge. *"Arkko!"*

"Arkko!" The *Twisted Cross'* first mate's name resounded behind the Jyotian, torn from Captain Iuonx's lips. "Arkko!"

"Nay! In the heart of this mountain Arkko died and was reborn as Ah-Banh-Cee. Ah-Banh-Cee—he who is destined to rule Raemllyn's oceans!" Arkko's words were those of a madman. "Bow to my will . . . or die!"

Bertam answered with raised arms. From his fingertips shot myriad miniature fireballs, each sizzling toward the figure on the crater's rim. Arkko's answer was a rain of spraying green. Again the magicks clashed, each devouring the other.

"Here it is! Just like I told you, Davin!" Glylina cried with glee. The Challing sat on the ground with Hel-k'lil's volume of spells open across her lap.

"Glylina!" Davin's frustration could no longer be contained. "There isn't time. We can escape while Bertam and Arkko battle." The Jyotian shoved Kulonna and Awendala toward the crater's exit. "Run! Don't stop until you reach the beach! We'll be behind you!"

"Arkko's guardian spell weakens. Can't you feel it, Davin? He was trying to renew it when we entered the crater. He didn't finish the chant. I can feel it, Davin! Now Bertam diverts the bastard's attention. The mist strains to break free." Glylina looked up from the tome, her face lit with glee. "All I have to do is . . . *arraggggahh!"*

Glylina jerked spasmodically; she writhed and twisted on the crater's floor like a woman beset by the falling sickness! Soft white flesh went flaccid, then rippled, expanding. Two beautiful jade eyes were replaced by a single eye and a dark socket. Flowing raven hair transformed into a shaggy mane of flaming red. Goran, not Glylina, once more dominated the changeling's body.

"Get Kulonna and Awendala out of here! Now!" The Challing waved his companion away when Davin stepped forward to help him from the ground. "Do it now, Davin!"

Davin took one step, then halted to turn back to his friend. Goran lifted the dead mage's grimoire and spread it before him on the ground. His lips moved as he repeated the chant written within. His bearded face lifted and his witch-fire burning eye turned to the rolling fog above the crater. "By the Goddess Minima who rules the winds, I set you free."

Davin stared in horror. As though an invisible barrier had been removed, the fog sank toward the crater's rim. Wispy tentacles of mist probed the air, groping and finding Arkko. They coiled about his torso, looped his arms and legs, then hoisted the screaming man skyward—into the waiting jaws of the beasts of the mist.

"Out of here!" Davin ran to the Challing and wrenched him to his feet. "The fog drops toward us."

"Nay, Davin. Look, they have what they want. They dine on the man who bound them to this accursed isle." Goran stared overhead, a delighted grin on his face while he watched blood and bits of human flesh rain from the churning cloud. "Better to have him torn limb from limb with my own hands, but this will suffice!"

Above, the cloud lifted. The golden glow of a setting sun filled the crater.

Davin stared to the horizon, watching fleecy white clouds scuttle across the sea. Somewhere amid the blueness cloaking Raemllyn drifted a cloud that wasn't a cloud but a murderous rent in the fabric separating the dimensions. He shuddered. They had escaped, but had not destroyed the horror Zarek Yannis created when he brought the Faceless Ones into this realm.

"It's frightening, isn't it Jyotian?" Bertam's words intruded on his thoughts. "It's still out there. It will be hard to look at a cloud and not shiver until the tear is closed."

"When will that be?" Davin looked at the mage who served Prince Felrad.

"Perhaps when the usurper is defeated and the secret of his power is discovered. Perhaps never." Bertam shrugged.

Another shudder worked its way up to Davin's spine. For generations magicks had been on the wane in Raemllyn. Now they threatened to tear the world apart at its seams.

"Of course she's seaworthy! We've spent a week making her so! But a lot of good that does us!" Captain Iuonx shouted as he climbed from the hold. "A ship's no good without a crew!"

"But Captain." Goran One-Eye followed him onto the deck. "There's a crew waiting back on the island."

"The women?" Iuonx pivoted and glared at the Challing. "Are you crazy? A ship with a crew of *women!* I'd be laughed out of every port in Upper and Lower Raemllyn. Besides, what do those lovely beauties ashore know about ships? Can't tell the wheel from the masts, if ye ask me!"

"I'm afraid you have no other choice, Captain," Bertam spoke. "The *Twisted Cross'* holds bulge with riches Prince Felrad has dire need of. We must make our way to Rakell with all haste."

"But *women!*" Iuonx roared.

Davin smiled. Iuonx really did have no other choice. Arkko's treachery had been bloody. Only two others of the crew survived the beasts in the mist. Those two now visited the village ashore.

"Without them, you don't have a ship, Captain," Goran added.

"And I suppose, ye want me to make you first mate?" Iuonx turned back to the changeling.

"Could anyone serve you better?" Goran's chest expanded until it threatened to pop the buttons on his shirt. "Who else knows the sea like I? Why, it was when I served as first mate aboard the Jyotian merchanter the *Opal Narwhal* that I lost my eye!"

"What?" Iuonx sputtered in disbelief. "Last night ye said it was a frost nymph that plucked your eye while ye made love to her atop an iceberg!"

"'Twas aboard the *Opal Narwhal* when the god Nalren himself rose from the depths—"

"No more!" Iuonx waved his arms and shrugged submissively. "If agreeing to the women will put an end to your tales, then go ashore and get the women!"

Goran beamed when he turned to Davin. "It's time to go collect our crew, friend Davin. We've been too long from a decent port, good food, strong drink, and other pleasures so sorely missed! So says the *Twisted Cross'* new first mate!"

# chapter
## 22

DAVIN ANANE SLOWLY drew a breath through his nose and released it with equal languor. A satisfied smile moved across his lips. The air contained a taste of spring. Even here along the upper reaches of Raemllyn, winter fled before the warmth that pushed its way northward.

Better was the smell of land that wafted in the Jyotian's nostrils. After the long months journey from Weysh, the aroma that blew across the waves was like an exotic perfume blended from rare blossoms brought from Lower Raemllyn's distant provinces.

"You have the look of a man who longs to be elsewhere," Tacllyn-lin-Bertam said with a hint of regret when he joined the adventurer at the *Twisted Cross*' rail.

"Aye, I can't deny it." Davin smiled. "There are beauties to Raemllyn's wilderness and her seas, but my heart lies with the cities."

"There is no way to persuade you and Goran to remain with us until we reach Iluska?" Bertam arched his eyebrows hopefully.

"Then Iuonx agrees with your plan to waylay putting in at Evara?" Davin glanced at the mage. Did the man prepare him for bad news? Captain Iuonx had assured Davin he and Goran would be put ashore at Evara.

"The possibility of the usurper's frigates being anchored in Evara's harbor is too great a risk with our cargo. The Isle of Rigden remains loyal to Prince Felrad. At Iluska the treasures we carry can be divided among several merchanters and slipped into Rakell."

Davin nodded. Fear of Yannis' many warships had diverted the *Twisted Cross* from entering the Bay of Zaid and making a direct run to Rakell on Isle of Loieter, or Loieterland as the island was often called. The treasure taken from Arkko's caves had a better chance, at least in part, of reaching Prince Felrad, hidden in the holds of a small fleet of merchant ships.

Hope remained on the sorceror's face. "Are you certain you won't continue to Iluska? You and Goran will be received as heroes."

Davin chuckled. "It's Arkko's treasures bulging the holds that will be well-received, not two unknown vagabonds. No, it's Evara for my friend and me—unless Captain Iuonx has made another change in his course and failed to mention it?"

"No, he will still see that you get to Evara. Or at least close to the city," Bertam answered. "That is why we sail so near the coast. As soon as night falls, the *Twisted Cross* will drop anchor and a longboat will be lowered over the side. You'll be put ashore about ten leagues north of Evara."

"A stout walk," Davin replied, unable to conceal his relief that Iuonx held to his word, "but one my legs will enjoy."

"Rakell lies west of Evara. An easy journey for two way-farers as experienced as Goran and yourself." Bertam's expression sobered. "Have you considered taking that journey? Prince Felrad has need of men with strong sword arms."

Davin was well aware of Felrad's fortifications on the Isle of Loieter. The prince's efforts would be futile unless the Sword of Kwerin Bloodhawk were placed in his hand. Davin intended to find Lijena Farleigh and reclaim the legendary blade before joining the rightful ruler of Raemllyn in his fight against Zarek Yannis.

"We can't divert to Rakell at this time." Davin pursed his lips. "But one day Goran and I will make that journey."

"Are you one of them?" Bertam asked.

"Them?"

"The deposed nobility. You have the look of a highborn about you, Davin Anane, in spite of your alleged part in all the cutthroat thievery the red-bearded one brags about." Bertam's eyes narrowed suspiciously.

Memories of Jyotis, the House of Anane, and its betrayal wiggled from just below the surface of Davin's thoughts, where their pain constantly waited. One day he would pay Lord Berenicis the Blackheart for his treacherous deeds.

"Highborn? Me?" Davin laughed harshly. "And don't put too much weight in Goran's tales. If any two men had done half of what he claims, they'd have lost their heads years ago."

Bertam didn't press the matter, but suspicion remained in his blue eyes.

"And you, mage, where are you bound after Iluska?" Davin asked.

"To my prince's side in Rakell," Bertam said. The sorcerer's gaze stretched across the waves to the shoreline and the approaching night. "There is a matter of certain coins that must be minted and distributed."

"And the rest of Arkko's treasures left hidden on his damnable isle?"

"I think Captain Iuonx can handle that," Bertam said. "For me there is another matter that Felrad needs to be apprised of."

Davin looked at the wizard. "Another matter?"

"I've studied Hel-k'lil's grimoire for long hours since we set sail from the isle. The man's knowledge was vast and his spells intricate. Had he managed to control the rent between the dimensions, he would have placed a weapon as powerful as Yannis' Faceless Ones in the usurper's hands," Bertam said. "Such a weapon would be equally powerful in the service of Prince Felrad."

Davin shuddered. "Control the beasts of the mist?"

"It may be beyond any man's power." Bertam shrugged. "Yet the possibilities must be explored."

*The possibilities must be explored!* Davin stiffened. How easily those words rolled from Bertam's tongue. Had the man forgotten so soon the fanged and clawed horrors that dwelled in the mist? The ways of magicks and those who wove their potent spells were not the way of Davin Anane, nor would he ever understand them.

The sound of heavy boots on the deck drew Davin from his reflections. He turned to find Captain Iuonx approaching. The man stopped a few feet away to scratch at his beard while he eyed the young Jyotian and then Bertam.

"Did you convince him that he is sorely needed aboard the *Twisted Cross*? That I've even learned to tolerate the red-haired one he calls a friend?" Iuonx's gaze shifted back to Davin.

"I tried and failed." Bertam shrugged.

"By Nalren's seaweed beard, I feared as much!" Iuonx walked to the rail and grasped it with both hands. He stared at the water while he spoke. "You *will* be sorely missed. In truth both of you have been worth the crimp's price—even though I paid it twice!"

Davin smiled. He doubted Iuonx would ever forget that night in Faldin when he discovered that he had purchased men he thought already securely aboard his ship. Nor was the Jyotian likely to let that memory slip away. The months aboard the *Twisted Cross* had taken him from Upper Raemllyn's western coast to her eastern shores, but Bistonia and Lijena Farleigh still remained half a continent away.

"I could use both Goran and you. To be certain, the women have proved to be an able crew—after they were trained—but a merchanter manned by women still doesn't sit right with me," Iuonx continued.

"Sorry, Captain, but as I explained to Bertam, I've been away from Raemllyn's cities for far too long."

"It's a poor choice of a city ye'll be dropping anchor in." Iuonx sucked at his teeth in disgust. "Like as not Zarek Yannis' troops will be swarming the streets everywhere ye look. Might make it damned difficult for a man of your chosen profession." The captain turned to Davin and lifted an eyebrow in question.

"Goran and I seem to manage well enough even under the most guarded situations." Davin's smile widened to hide the doubts that niggled within his mind. A city full of soldiers wasn't exactly his idea of the perfect location for thieves grown rusty at sea.

"Well, I don't know about that. I don't like setting you two ashore empty-handed after all ye've done for the *Twisted Cross*." Iuonx turned from the rail and hailed a passing brunette. "Natti, there's a pouch sitting on my desk, go and fetch it for me, lass."

With a bright smile the woman trotted off to Iuonx's cabin and returned moments later to hand the captain a heavy cloth sack. Another beaming smile and she returned to her duties, the captain's eyes following her every move.

Davin grinned. Although Iuonx bellowed and roared about his crew of women, it was more than obvious he took unspoken pleasure in those serving under him. Natti's beauty made that reason equally obvious.

"Here." Iuonx turned and shoved the sack into Davin's hands. "This is the sum ye paid that son of a sea slug Elozzi for passage—four hundred gold bists. Real bists, mind ye, not those glittering pieces of lead we'll be spreading to undermine Zarek Yannis' treasury!" Iuonx winked shyly and laughed. "And should ye ever need passage on a fine seaworthy vessel, all ye need do is look up Haigex Iuonx, and ye'll have a deck on which to sail."

Davin hefted the weight of the sack and drew a pleased breath. He had never expected such a show of generosity. "Captain, I'm not certain that I know what to say."

"I do!" Goran boomed out. The Challing approached with Kulonna and Awendala at his side. "It's not enough! We've spent months slaving on this leaky bucket. Months! And now we're no better off than when we started!"

"Aye," Iuonx nodded in agreement. "I considered adding fair wages to the sack, then I remembered each and every one of your lying yarns about that lost eye. I figured the patience I displayed and my restraint from having the hide peeled from your back was worth the wages!"

Bertam spoke before Goran could answer. "It's dark."

Iuonx signaled, and four women lowered a longboat over the side, then climbed down and manned its oars.

"The gods be with all four of ye." Iuonx grasped Davin's shoulder and squeezed it. "And may fortune go before ye."

"Four?" The Jyotian's eyes widened, and he turned to Goran. "Four?"

"Aye." Goran shrugged as though helpless before the Sitala. "I tried to talk them out of it, but they insist on coming with us. I think they hope to help spend the contents of that sack."

"I have to arrange passage to Rakell," Kulonna said defensively. "I still am an emissary to Prince Felrad for my father."

"And I must find a way to Yaryne," Awendala added. "Though my parents be dead, I still have family in that city."

A perplexed expression clouded the Challing's face. Davin shook his head. "We'll see both of you safely on your way."

"Although"—Awendala leaned to Davin, her emerald-green eyes rolling up to meet his—"if you seek companions to help lighten that pouch, I am certain both Kulonna and I are willing to discuss your plans."

Laughter rolled up from Davin's belly and echoed out across the Oceans of Kumar. His right arm encircled Awendala's slim waist and drew her close, guiding her toward the longboat. "Come, there is much we have to discuss on the way to Evara!"

"Perhaps we should have the same discussion?" Goran looked down to Kulonna.

"As long as there's not too much talk." The young woman took the Challing's meaty hand and led him to the waiting boat.